Mindrider

by
Graham Storrs

Canta Libre | Queensland

Doulos and Jura fonts used under the Open Font License.

Interior Design by Steven Saus

Cover design by Kate Strawbridge, Dwell Design & Press.

Mindrider
Copyright © 2016, Graham Storrs
ISBN: 978-0-9945899-2-7
Published by Canta Libre, Queensland, Australia
August 2016

10 9 8 7 6 5 4 3 2 1

Table of Contents

Dedication

This book is dedicated to my daughter, Dr. Katherine Rebecca Storrs, who is just about to begin her fourth decade of making me the proudest father in the history of the Universe.

Chapter 1

I can't stand it when they argue. I want to make them stick their heads in the oven. There, she's screaming again. It's like a roaring flame. I cringe away from the glare and heat. It blisters my skin, dries my eyeballs.

Not that I have any – skin or eyeballs that is – but sometimes it feels like it.

I've had enough. Either she goes, or I do. All it takes is a little tweak, a minor adjustment in her mind, a cascade of synapses here, a burst of neuronal firing there.

"I've had enough!" she shouts. "I'm leaving."

Dave looks gobsmacked, the poor sap. He starts blustering and stammering as she runs about grabbing her coat, her bag, throwing things into a suitcase. I don't need to do any more. She's on autopilot now.

But then, "I didn't mean it," Dave pleads. "Don't go. I'm sorry. Please, Jen."

Uh oh. She's wavering. I feel her empathy as she looks into his wounded, puppy eyes. She's beginning to wonder why she's being so mean, why she's over-reacting like this.

So I make Jen go over and lay a hand on Dave's arm and I slip across into him. I've never liked it in there. I don't know why. Some rides are just more comfortable than others. "Well clear off then, you stupid cow," I say through Dave's mouth. "I'll be better off without you."

I feel the shock in him at what he's just said. He's horrified. But maybe not so much as Jen. With an incoherent wail of dismay, she grabs up her half-packed case and bolts for the door.

She's going to her mother's. I know that because I felt the plan form while I was still in there. Dave is overwhelmed with re-morse and completely confused by what's going on. *Let her go*, I whisper into his inner ear. *Now you can screw that Maggie from work. She's always fancied you. You should call her tonight.*

Of course, I have no intention of letting him have sex with anybody. The whole sex thing makes me nauseous. Can you imagine what it's like in here while that's going on? But the idea gives him pause, long enough for Jen to run weeping from the house, slamming the door behind her.

Dave's mind is now a soggy mess of emotion but I soon have him sitting quietly in front of a football game, sucking cold beer from a bottle, feeling quietly sorry for himself – and daydreaming about the voluptuous Maggie.

The real work will begin very soon. My sniffers are out prowling around. They've felt the nightmare – just hints, but it's out there somewhere. So I ready my defences, I dig myself in, and I wait.

Being bait is ninety-nine parts hanging around. So that's what I do most of the time. I go where the Vaticinatrix says, then I hunker down and wait. It's how I serve the Colony, hanging round on the fringes, waiting for a nightmare to sniff me out.

You get to choose your own billet on a mission like this one. That's why I'm here with Dave and Jen. They're simple people – unlike some humans. Most of us mindriders like quiet minds, simple minds, nothing fancy.

There is a knock at the door. Dave gets up to answer it, wondering if maybe it's Jen and she left her keys. I don't pay much attention – Dave and Jen are sociable types and they always have friends and family coming round – until the door bangs open and Jen bursts in with a huge hunting knife in her hand. She lunges at Dave, who would have stood there like a dummy and had his guts ripped out if I hadn't taken charge and made him dodge the blow. Jen stumbles past him, off-balance. She turns, her eyes wide with insane rage. I make Dave grab her arm and I try to slip across into her before she can do any damage.

But I have to pull up sharp. She's already occupied. The nightmare is in there and I recoil as it lashes out at me.

"Jen?" Dave says, dazed and frightened, retreating across the room. "What's got into you?"

Jen laughs out loud, or, rather, the nightmare does, as if it appreciates the unintended irony of the question, and comes at him again with the knife. I let Dave stumble back another pace until he is beside the dining table. Then, with a ferocious wrenching of muscles – far beyond the limits to which his own mind would ever push his body – I make him grab a wooden dining chair and swing it at Jen. He cries out with the pain of straining tendons and tearing muscles but the chair smashes into Jen so hard it knocks her sideways. She goes sprawling across the floor and I make Dave go after her, ready to knock her down again. But there is no need. She is groaning on the floor, her eyelids fluttering, with a deep cut on her temple and an arm that might be broken in two places.

Now the real fight will begin.

As Dave bends over his fallen lover, his mind such a clamour I can barely hear myself think, the nightmare comes bursting out of Jen straight into him. I don't even bother trying to resist it. It is way stronger than I am. Instead, I flee into the depths of Dave's mind, flying through caves and tunnels into subterranean darkness where Dave himself has barely any access or awareness. Behind me, I hear feral screeching as the nightmare follows my trail.

The thing about nightmares is, they're not very bright. Cunning as all hell though. And strong. This one is a bastard. It is snapping at my ass all the way down and I only just make it to the caves I've prepared. It almost has me in its talons.

I wish again that I'd stayed in Jen and made Dave leave. Jen's mind was great, full of stuff I could use. Dave is dull, unimaginative. All there is in here are clichés and a few childhood dreams. Not a lot to work with.

I make my way through the narrow tunnels I've set up, hearing the nightmare screeching with rage as it tears down walls. Soon I come out at an opening in a cliff wall. Fields and hamlets spread out below me and there, dozing quietly on the ledge, is the most unsubtle dragon you've ever seen in your life. It is green, scaly and has a bog-standard crocodile-style head. Where Dave picked it up I have no idea – a kid's story, a Hollywood B-movie, who knows? – but it's mine now. I put it on like an overcoat, flex its mighty wings, and leap into the air.

I soar out and up, a couple of powerful beats of those leathery wings pushing me high into the cloudless sky. Wheeling around, I turn back to the cliff just as the nightmare emerges from the caves. Its angry eyes narrow as it sees me. I narrow mine right back at it and shove powerfully at the air, throwing myself into a power-dive, feeling the fire boiling in my belly.

I'll give it this, the nightmare isn't the least bit intimidated. As I shoot through the sky towards it, it crouches down, bracing itself as if to catch me. *Up yours*, I think, pulling up hard to hover just metres from it, and hose it with excoriating fire. I keep belching out flame until I am empty. It is only after the blaze and the smoke have cleared that I can see what effect my attack has had.

None whatsoever.

Shouting expletives, I flap frantically away from the thing and dive straight down to the fields below. Looking over my shoulder, I see it leap from the cliff-face, coming right after me.

That was supposed to have been a killer blow. I was supposed to be dragging its crispy-fried corpse back to the Vaticinatrix for a pat on the back, not fleeing for my life with it howling and screaming behind me. This critter is one tough little puppy!

Fortunately, I have a backup plan. I always have a backup plan. That's why I'm still out there doing my job while many another mindrider has ended his days with his psyche shredded and devoured.

And there it is. Out of a misty valley-bottom, dark shapes are appearing – forming, actually, as I dredge them out of Dave's mind. With a twitch of my wings, I head straight for them.

The mists clear to reveal a column of tanks. Not just ordinary, real-life tanks, these are super, sci-fi, beam-weapon-wielding tanks from some stupid film or game that Dave must have seen once. When I first came across them, rooting around in the depths of Dave's unconscious one day, I knew they were just the kind of thing I needed. The sheer awe and admiration he feels for them enhances their power a hundredfold. Now all I have to do is get inside them before the damned nightmare has me for lunch.

It is a tricky manoeuvre. I shoot past the tanks at high speed, dumping the dragon and grabbing onto a tank just as the nightmare sinks its claws into the dragon's back. It must feel me slip away even in the instant it thinks it has me. With a howl of rage, it tosses the empty dragon aside and lashes out at the tanks, smashing three of them to pieces, raking its talons across the column.

Working with desperate speed, I line up all my guns on the beast as it swings back to finish me off. Blinding, crackling energies blast at it from a dozen muzzles, catching it full in the face as it comes roaring towards me. I flinch at the destructive power I have unleashed, the beams splashing off the nightmare's hide, bathing everything in deadly energies. The tanks closest to the beast begin to buckle and melt. Channelling all Dave's belief in the power of the weapons, I ramp up the attack, but one by one, the beams are failing, the tanks slumping into the scorched ground.

The nightmare doesn't turn away, doesn't run. It just keeps coming, slowly, relentlessly, pushing against the forces I am blasting it with.

I begin to feel real fear. I've never seen power like this before, never knew it existed. I ratchet up my onslaught with every ounce of my strength – every ounce of Dave's too. Let's face it, what is the point of him surviving if I let the nightmare live? It would devour the pair of us. Yet I can feel myself failing, the life draining out of me. Still I pour everything I have into destroying the beast. There is no second backup. This is all I have left.

Dizziness overcomes me, darkness creeps in around the edges of my mind. The energy beams that play on the nightmare begin to weaken and wander off target. With a sob, I hang on, forcing myself to concentrate, willing the creature to die. And then, as the beams begin to wink out, the nightmare gives a wail of despair and falls to the ground.

I let the tanks fade away, the beams die. I cannot move. I can barely see the blackened ground before me. A terrible weakness sets me trembling. Exhaustion fogs my mind. Yet I force myself to move forward, to inspect the body of my fallen enemy.

It lies on the ruined earth, charred and broken, yet still clearly the monster of fangs and claws it has always been. I watch it without the usual feelings of triumph and elation. The damned thing has cost me too much. I just want to leave it there and climb into a quiet hole while I get my strength back, but I have to verify the kill and let the Vaticinatrix know what has happened.

I limp a little closer and prepare to probe it for signs of life when it raises its head and looks at me. It is so close it could lash out and impale me with its claws, yet I can't move, can't run. Fear and exhaustion root me there, and I wait to die.

A weak and crooked smile crosses the creature's face. Then, against all the laws of the divine and the mundane, it speaks. "Don't worry little mindrider, you are safe." Its voice is dry and unspeakably weary. "I am dying. If I had the strength to kill you, you would already be dead." Its head falls back to the ground and its gaze sags. I can see it has very few words left in it. Yet even the few it has spoken have been miraculous.

I've seen a lot of nightmares in my time on Earth and every one I've seen I have fought and killed. They were all big and powerful, vicious and cunning, but they were all what they were supposed to be: animals. They screamed, they roared, they killed, but they did not speak.

"How can you do that?" I ask. "What's going on? You're not a proper nightmare. You're... You're... What are you?"

The creature doesn't raise its gaze but it answers me in a gravelly voice. "Why did your people come here, to this planet? Why pick us? We've done nothing to deserve this... assault."

I wish I could think more clearly. My own exhaustion makes it almost impossible to get my thoughts straight. This planet, Earth, is part of our colonisation program. It was uninhabited when we came here. Just billions of human minds for our people to settle in and farm. No indigenous life of any higher order. "You nightmares arrived later," I protest. "Predators that destroy the minds we live in and destroy us too when you get the chance. Just a mindless pest that we hunt and eradicate."

The nightmare is silent for so long I think it has, at last, died. "Not mindless," it wheezes. "Warriors, yes. Indigenous, yes." Its voice is a whisper. I move closer to catch its words, forgetting whatever danger there might be. "Our culture... under attack. Our women... murdered." Its last words are barely intelligible. I press close to hear them. "Invader!" it snarls, denouncing me with its dying thoughts. "Murderer!"

It is a long, long while before I recover enough strength to drag myself out of the depths of Dave's mind and back up to the higher levels. I leave the nightmare where it fell. For some reason I can't bring myself to handle its corpse.

Dave is in the back of a car when I finally surface. He is in handcuffs. There is a police officer driving and another in the passenger seat.

"And after I killed her I had the strangest dream," he is telling them. "There were dragons and tanks and a monster," he says.

"Don't waste it on us, buddy," the driver says. "Save the crazy act for the medical examiner."

Dave ignores him, lost in the strangeness of what has happened to him. "It was so real," he tells them.

His mind is shot. I can feel the many fractures. He will be useless to me now, so I move across to the man in the passenger seat. As soon as I am in him, I feel the horror he felt when they found Dave slumped beside his dead wife, blood all around her head.

"I think there might have been two monsters," Dave says. "Two monsters in my head. I can't be sure."

Nor can I, I realise. Not any more.

Chapter 2

We drive through moonlight. I'm still riding the policeman, whose name is Frank, Detective Frank Taylor. Frank is a human word meaning honest. A tailor is someone who makes clothes. Honest Tailor. My people do not give our children names that mean things. We give them names that signify type, rank and genealogy. Names are for children and lovers – crèche names, pet names – private names. Our names are very complicated but they are rarely used. A soldier is a soldier, a tender just a tender. Only the Vaticinatrix is unique.

Yet, as I watch the moonlight through Frank's eyes, I feel how different I am becoming.

Difference is not the same as pride. I have always been a good soldier – one of the best. That is my genealogy. I come from a long line of good soldiers. Pride comes from fulfilling your role well and serving the Colony. Difference comes from knowing things you should not. Thinking things you should not. It comes from doubt, from a growing, niggling mistrust of your leaders.

That's what I think as I let Frank drive me through the city in his vile-smelling police car. I need to talk to the Vaticinatrix. I need my doubts assuaged. I need to feel I belong again.

I urge Frank to drive the long way, through the park, so I can really see the moonlight. Frank wonders why he is so interested in it. The Moon fills his mind with dark, disturbing images. Nothing real, just stuff he has seen on TV. Vampires and ghosts and werewolves. The reality is much worse than he imagines. Yet I wonder why the delicate silvering of the trees, the pale wash on the parkland, brings out such anxiety in him when it is so very beautiful. He should be grateful to have a moon like that, so large and bright. On all the planets I have visited, this is the first I have seen that is so blessed. Yet Frank never gives it a second thought. It's just the Moon to him. Most nights of his life, he never even looks up at the sky.

We leave the park and wind through the barren canyons of the metropolis. I leave Frank to get on with it and let my thoughts wander.

The Vaticinatrix told us this world was uninhabited – by cognophytes anyway. She told us the nightmares were invaders. The humans, she said, were perfect farm stock, simple, unevolved creatures, just beginning to develop a pre-space technology. But that wasn't quite right either. Some of them are not simple at all. I believe I have noticed an advanced strain among them. There may even be some who would notice our presence. The very idea of being in the mind of someone who knows you're there makes me shudder. It's an unpleasant, creepy idea.

When I make my report to the Colony, speaking to an administrator through Frank's mobile phone, I tell the whole story of my encounter with the nightmare. I report every impossible word it spoke. The response is silence. Then the administrator says, "Thank you, soldier," and hangs up.

-oOo-

Frank lives in a two-room apartment near the police station where he works. The neighbourhood is beat up and worn out, not rough or dangerous, just tired. His apartment is like that too. There is a sagging sofa of indeterminate colour in front of a TV from a decade ago. The place is clean and tidy enough, but it looks like no one would care if everything in it was rounded up tomorrow and driven to the city dump. There are no photographs, no paintings on the walls, no books.

I haven't been paying much attention to Frank but I take a moment to have a look around. Inside, he matches his apartment: tired, sad and sparsely furnished. Out of curiosity, I peer down a layer or two and jump back, reeling. Beneath his placid surface, this man is a roiling mass of self-loathing and despair. His silent screams racket around my mind. Scenes from his tortured childhood leak through the opening I made, sliding out with the everyday horrors of a city cop's memories, merging and darkening everything.

Frank groans and curses and reaches into the freezer for a half-empty bottle of vodka. I move away from the turmoil I have let loose and watch as the walls of Frank's mind doggedly rebuild themselves.

Frank is a man on the edge.

I don't think I'll be staying here long. Yet the small fortress he lives his life inside is at least a quiet place for me to stay while I think things through. I guess he has few friends and expect an un-interrupted night.

When the doorbell rings, I jump as much as Frank does.

We peer out through the spy-hole at the pizza delivery boy on the landing.

"I didn't order a pizza," Frank shouts.

We see the delivery boy check the docket on the box top. "Frank Taylor. Four seasons with extra olives."

I feel Frank's uncertainty. He's done this before, forgotten things he's done, ended up in embarrassing situations. But that's only when he drinks, and he hasn't touched the burning-cold bottle of vodka still in his hand.

"Get lost, kid."

The delivery boy looks annoyed. "Look, Mister Taylor, some-body ordered you a pizza. It's already paid for, so why don't you just let me hand it over?"

I feel a familiar disturbance in my mind. A sniffer, but not one of mine. Another soldier must be around here somewhere.

"I said, get lost," Frank says. "Give it to a homeless guy." He heads to the kitchenette to find a glass for his vodka, dismissing the pizza from his thoughts.

But the boy persists. "You got to sign, Mr. Taylor, or I get into trouble back at the shop."

Sniffers are cognophytes too. They live in the minds of other creatures, just like me. They're stupid, but they're easily trained, and they have an exquisite sensitivity to electromagnetic fields. On Earth there are many animals with sensory abilities so far beyond humanity's that they seem incredible – the hearing of bats, the eyesight of eagles, fish that detect electric currents, birds that feel the planet's magnetic field. Sniffers are like dogs, like bloodhounds. They have a sensitivity to electromagnetic fields that is millions of times beyond my own. They can feel and identify the minute disturbances a single mind makes, even in the EM clutter of a human city. All that radio noise, the power lines, the engines, the magnetic fields, and they can still pick out a single mind if they get within a few hundred metres. And, when they get very close, they can actively probe the field for their prey. That's when even my kind can sense them, like a bad smell on the wind.

Every soldier has a pack of sniffers – a family group of three to five usually. We use them to give us early warning of intruders, and for hunting nightmares. But this is my territory. There shouldn't be another soldier anywhere near here.

My attention snaps back to Frank as I realise he is angrily yanking open the door. I make him stop, flood him with alarm and adrenaline, but it is too late, the door is ajar and the kid out-side kicks it so hard it knocks Frank back. Through Frank's eyes, I see the delivery boy, a scrawny teenager in an ill-fitting red-and-white uniform, throw aside the pizza and snatch up the shotgun that had been resting out of sight beside the door.

Even though Frank is confused and shocked, I get him to focus on his weapon. It is there on the sad old sofa where he tossed it. If he can get there in time, we might just survive. On his own ini-tiative, he hurls the vodka bottle at the kid's head.

Nice one, Frank.

He twists towards the gun, lurches into motion. The boy has to dodge the bottle and his first shot goes wild, smashing up the kitchenette behind us. Frank takes a pace, another one, then dives for the sofa as the boy pumps a new round and swivels the gun towards us. We're not going to make it. I push Frank as hard as I can, but the gun is still too far away.

I feel the hard metal on Frank's fingers, the butt on his palm, one fingertip finds the trigger. The shotgun explodes behind me and the shot slams into Frank's back like a sledgehammer.

He is stunned. His thoughts fragment into fear and shock, but I hold onto him. As he flops onto the sofa, his face pressed into the musty, greasy fabric, I make him pull the gun from its holster, force his eyes to stay open. Out of sight, I hear the delivery boy pumping another shell into the breach. Frank's hand and the gun are under him. Judging it only by the sound, I push the hand out to the side, turn the gun to point behind him, and fire blind. I keep him pulling the trigger until the gun is empty.

Chapter 3

As Frank slowly drifts back to consciousness, so do I. I have been dreaming. I was a hatchling again, flying through a world of mountains and lakes, castles of green stone erupting like geysers from high peaks, my litter-mates squabbling and tumbling all around me, and the gentle, loving presence of the Vaticinatrix filling my whole world. Mother to us all. The very core of our existence.

Ekkri is there with me, my friend, my crèchemate. We fight and swoop and laugh. We go wild among the wide and beautiful spaces of a Treforgan mind, absorbed with the game, fuelled with excitement, racketing among the mountains without a care, being focused on the moment.

Yet, even as I realise how happy and free I am, the dream fades. It thins and disappears and the harder I try to hold it, the more quickly it dissolves.

I wake to whiteness. Whiteness and a dull pain. Then comes memory and the realisation that I am still alive. Alive! I savour the fact with a fierce triumph, as if I am a child again, crowing over a playmate's defeat. Whoever had tried to kill me, I got them first. I killed them. I won. Childish, I agree, but it is a deep and spiritual pleasure to know your enemy is dead and you are not. Especially when it could so easily have been the other way around.

I examine my ride to check what state it is in and find Frank's thoughts in jarring counterpoint to my own. For a moment, I am awash in his bitter disappointment. I feel his tiredness with a life he sees as nothing but pointless endurance. A random death by an unknown assassin would suit Frank just fine. Waking up alive in a hospital bed strikes him as just another cruel trick that life has played on him.

Then he pushes all these thoughts away with a snarling violence and his mind is stark and empty once more.

Jeez, this guy is about ready to be fitted for a padded cell, and I'm way past ready to move on. I don't want to be in here when all that crap he's been suppressing finally erupts. More to the point, I don't want to be lying in a hospital bed when my life might be in danger.

The delivery boy was clearly being ridden. If that was a nightmare in there, it was like nothing I'd ever seen before. They're not the kind to bother with making their rides blast you with a shotgun. They usually just grab you and jump aboard, fangs bared.

Yet maybe I don't know nightmares as well as I thought I did. Maybe I don't know them at all.

And what was with the sniffer? I'm pretty sure that was a sniffer I felt. Are there indigenous cognophytes that have that EM signature? Things we've never encountered? Maybe, but it sure felt like one of ours. And if that was a Colony sniffer, maybe there was a mindrider in the delivery boy...

"Detective Taylor?"

Frank looks across at the person approaching the bed. I see a human female. From his autonomic reactions, I can tell Frank sees an attractive woman. For some reason, his mind flashes pain, loss, regret. It is gone as soon as it appears. Definitely time to go.

"I'm Doctor Nielsen," the woman says, standing by the bed, smiling down at him. "You had a close call."

"I still had my vest on," he says and barks out a bitter laugh. Pain shoots through his upper back and I damp it down.

A tiny frown creases the doctor's brows, but she keeps her expression pretty much under control. "You've got some very bad bruises there, but by some miracle nothing is broken. I'd like to keep you in for a day or so in case there is anything we missed. You need to rest anyway."

"No, I need to get out of here." Frank sure is one tough SOB. Even I seem more worried about his health than he does, and I don't give a damn whether he lives or dies.

He pushes back the sheets and tries to get up. The pain hits him with a blinding fierceness and he slumps back onto the bed.

The doctor leans in to help him and I take my chance. I grab her arm with one of Frank's big hands and clamp it there so I've got a good connection. Then I flow through their bodies' electric fields, leaving Frank and entering Nielsen.

Lights flash and alarms sound. I am in a place of whirling, dizzying complexity. A face appears, a mile high. It is the doctor. She is screaming in terror, yelling at me to get out. Bars spring up all around me, cage upon cage upon cage, until I am buried in metal and blackness. The horrified screaming goes on and on until, recovering my wits, I pull back out of her as fast as I can manage.

I make Frank release her arm and she staggers back from the bed. Horror is in her wide-open eyes and her gaping mouth. She goes back three paces. Four.

"What...?" she gasps.

Frank, who doesn't have a clue what just happened, stares after her.

"What was that? What the hell are you?"

"What the...?" Frank says. He looks at himself, trying to see what the doctor is so terrified of.

Nielsen takes another pace backwards and then turns and runs.

"Wait!" I shout through Frank's mouth, but she has gone. I hear her footsteps running down the corridor. All I can think is, *She knew I was there. She felt me go into her.*

"Frankie, you old dog!"

The man who has just entered the room is an overweight, scruffy-looking individual in his early forties. He carries a cup of coffee in one hand and a paper bag in the other. He is grinning unpleasantly.

"I saw that pretty young thing come running out of here like her ass was on fire. What did you do to her? Tried to feel her tits, right?"

Anger flares inside Frank. The grinning man is Detective Nick Patros, Frank's partner. Nick thinks Frank is a prig with a broom up his ass and he likes to tease him. Frank hates him for it, but never says a word. It makes Frank feel guilty that he hates his partner, but he can't help himself. I get all this in the instant Frank sees Nick.

"I didn't touch her," Frank says, left off-guard by the doctor's behaviour. "That is..." He looks at his own hand, unable to understand what happened. "...I grabbed her, but..."

"Grabbed her butt, eh?" Nick throws the bag into Frank's lap and it opens to reveal grapes inside. "There may be some hope for you yet, old man." Frank is, in fact, ten years younger than Nick, but that's another way that Nick likes to tease him.

"So, you ready to tell us what happened, buddy? Seems the guy you shot..." Nick pulls a notebook out of his jacket and flips it open. "...was a seventeen-year-old kid called Rearden. Want to tell us why he came gunning for you?"

Frank hasn't had a moment to think about it. He shakes his head. Robbery? Vengeance?

"So who is the little punk? Did you know him?"

Frank shakes his head again. "Never seen him before. Never heard of him."

I leave them to their unsolvable mystery. I've got imponderables of my own to chew on. Like how in all space that doctor could have known I was riding her. I need to talk to her. In the space of a few hours so many mysteries have piled up, I am feeling disoriented. I need to nail down at least one of them.

I get Frank to grab Nick's arm, intending to jump across to him and find Dr Nielsen, but I hesitate.

"Hey, you coming on to me or what?" Nick asks.

Frank rationalises his actions. They always do. Whatever crazy stuff you make your ride do, they always work out some reason why they should be doing it. Confabulation is what their psychologists call it. I call it damned convenient.

"Internal Affairs doesn't just think I shot some kid for no reason, do they Nick?"

"Shit no. There's too much forensics says you was the victim here. All we don't have is a motive that would make any kind of sense."

Riding Nick wouldn't get me anywhere. Why would the doctor talk to him about feeling a stranger step into her head? From the way she reacted, she probably thinks she's gone completely nuts. I need someone she confides in, someone she trusts. Failing that, I need Frank.

I give his mind a poke. I can't just lie there. What if somebody tries to kill me again? "Get me out of here, will you?" he says, struggling out of the bed. This time, I'm ready with the pain relief and he makes it to his feet.

"Now, wait a minute!"

"I can't just lie here, Nick. What if someone else tries to kill me? What if it's one of the nurses this time, or a visitor on the ward? This thing has got me freaked."

"Frank, you crazy bastard. You just took a shotgun round at close range, you should-"

I should talk to the doctor.

"Will you get me my clothes? They're probably in that cupboard there."

Nick goes for the clothes, but he's still protesting. "This is stupid, Frank. How the hell are you even standing up? You should be in your bed, on morphine or some shit like that."

"Yeah, I should talk to the doctor." He takes his clothes and starts to dress. "Look, I'll see the doctor before I go. OK? I'll square it with her. Happy?"

I need to get rid of Nick.

"No."

"Well that's tough. Look, Nick. Thanks for coming over, but I don't need you holding my hand. I need you out there working the case. I want to know what happened. I want to know if I'm a target or something. Yeah?"

Nick's long-time habit of thinking of his partner as a screwball comes to my rescue.

"You're a strange guy, Taylor," he says. "What are you going to do?"

"I'm going to find a little hotel room somewhere and lie low until you've worked it out and I know I'm safe. I can't go home, right? The place is a crime scene anyway. Help me find the doc, and then you can leave me to it."

"Sure."

Nick disappears for a few minutes and comes back with a piece of paper and hands it to Frank. I see it has a mobile phone number written on it.

"The doc's gone missing," he says, "but the little cutie at the desk says this is her cell." He grins. "She also says she's busy tonight, which I assume is a lie. You're going to stay here until the doc turns up, yeah?"

"Yeah. Don't worry."

As soon as Nick has gone, I make Frank call the number. It rings for a while before the answer machine cuts in.

"Doctor Nielsen," I say, through Frank. "This is Frank Taylor. We need to talk about what just happened. Call me." I give her Frank's number and hang up.

I wait, looking down at the phone in Frank's hand for maybe two or three minutes before it rings.

"This is Dr. Nielsen."

"Can we meet somewhere, please? Something very strange happened when you came to my room. I want to try and understand what it was. This is very important, Doctor."

There is a long, long pause. "There's a café by the main entrance. I can get a nurse to put you in a wheelchair and take you there."

"That's OK, I'll walk. I'll see you in five minutes."

I hang up before she can argue and set off.

-oOo-

It takes me more than five minutes to reach the café, changing levels, crossing between buildings, travelling endless corridors. When I arrive she is already there. I weave between tightly-packed tables and take a seat opposite her.

"Thank you for meeting me," I say.

She is frowning at me. "How can you possibly be walking around?"

I make Frank smile. "I have exceptional willpower." Sometimes I forget to do all the facial expressions when I take complete control of my ride. It tends to creep other humans out. But today I am on my best behaviour. I don't want the doctor to run off again.

I can see her ponder this for a moment and then dismiss it, making herself focus on what's important, I suppose.

"You wanted to talk," she says.

The café is full and noisy, all the chattering people lean towards one another, competing with the babble and the hissing, screeching cappuccino machine. We won't be overheard.

"When I touched you..." She flinches at the memory, drawing back a little, as if I might reach out and grab her again. I carefully move Frank's hands off the table and put them in his lap. "...you felt something. You felt as if I was there with you, inside your head."

Her eyes are wide and her nostrils flaring. "How could you know that? What did you do to me?"

"Have you ever felt it before? Has anyone else got inside your mind?"

"No. No, of course not!"

"Have you ever been able to go into other people's minds?" I am groping for anything that might help.

"It was some kind of trick," she says. "You... You hypnotised me, or something. Who are you?"

"It wasn't a trick. I promise you. I can move between..." This is hopeless. How do you begin to explain to a human how a cognophyte lives? "Look, I need to understand how you knew I was there. It is very important." *All right. How about a demonstration?*

"I want you to pay attention to the woman sitting to my right." I reach out a hand and take the woman next to me by the shoulder. In a moment, I have flowed into her. I make her turn to look at Dr. Nielsen and say, "I can move between minds..." I make the woman touch a man to her right. He turns to Nielsen and says, "...as easily as you walk between rooms." The man touches a child and the child steps up to our table. I make him say, "No one whose mind I have entered ever knew I was there." The child puts his hand on Frank's and I am back where I started. "Until I tried to enter you."

The doctor jumps to her feet, knocking the table and spilling her coffee. Her chair clatters back into someone else's. She raises a hand to her mouth, staring in horror from one to the other of the players in my little demonstration. With a small, stifled cry, she pushes through the room and runs for the exit.

I let her go, kicking myself for being such an idiot. Warm coffee is dribbling from the table onto Frank's lap and people all around are looking at him and murmuring to one another. I yield control of Frank and let him deal with getting himself out of there. I need to be alone to think for a while.

Chapter 4

How do you know who you are when everything that defines you is called into question?

I sit in a tiny room in a tiny hotel calling itself Miramar or Bayview or somesuch. Frank brought us here and paid cash for the room. I'm glad he's able to look after things like that on his own because, honestly, I'm starting to feel a bit low.

I have three astonishing facts to ponder, any one of which would be enough to upset my equilibrium. The nightmares – or some of them, anyway – might be more than the simple brutes I had always been taught to believe they were. There is at least one human – so there are probably others – who is self-aware enough to know when one of my kind enters its mind. And, most unsettling of all, a soldier from my own colony tried to kill me last night.

I don't know what any of these things mean. I feel as if I don't know anything for sure any more. Everything I thought I knew is a lie.

I keep my sniffers close. They surround the hotel. But what good is that if my own people are trying to kill me?

We came to Earth from a world called Treforga. My people had done well there. We had spread and multiplied until almost all two hundred million Treforgans hosted a mindrider. As ever, when this stage is reached, new colonies, or fast-growing colonies, were under pressure to move off-world. Mine was a young colony and a vigorous one. Our Vaticinatrix decided we would do better on a new world than trying to grow our numbers on Treforga.

Treforgan technology was pushed forward. Their scientists and engineers were given the necessary clues to drive their simple, in-system space technologies towards true interstellar capabilities. And so we left, on a shiny new Treforgan starship. Eventually, we found Earth. Luckily, planets with suitably-intelligent hosts are plentiful.

Planets like Earth, however, are rare indeed. Seven billion hosts and not an indigenous cognophyte in sight! It represented riches beyond our wildest dreams.

Hang on. What's Frank up to? He has strapped on his shoulder holster with the big police-issue Glock pistol and is heading for the door, his teeth clenched against the pain of putting on his jacket. I glance around inside his head, to see what he's up to.

He's going to the police station to talk to Nick about how the investigation is going.

Should I let him go?

Why not? It's not as if I care what he does, as long as it doesn't get me killed.

He leaves the room and locks it behind him. He takes the stairs down to the lobby, even though the lift would have been kinder on his back. He takes a second to check with the guy on the desk that no one has been asking for him. Then he steps out of the doors, pausing to give the street a casual but expert appraisal before he strides out into the street and on his way.

You know? I could have picked a worse ride than Frank. He's careful, a bit paranoid, streetwise, and armed. And that's pretty much just what I need right now. I decide there and then to stick with him a while longer. And that means doing an inventory of his soul to see what kind of junk he has lying around in his psyche that I can use.

Like any good rider, I need to know my ride. Like any good soldier, alone in enemy territory, I need to understand the terrain and identify useful materiel. I need to know where I can run to, where I can lay ambushes, where to make a stand, and where the exits are. I've already had a taste of Frank's inner mind and it wasn't pleasant, but I'm ready for it now. Steeling myself, I plunge below the surface.

It is dark inside Frank. Dark streets wind between looming buildings. Every doorway is a shadow, every alley a black void.

There are people, barely glimpsed as they pull back out of sight. Small things scuttle in the corners of your eye, too quick to see. There are monsters too, bulky, powerful creatures that lumber through the streets, vague and menacing. The threat of violence and death hangs like smoke in the damp air.

OK, not exactly Disneyland, but not so bad, really. Somewhere below this murk, I expect I'll find where the monsters come from. Frank isn't so different from other humans I've ridden, just a bit more extreme is all. I blame it on them being mammals. All that dependence on a pair of parents for all those years. It's got to do strange things to a kid's mind. Then that damaged child grows up, meets another twisted human and they raise kids of their own. It's a miracle this species survives at all. Lucky for them, nature doesn't care how crazy they get, just so long as they keep pumping out babies.

There is a blasted ruin up ahead. It might have been a magnificent cathedral once, but now it is all crumbling walls and shattered towers. I look inside and find only wreckage and decay except in the corner of a small chapel where the ground has been cleared and swept clean. There I find a slab set into the floor to mark a grave. There are fresh cut flowers – fresias – on the slab and the inscription says only "Janey". The scent of the flowers is wonderful after so much dank and putrid staleness.

Well, Frank, I think we've established you're a morbid and depressive type but I haven't found much I can use yet. I keep on looking. In a row of shops I find a gunsmith selling the most improbable, outsize weapons. The fact that the shop is in good repair tells me Frank goes there from time to time to find something to help him face his demons. I note where it is and move on.

There is light ahead of me and I head for it. A nicer part of town, maybe. I can hear traffic and the sounds of people in the streets. I hurry on, puzzled by it. I didn't expect anything clean and bright and vibrant down here. What could it possibly mean?

A massive, dark figure steps into the street ahead of me, blocking the light, towering high above the parked cars and street lights. The figure is a man, powerful and evil, with fixed, staring eyes and clenched fists like granite boulders. A thought flits by and I snag it. *Father.*

Now that's more like it! At last I've found what I need, the monster in Frank's unconscious that is so bad, so mean and so fearful, that nothing could stand against it. It is built of purest fear and endowed with a lifetime of acknowledging its unbeatable, unstoppable malevolence. It is the perfect monster for me to use against all comers. Anyone or anything tries to take me on in here and Frank's dad is my new best friend.

Cheered up immensely, I head back up to the surface to see what my ride is up to.

Frank is having some kind of argument with his boss at the police station. They are both angry and trying to remain professional about it but it is clear that they are both very emotional and neither is the least bit happy.

"Just go home and rest for chrissakes Frank. Jesus, you should still be in hospital from what I hear."

"I don't want to sit around doing nothing when I could be out working the case."

"Working the case? Are you nuts? For a start, people are telling me I should arrest you for murder."

"Murder? What happened to self-defence?"

"Tell it to the DA's office, Frank. They've got some punk kid hotshot who's got you painted as an unstable psycho who needs to be dragged off the streets in the public interest. All kind of shit is floating to the surface, Frank."

Fury crashes through Frank's mind like a small tornado. I get a flood of memories from a time about two years ago. They have Frank in a psychiatric ward. He's a voluntary patient but he's scared about something he did, about things he might yet do.

"It was a brief episode, Al," Frank says, barely holding his voice steady. "You were there. You know what was going on. That's all behind me now. I've moved on."

Not from where I'm sitting, Frankie boy!

"Yeah, yeah!" His boss is conciliatory, a bit embarrassed per-haps. "I know, Frank. But it's there on your record. It's not going to look good if some prosecutor reads it out in court."

Frank's anger is getting the better of him. He isn't thinking clearly and I'm beginning to think I should just get him out of there – or switch rides. But I need to see that doctor again.

Nielsen. I need to try to talk to her one more time. So I stick with Frank.

"So what now, Al? You going to just hang me out to dry? You going to leave me sitting at home chewing my nails down waiting for a couple of uniforms to come and pick me up?"

"Frank, it isn't like that. All I'm saying is questions are being asked. Some people got opinions. No one here thinks you did anything wrong. It just... None of this makes sense. That kid with the shotgun, he was a frigging boyscout. No record, good grades, reliable worker, good family. Shit, that whole family is so clean you could eat off them. Then, one day, he steals the gun from behind the counter at the pizza place where he works and heads over to your apartment. Does that make sense, Frank?"

Frank shakes his head. He's been telling himself the kid held a grudge, maybe Frank had put away the kid's old man, or his brother, or something. Maybe he was in with some street gang, doing his initiation, or settling a score for them. But if the kid was clean, the whole thing looked personal – like a lover's tiff, or some kind of deal gone wrong. He could see just how it would look. The same thoughts must be going through Al's mind as are going through his own.

"I'm the victim here, Al. I don't understand it any more than you do, but I'm the victim. People got to remember that." Fear is starting to replace anger in Frank's mind as it becomes clear just what kind of a mess he is in. He wants to ask for his gun and his badge. They'd taken the gun as evidence and his badge hadn't been with his clothes when he got dressed at the hospital. Now he can see it would be impossible to get them back. As long as he is recuperating he is OK, but the minute he is fit for duty, they will suspend him. Without Al's cooperation, there is no way he can work the case. Even with it, he will be lucky to avoid being arrested for murder.

The silence drags out.

"Internal Affairs want to talk to you when you're ready," his boss says. His tone is sympathetic.

"Yeah. Right." Frank is defeated. He wants to be alone. "I'm going home to rest, OK?" I nudge a thought into his head. "Maybe I'll go back to the hospital. I feel like I was hit by a truck."

"Don't worry Frank. You got friends here, you know? Just remember that. OK?"

Al's tone is kind, affectionate even. The man really does like Frank. I can't see why, myself, but maybe there is more to their history than I know yet. Not that it is any interest of mine. I am more concerned about what to do next to sort out my own problems. Al asks where Frank is staying and I make Frank write down the wrong hotel and the wrong address.

-oOo-

Back in the street, I call my sniffers to me and get them organised to keep a box around Frank as he walks towards the hospital. He is still twitchy and is scanning the street constantly. I consider for a moment taking the idea that he is in danger out of his mind. It's sort of irritating when your ride is so anxious. Yet, even though Frank would be no good at spotting a nightmare or a mindrider, he seems to be well trained at spotting human dangers.

I watch him work for a while. He is noting people in the street, checking how they move, what they look at, how their position changes relative to himself. He stops to tie his shoelaces, checking reflections in a shop window, he steps suddenly into a shop and stands inside watching what people do in the street outside. It is interesting. I've never ridden someone with Frank's training before. I can see how his skills could be useful, if you were stuck without any sniffers, say.

I suppose I am just passing the time, letting myself be distracted, so I don't have to think about what it means that a mindrider has tried to kill me. Was he sent by someone? Someone in the Colony? It is such a ridiculous notion that my speculations veer off in all kinds of crazy directions. Can there be a second Colony here on Earth, one we don't know about? Can the nightmares control the sniffers somehow? Can they even control a mindrider? There isn't a single idea that crosses my mind that doesn't scare the hell out of me.

So when I feel a jolt of fear pass through Frank, I am disoriented for a second, as if he is feeling my own emotions.

Frank has been watching for people trailing him in the street, so we're both surprised when a black van mounts the kerb right in front of us and three men jump out of the side door. Two of them grab Frank in a quick, coordinated assault, while the third stands ready at the van. He is holding a syringe and Frank bucks and kicks at the sight of it.

Long before they can drag him the two paces to the van, I have jumped across to one of the men holding Frank. I'm ready for trouble, ready to meet the mindrider or whatever is inside him, but I find myself alone. I search around quickly for some clue as to what is going on, but this is just an ordinary human. Well, maybe not quite ordinary. He is part of the human military, a member of a special ops team, and he has orders to capture and kill Frank.

Astonished by this new revelation I almost let the guy with the syringe stick it in Frank's neck. I make my new ride reach out and grab the man's arm, twisting it hard so he drops whatever he was about to jab Frank with. Both of the other attackers are now watching my ride with shock in their eyes. My man is carrying a handgun, so I draw it quickly and shoot both of them. They fall dead in the street. My ride is a good shot.

A woman screams and I glance around. Several people are staring at us. One is reaching for his phone. Frank is looking dazed and frightened, probably thinking he will be next. I grab his arm and shove him into the van shouting, "Get in! I'll explain ev-erything once we're moving." He stumbles into the van and I slam the doors on him and run round the van to the driver's side.

As I round the back of the van, I find the driver crouching there beside the vehicle. He has a gun pointed at me.

"Jesus, Brad, I nearly shot you! What the fuck is–"

My ride drops him with a single shot and I get him into the van and drive away from there as fast as I can safely go. I glance in the back at where Frank is bracing himself against the van's erratic motion. His face is ashen and I realise that, without me to damp down the pain, his back must be in agony again.

"Don't worry," I shout. "You're safe now."

It isn't quite true. The cops will be tailing this van within minutes and, for all I know, Brad's army unit is tracking it too.

I make Brad take a complicated route through the city centre and about ten blocks on, park the van in an underground garage. We all get out and run for the exit.

Chapter 5

Humans are not like us. Their awareness is adrift in a sea of emotion. Their consciousness bobs around on massive waves of primitive need, like a storm-tossed ping-pong ball. And their minds are fragile, and fracture easily. These people damage one another, they damage themselves, just being alive damages them, sometimes beyond repair.

Frank is a case in point. His mind is a black and ugly place and his awareness skates over the top of it, always on the edge of being sucked in. It would take very little to break that delicate crust he is standing on and have him disappear below the surface forever. So I watch him across the café table and I try to pick my words carefully. It helps that he believes my ride will shoot him if he tries to leave. It keeps him focused.

And I need him focused. I need Frank to understand what kind of danger he is in so that I can keep him safe. And I need him safe so that I can use him to approach Dr. Nielsen and get the answers I want from her. I don't know why, but I suspect her awareness of my presence in her mind is an important clue to the mystery that surrounds me.

But what can I say to this human to make him understand what is happening, especially when I do not understand it myself? Whatever it is, I need to get it over with quickly. It is tiring having to control a ride completely for as long as I have controlled this one. Mostly you control a ride with little nudges of motivation, the surreptitious insertion of ideas, a quick lash of fear or desire. To take them over completely, to direct every muscle, to suppress or disconnect their thoughts, is easy enough with training and practice, but it requires a lot of concentration and you soon get tired. I could already feel my strength ebbing. Another ten minutes or so and I would start slipping, making little mistakes. Five minutes after that and I'd have to set him loose.

"What the hell is going on here?" Frank says through gritted teeth. He is keeping his voice low and trying not to seem too agitated. Having ridden him for a while I can tell what he is thinking. He doesn't want to start a fight, to cause me to start shooting here in this café where innocent civilians might get hurt. That's why I brought him here.

"This man is a soldier," I say. "Part of a special ops team sent to kill me."

He looks side to side then back at me. "What man?" he asks.

I curse my stupidity. Twice in two days now I have tried to tell a human about myself. If I'm going to keep breaking the Colony law, I should really try to make a better job of it.

"Frank, do you believe that aliens could visit the Earth?" I already know the answer. He believes in ghosts, vampires, evil spirits, all kinds of nonsense, but the one thing that it is actually reasonable to believe in, he thinks is total rubbish. "Well, it's happened."

He is watching me warily, trying to decide what kind of nutcase he is dealing with, I suppose.

"I am not human," I tell him, flatly. "I am a soldier from another world, part of a group of colonists who have come to settle your planet."

"What the hell is this?" he says, his face a snarl. "Cut the bullshit and tell me who's trying to kill me."

In one ear and out the other. Typical bloody human!

"Frank, I saved your life back there. You could at least listen to what I'm saying."

He glares at me resentfully. "A special ops unit, you say?"

So he was listening. "This body, this man you see in front of you, was one of them. I'm riding him. I'm inside his head controlling his every action. I know who he is, who his bosses are, where he's billeted, where he trained, his whole life story if I want it. He is a legitimate member of your government's armed forces. He received orders to kill you through the regular chain of command."

Frank is still looking at me like I'm about to run amok. "Do you believe that shit you just said?" he asks. "About being an alien inside this man's body?"

"Look Frank, you don't have to believe me. I'm only telling you this as a courtesy. I shouldn't be talking to you at all, but it's like this: these people are not after you. You don't matter a damn to anyone. It's me they want to kill."

Frank looks angry. His hands have moved to the edge of the table and I suspect he is getting ready to shove it at me and make a run for it. "The Army wants you dead," he says, clearly stalling. "Not you the big dumb ox with a gun pointed at me, but you the alien invader inside his head."

"Frank, don't try to run. This big dumb ox is a trained killer. He is faster than you and he is a very accurate shot. I can easily use him to kill you if you try to escape."

A snarl of frustration crosses his face but his body relaxes and he sits back. "So what's all this got to do with me?"

"I've been riding you... I've been inside your head for the past couple of days, ever since you and your partner took that call on Brooke Street."

"The guy who killed his wife."

"That's the one. There's a war going on, Frank. My people are peaceful colonists. All we want to do is settle here and live quiet lives, but there are others like us – other cognophytes – on your planet and they're fighting us."

Frank shook his head rapidly, as if trying to shake off all the crap I was dumping on him. "You still haven't told me what any of this has got to do with me."

"That kid who shot you–" His eyes widen and become fixed. All his attention is on my ride. "–was trying to kill me too. He was being ridden by one of my own kind."

It isn't the information he's looking for. He can't take this back to his boss. "By one of these enemies of yours, right?"

"No, by another colonist. Frank, I don't have much more time. I've got to ditch this guy soon and get back inside you. There's something weird going on. My own people want me dead. Your government wants me dead – and they shouldn't even know I exist – and that doctor of yours, Nielsen, might have some of the answers."

"Nielsen?"

His question is so stupid and confused I pull up short. Why am I talking to this man? What am I thinking? I should be doing something useful, tracking down the information I need, not chatting away to the farm animals. The attack by the humans must have upset me more than I know. I search my motivations and to my surprise I discover how scared and alone I feel.

I make my ride stand up and signal Frank to do the same.

"I'm sorry, Frank. Forget it. I just needed someone to unburden myself to, and it seems you're the only one I've got. OK. I need to dump this guy now."

I take the gun out and hand it to Frank, butt first. He looks at it stupidly for a moment, then takes hold of it. As soon as he has a firm grip and his local field is connected to my ride's, I transfer myself across to him, leaving behind a strong suggestion that the guy should run for his life.

And he does. He takes off like a scalded cat, leaping across tables and barging through surprised diners until he is out of sight. Frank, considers chasing him, but only for a moment. His back is in agony and he is in no condition for a sprint across town. He looks up and notices all the alarmed people staring at him and backing away.

"It's all right, I'm a cop," he says, reaching for his badge. But the badge isn't there. Nevertheless, it seems to calm people. Quickly, he pockets the gun and leaves the café.

-oOo-

From the inside, it is clear that Frank doesn't believe a word I told him about myself. The only way he can rationalise what has happened is if it is all a case of mistaken identity. The kid with the gun, the wet team in the van, they were after some other guy. The fact that one of his would-be assassins was a certifiable, raving nut-job was just pure luck. Baffling, bizarre, blind, beautiful luck.

But now he has to call his boss and report three homicides and a raving madman on the loose. I leave him to it and take a rest. Controlling that soldier was tiring work and I need to recharge.

-oOo-

Next time I pay Frank any attention, he's in the police station again with his partner and his boss.

"Didn't I tell you to go home and rest?" the boss is saying. "Jesus, Frank, you look like shit. And now what have we got? We've got three more homicides and your prints all over the murder weapon, that's what we've got."

Frank stirs himself to a mild irritation. "That's bullshit, Al, and you know it. There were a dozen witnesses on that street who saw me grabbed and then saw that big, crazy bastard shoot the others. Don't tell me nobody called it in. Don't tell me you haven't been checking up on that son-of-a-bitch."

His partner, Nick, chimes in. "All Al is saying is, what the fuck is going on, Frank? You gotta know something. Why are all these guys suddenly queueing up to bump off an insignificant nobody like you? No offence."

Frank is tired of going over the same ground. The case has been taken out of Al's hands and given to a different section and neither Al nor Nick likes the implication that they can't be trusted. It's making them mean.

Since getting back to the station, Frank has been interviewed by a couple of hardasses from Homicide and by a different hardass from Internal Affairs. The whole thing is getting out of control and it is clear to Frank that nobody has a clue what is happening.

I am surprised to discover that Frank chose not to tell his interviewers about what I told him in the café. He reckons he is in enough trouble without making himself a laughing stock by talking about alien invasions.

"You're on suspension, Frank," Al says. "It's official. Nothing to do with me. It came down from above." As an afterthought, he says, "Sorry."

Frank gets up and heads to the door. "You know what? I don't need this shit. The whole Department is treating me like I'm a mass-murdering psycho. I thought after fifteen years in the job I'd be entitled to some kind of respect."

Nick seems genuinely hurt. "Don't be like that, buddy. You know we got your back."

Frank does not deign to contradict him, just leaves, feeling sorry for himself, and heads off home. I pop Nielsen's name into his head and he remembers the nut-job with the gun telling him that the doctor might have some of the answers. He hails a cab and heads for the hospital. To Frank, this makes less sense than it does to me, but the fact that I mentioned Nielsen is a puzzling fact and he latches onto it, elevating it to the status of his only lead.

The skies are darkening as evening approaches. The cab grinds its way slowly through the rush-hour traffic. The cabbie starts up a conversation and keeps it up in return for the occasional grunt from Frank. The gathering gloom reveals that lights are on in the shops and office blocks we crawl past. By the time we reach the hospital, the street lights and car lights are on too. Frank gets out and I make him look up for the Moon, but it is nowhere in sight.

-oOo-

The hospital has a huge reception area. Padded bench seats form rows in front of a long reception desk, making the place look a bit like an airport terminal. There is just one person at the desk. It is out of office hours and no one is arriving for appointments.

Off to the left is a café, closed and gloomy, and ahead is a broad corridor with elevators along one wall. Frank ignores the reception and heads straight for the board listing all the consultants and their office locations. Nielsen is listed as a Consulting Orthopaedic Surgeon and has a string of letters after her name.

"Frank?"

He turns sharply, sending a jolt of pain through his back. A woman is rising from one of the bench seats, grabbing up her bag and a magazine, hurrying to catch him. She is a small woman of about Frank's age, delicate and large eyed. He watches her approach with something like despair. Memories flip out from the dark cracks Frank has stuffed them into and hurt him more than his back does.

For an instant his mind is full of the need to run, to get away from this woman, to hide somewhere, but thoughts of flight are quickly scattered by a sense of overwhelming, miserable defeat. There is no escaping this. There is only passive endurance and the hope that the misery won't last too long.

"Hello, Tess," he says.

"Frank, are you OK?" She bustles up to him, inspecting him. She is Tess Corrigan, I see from the memories flying loose and loud in Frank's head, Janey's sister. Janey. Frank's wife. Frank's dead wife, who died...

A massive wash of pain cuts off all coherent thought of Janey. But I catch glimpses. She looks a bit like the woman looking up at Frank with concern in her eyes. Younger. Smiling. Then I see her in a bedroom, tied to a bed, cuts across her naked body, blood soaking the sheets, smeared across her body, across the walls. And the same scene in police photographs, caught from every angle, sharp and clear.

"Al called me and said you'd been hurt," Tess says. She puts a hand on his arm and he has to fight not to flinch. "He told me an address, a little hotel, but they didn't know you there. Al said to try the hospital.

"What's going on Frank? Why are you walking around? You just got shot. You should be in bed."

From her enormous desk, the receptionist watches them over the top of her book.

"I'm OK, Tess. It was nothing. I had a vest on. It's just bruises. You shouldn't have come all this way." Tess lives right across town, with her husband Jack and their two kids whose names Frank never learned.

"Do you think Janey would ever forgive me if I heard you were shot and just ignored you?"

"Janey's..." Dead. Dead, dead, dead, dead, dead.

"I gotta go, Tess."

He walks towards the elevators and Tess follows him.

"If it's Doctor Nielsen you came to see, she's not here."

"What?"

"She went home. It's late, Frank. I talked to the nurse at the desk. Doctor Nielsen went home."

The stupidity of what he is doing hits Frank hard. How could he have thought she'd be here? He looks at his watch. It's nearly seven.

"Frank?" Tess touches him again. Her big eyes are troubled. "Frank, you look like you need a good sleep. A hot bath, maybe? Take it easy for a while. Why don't you come home with me? Jack would be pleased to see you. And the kids. You could stay a few days, until you're feeling better."

He shakes his head. What she is suggesting would be torment. Can't the woman see? He moves past her, letting her hand fall away, and steps across to the desk.

"I need Dr. Nielsen's home address," he tells the receptionist. "It's important that I see her."

"I'm sorry sir, but we can't give out that kind of information."

"I'm a cop," he says, reaching for his shield. "I need to talk to her on an urgent matter." But the shield still isn't there.

Anger flares inside him. More stupidity! He turns away from the receptionist, who is eyeing him nervously. Tess is there behind him, anxious and uncertain. He makes an effort to pull himself together.

"I'm sorry, Tess. There's a lot going on. It's... It's good to see you, but Al shouldn't have made you come all this way for nothing. I'm fine. I'm just... I've got a lot on my mind. I need to get to the bottom..." He draws a breath, trying to steady himself. "You go on back to Jack and the kids. Say hi from me. I'll... I'll try to get over some time."

For some reason Frank can't understand, there are tears in Tess's eyes. "What happened to Janey..." she says, and alarm bells go off all over Frank's mind. Shutters slam down. Defences go up. "...it was a long time ago, Frank. You've got to let it go. She wouldn't want this."

"Yeah," he says, too loudly. "You're right. Look, it was great to see you." He strides past her to the big, sliding doors. The doors roll open and he beckons a cab that is waiting there. The only one on this quiet evening. "Let me get you a cab to the station. You should be heading back. It's quite a trip." She follows him out and up to the cab. He holds open the door for her and she stands beside it, looking up at him. There are tears on her cheeks and her eyes glisten in the light spilling out from the foyer.

"Goodbye Frank," she says, softly.

He puts a smile on his face. "Have a safe trip back. Thanks for coming to see me, but I'm fine."

She nods and lets her gaze fall, defeated. She gets into the cab and Frank closes the door on her.

"Bye Tess," he calls as it pulls away. She doesn't turn to look at him.

Chapter 6

I've mentioned how fragile human awareness is. Well, here's another example: they can lose their consciousness. In fact, they loose it at least once a day. Mostly, it is because of what they call sleep, but many kinds of physical, chemical or electrical trauma can cause it.

None of us from the Colony have experienced sleep before and the Metacolony has only one other example from a previously-encountered species. It is hard to get used to.

When your ride loses consciousness, much of its brain activity decreases to a minimal level. That means it's hard to stay alive in there. You have to retreat into whatever parts are still active, store non-essential functions, and hope that you can keep your core alive until the ride wakes up. It's scary when it first happens, even when you know it is coming and you've been trained in how to survive it.

The worst thing is how vulnerable it makes you. Some of us hate it so much they switch rides every night, always finding someone who will stay awake. A trip to an all-night diner is a favourite tactic. You'd be surprised how many of the staff in those places have got mindriders in their heads after dark.

Some of us are more relaxed about it. Sleep isn't just on or off. There are many degrees of it, and for most stages of sleep you can get along quite happily. It's only the really deep phases, blocks of about twenty minutes about four times each night, when you have to hunker down and wait it out. With some humans it's not even that bad. Take Frank, for example. He's such an insomniac he barely sleeps four hours in every twenty-four.

So I let him go back to his crummy hotel, fall face down onto his bed, and pass out.

-oOo-

In the small hours of the night, I get a yelp from my sniffers. Something is coming.

I take Frank's emotional centres by the neck and give them a shake. In moments, his sleeping brain is flooded with fear and his sluggish adrenal glands are pumping epinephrine through his veins. As the lights come on across his fuddled brain, I kick and shout and pile on the anxiety. *Wake up, damn you!*

With a gasp, he starts into consciousness, sitting up in bed and looking wildly around the room.

In the shadows by the door, a man is standing. He is bulky and shapeless but I see his hands are hanging loosely at his sides. No weapon is visible. The sniffers are going wild, telling me there is a nightmare nearby. I shut them up with a command.

Frank turns on the light and I give him a moment to inspect the intruder and recognise him if he can. Frank's mind is fuddled with sleep and with all the fear I've been filling him with, but it is quickly obvious that he doesn't know this man.

The man is scruffy. In fact, his clothes are rags. Even from across the room I can smell him. He is whiskered and his skin is weathered. He wears so many layers of clothing it distorts his shape.

"You are one of the murderers," the tramp says in a flat tone. His expression is blank. Whatever is riding him is making no effort to pretend this is a normal human. "You are the one who killed Berreg."

The tramp stands silently waiting for an answer, as lifeless as a puppet in a shop window. I let Frank grab his gun from the bedside table and line it up on the man. Once he has him covered, Frank relaxes a little.

"Who are you? What do you want?"

The tramp remains motionless. I set Frank aside and take control.

"You are a nightmare," I say. Its mind creates such a distortion in the local field it smells worse than the vagrant it's riding.

"Murderer," the thing in the tramp says. Its voice is full of hatred, despite the human's expressionless face. "Invader."

"Here I am, if you want to try your luck." Despite my bravado, I am tense and anxious. I face another impossible nightmare that can speak, a sentient being like the other one, the one that had been so hard to kill.

"I could have killed you," the tramp says. "I could have killed you while your host slept. I wanted to. I wished that I could. Remember that, Invader." He turned to the door and opened it. "Now come with me."

He leads me out of the hotel and into the street. There are two more vagrants waiting. They also smell of nightmare, but they do not speak. Together we walk through the quiet city to a deserted alley. Six more tramps emerge from the shadows as we near them. I am so grossly outnumbered now that there is no hope at all of surviving a fight. I keep Frank's gun cocked and ready just in case. If I do not survive this, many of them will die with me.

The nine tramps move stiffly like wooden soldiers into some kind of formation, all facing me. I realise it is a diamond, with me at one of the points. The guy at the back puts his hands on the shoulders of the two in front. They put their hands on the shoulders of the three ahead of them, who also do the same. In moments they are all connected, back to front, hands to shoulders. Then the one in front of me raises a hand towards my shoulder. Alarmed, I step back, out of reach. His hand hovers in the air.

"If we wanted to do you harm, we could have done that easily by now, Mindrider."

The whole group waits silently while I make up my mind. Run? Or step forward into who knows what danger? How I long for the chance to rejoin the Colony and share my fears with my people. But I am alone. I dare not return to be among those who have tried to kill me. Not until I understand more. Alone, uncertain, growing apart. Scared of my own people, scared of these sentient nightmares, scared even of the humans and what their military might know.

I need answers. I need answers more than I fear for my life.

I step forward.

The vagrant lowers his hand onto my shoulder and the dark alley is gone. I am in a place altogether darker.

An endless plain. Grey, cindery dirt beneath me and oily, black clouds above. The clouds churn. They are streaked with red, as if a great fire burns within them. Nothing is alive. All that marks the plain are the charred stumps of trees. A thin wind carries flakes of ash, or maybe snow. Despite the burning clouds, it is cold.

The nine nightmares stand in a circle around me. Their black hides make them impossible to focus on in the gloom. They are huge. Bigger than any I have seen before until the last one I killed. They shift on clawed feet, writhing like snakes, their faces all teeth and snarling hatred. Their leathery wings lifting and rustling, ready for quick, violent action. From the narrow slits of their orange eyes to the vicious spikes along their spines, everything about them speaks of power and strength. Their gyring restless movements speak of a barely restrained yearning to tear me to pieces.

Could this all be taken from the tramp's mind? Or have these creatures some way to impose their own mental constructs on the inner landscape of a human brain? And if so, why choose to create such a bleak and blasted world?

"You have killed many muliebri," a voice behind me says.

I turn to face it. It looks as ugly and cruel as the rest. "Is that what you call yourself? The Muliebri?"

"It is a fool," says another.

And another wails, "They do not even understand what they do."

"Enlighten me then," I say to the first speaker. "I thought – we all thought – that you were mindless animals. Worse than the humans. We were told that you were the invaders. A plague of vermin, to be eradicated lest you spoil our harvest."

"It lies!"

"Destroy it!"

The first speaker glares around at its fellows. "Silence! You know the law. This one defeated Berreg, Chief Warrior of the Drokkan. It is owed a clandebt."

"The law is for The People, not creatures like this!"

"Silence, I say! I am Chief Warrior now. I enforce the law. Will anyone dispute that?"

The challenger ducks its head in an unmistakeably subservient gesture, but it is still snarling, and its baleful orange eyes fix themselves on me.

With a final glare at the others, the Chief Warrior turns again to me. "This is how we pay our debt, murderer. We give you a warning. We give you information." The others hiss and growl. "Your invasion is two years old now. We watched you arrive. We know where you settled. We watched you deploy your soldiers. We fell back as your slaughter began. Only the muliebri were foolish enough to keep returning to the territory you had taken. The rest of us waited for you to take enough, to stop and be satisfied. The Council of Clans drew a line around you. If you stopped within that line you would be allowed to stay. If not, the Drokken would act to contain you. Or to eradicate you."

We should not be here on this planet. It is against our own laws to settle a world already inhabited by intelligent cognophytes. Yet the creature's talk of containing or eradicating my people fills me with indignation. Who were they to presume to threaten the Colony? I fight down the urge to challenge them. Something is very wrong. Some part of me can see that we are not on Earth by accident, that the Vaticinatrix could not have made such a mistake.

"You should talk to my leaders," I say. "This is a matter that should be resolved through negotiation, not by fighting."

"You've scared it," says one.

"Suddenly it wants to talk," says another.

The Chief shouts over them. "There will be no more talking. The debt is paid, invader. You have your warning. Justice has been done by you."

"No, wait! At least tell me where this line is. At least let me pass that on to my people."

"The line is here, invader. Be careful not to step across it."

-oOo-

I am back in the alley. The darkness is just darkness. The oppressive gloom of that terrible wasteland lifts from me like a clearing fog. The nine vagrants look confused and surprised. They shuffle out of their formation, marvelling at being there. They are moving like people now, not automata. I set Frank walking back to the hotel and then drop my control of him. He comes to himself out in the street, clutching his gun.

Chapter 7

The morning finds me in a rented car heading out of town. Frank is driving. His mental state is delicate to say the least. So many unexplained events crowd his anxious thoughts. So many gaps in his awareness from which he has woken in bizarre circumstances with no memory of how he got there. He feels hunted, paranoid, he's about to lose his job and his livelihood. He's starting to crack up, and no wonder. I need to get rid of this guy as soon as I can, but right now I still need him. As soon as I've visited the Colony, I will be back on the trail of Dr. Nielsen.

This is how a Colony works.

We find a planet with intelligent animals on it but one that is uninhabited by cognophytes. There are ancient laws that stipulate that we do not trespass on another species' territory. Sensible laws that are there to avoid conflict and allow us to expand in peace. After all, it is a very, very big Galaxy. There is more than enough room for everybody. Some other parts of the Galaxy are also taboo. There are two main reasons for this.

One is that the body-bounded in those places have reached levels of self-awareness that would make them aware of our presence. Again, this is a good, practical injunction, as well as having a strong ethical basis: why would we want to quash the birth of a new race of cognophytes? Such an emergence is rare and precious and we feel strongly that such species should be protected and allowed to grow.

The second reason is that some of the body-bounded have developed technologies that can detect us and even harm us. As repellent as it seems to us that such races be allowed to survive, it is the wisdom of the Metacolony that we avoid them. The body-bounded do not always feel the same. Some of their most technically advanced species see us as abominations and have waged long and bitter wars against us. We have always survived these genocidal crusades, but we have learnt not to provoke them.

We arrive at a new world with few people and resources. Only about two thousand of us arrived on Earth in a single Treforgan spaceship. A Seed Colony like this comprises a Vaticinatrix, Her staff, a small military unit, and a variety of other specialisms. It is a great privilege to be part of a Seed Colony, a gift not given to many generations. We settle in and spread. Eventually, new Vaticinatrices are born and begin their own sub-colonies. And so we multiply and grow.

Earth is a rich planet with billions of hosts. It will take us many centuries to fill all the available space. As we do, we guide and manage our herds as is only proper. We keep them from self-destruction. We help them multiply too. We promote technologies that will extend their lives and keep them healthy, that will feed them all and make them happy. When there are enough of us, we help them avoid war and other conflicts. We bring peace and health and plenty to any species we farm.

In the end, when we have spread into all the hosts we can, and our own growth is becoming limited, we give them the technologies for interstellar flight. When that day comes to the Earth, there will be a diaspora. Ships will spread from here to all parts of the Galaxy. Some of them will be the seeds of new Colonies on suitable planets.

And so it goes on. We are a benign influence in this Galaxy, bringing stability and prosperity wherever we go. It is the source of deep and profound satisfaction to me that my people are such a force for good.

Traffic is light as we head away from the city. The rising sun is behind us. It flashes on the windscreens of the heavy inbound traffic. Frank is under the impression he is chasing down a lead on the people who have been trying to kill him. It is almost true. True enough anyway. He drives with a grim intensity, hands tight on the wheel, shoulders hunched. Now and then, he says things aloud. "Fifteen years," he says, thinking about Al and Nick, resenting what he sees as their betrayal of him, their lack of trust. "What the hell do you think you can do?" he says, remembering his sister-in-law at the hospital. "You just make it worse."

Much later, as we leave the highway and turn into small, rustic roads, he shouts, "In the fucking street! Waving my fucking gun like some goddamn punk on crack!"

At last, we reach the mansion. It is big and it is secluded. It is owned by a human billionaire that the Vaticinatrix now rides. His family and servants are all occupied by mindriders. None of them is the least bit aware of what has happened to them, or that their sudden preference for remaining on the estate nearly all the time is at all odd. Neither have they noticed the enormous Treforgan spaceship under camouflage nets in the gardens, even though some see it every day. The billionaire is having a hangar and an airstrip built near the house. The sooner the ship is properly hidden, the better.

The mansion is set in extensive grounds and the company that owns it all has manufacturing and research facilities there too. It is, in effect, an industrial park, a sprawling campus, where about two thousand people work. The perfect headquarters for the Colony.

There is a buzzer at the gate and cameras which turn towards me. A speaker crackles and a voice says, "How can I help you, sir?"

I take full control of Frank and speak the necessary passwords.

The gate opens and two security guards appear. They are armed and their weapons are drawn. Either I am who I say I am, or I represent a serious security threat. I get out of the car and wait for them. One watches me while the other studies the car, checking for passengers. There is a sniffer in the bushes nearby. I cannot see it but I feel it touching my mind. I keep still and let the two guards approach. They put the barrels of their guns close to my head. It is all standard procedure. At last one of them reaches out and touches me and my identity is confirmed.

"You may proceed to the house, soldier," he tells me, lowering his weapon. "Welcome home."

-oOo-

Ekkri meets me at the door, riding a household maidservant. We touch and share. Our friendship is old and strong. The pleasure of being with my old crèchemate is sweet beyond all others. The familiar fit and rub of his mind is a balm to me. After so much loneliness and concern, I almost weep at the joy of seeing him again.

"Welcome home," he says after a while. "I miss you and worry about you when you are at the front. How long are you back for? I thought you weren't due for rotation for another two weeks."

Ekkri is an administrator and is privy to all the Colony's troop deployments. He makes sure he knows when I am due for rotation.

"I've come to see the Vaticinatrix. I've discovered something odd and I need to discuss it. You must have seen my last report."

"Your report?" He is clearly confused. "Your report said you had killed another nightmare. Nothing unusual there. Not for you, anyway."

"And the talking didn't surprise you?"

"Talking? I only saw the transcript. I didn't hear the recording."

"Are you saying there was nothing in the transcript about what the nightmare said to me?"

"Said to you?"

"Yes! I..."

He does not pry, although I feel his puzzlement and his concern. I feel something else too.

"What's wrong? Is the Vaticinatrix all right?"

"She's fine," he says, a little too quickly. "Only..."

And this is another disturbing thing, this reticence between me and my friend. It is as disturbing as anything else that has happened of late.

"I don't think you will be allowed an audience," he says. "Things have been tense lately. Celedorn handles most matters himself now, he says the Vaticinatrix must concentrate on the war with the nightmares."

"Well, this concerns the war." Celedorn is another administrator, a high level functionary. How can he deal with the Vaticinatrix's business? I feel a sudden surge of disquiet, an overwhelming sense of everything being out of kilter, everything warped and wrong. The foreboding that fills me spills over so that Ekkri notices it.

He draws back in alarm. "What is it? You know something terrible, don't you? By all the stars that shine! What could be so bad?"

"I don't know. And I can't tell you." Whatever it is I know, or think I know, it has marked me for death. I dare not put that mark on Ekkri too.

"Come on," I say. "Why don't you take me in to see the Vaticinatrix and fill me in on all the court gossip as we go? You know how bored I get out there, with only the humans for company."

We walk, hand in hand, into the great building and Ekkri does his best to keep up a stream of chatter as if everything were normal. The Vaticinatrix's office is far back in the immense building and we pass many other colonists along the way, each reaching out a hand to touch and greet me.

We stop at a large door that stands open. Inside I see more of the Colony's staff. Ekkri draws me aside.

"Promise me that you will be safe," he says, dropping the pretence of normality.

I make myself smile. "I am a soldier, you dimwit. How can I promise that?"

"Your thoughts are so dark. I have never seen you like this before."

I try to compose my thoughts and to project as much comfort as I can, but it is a vain attempt and I abandon it quickly. On an impulse, I pass him Frank's mobile phone number. "I will be riding this one for a while longer. If you need me, you can call."

"Need you? Why would I–?"

But a functionary comes out and speaks to us. "Celedorn will see you now."

I feel a surge of irritation and realise it is born of my disquiet. Nevertheless I say, "You have made a mistake. I came here to see the Vaticinatrix."

"There is no mistake. No one sees the Vaticinatrix without first seeing Celedorn so that he may judge the weight of the matter."

Now I am angry. "Who are you? Show yourself."

The functionary steps forward and touches Frank's hand. It is another administrator.

"Access to the Vaticinatrix is everyone's right," I tell him. "It is a tradition that pre-dates our time on Treforga. The Vaticinatrix must see me." It occurs to me that I can't remember when I last saw Her. It could be months. Years. Surely I have spoken to Her since we reached Earth. But have I?

"Traditions change."

We all turn to see the speaker, a tall man in a dark suit.

"Celedorn," the functionary says, releasing my hand and moving away. He stands facing the administrator and appears tense. "This soldier is being difficult about the new protocols." He sounds merely irritated and a little nervous. Yet, just before he broke contact, I felt a jolt of fear pass through him when he heard Celedorn's voice.

Fear! Of one of our own!

"Soldier, you say?" He turns to me. "You must be the famous Arramar." Arramar is my comrade-name, a name used by close friends. This administrator has no right to use it. He reaches out a hand and I touch it. We exchange identities, but his mind is guarded and reveals nothing else. I cloak my own thoughts, following his example instinctively.

The functionary turns and leaves us. Ekkri stands apart, seeming unsure about whether to stay or not. Celedorn looks at Ekkri briefly and nods, and my friend, with a quick, troubled look my way, leaves too. Celedorn takes away his hand from mine. We will be speaking through our rides, it seems.

"You have come to escort me to the Vaticinatrix, I assume." I already don't like this guy.

"The Vaticinatrix is busy. She has asked me to talk to you in Her stead."

"I will wait for Her to be free. The matters I need to discuss are important."

He regards me for a moment.

"You have been at the front for a very long time, Arramar. There have been some organisational changes you may not be aware of."

"I must have missed the memo."

He laughs. "The memo! You have an excellent grasp of human vernacular, I see. But then I suppose you are pretty isolated in your line of work. No one to talk to but the livestock. Do you know you have hunted down and killed more of the enemy than any other soldier in our army?"

"I've done my duty to the Colony."

"Yes, indeed! But you may be growing tired. You deserve a break, I think. A bit of time off. Long periods of combat can make a soldier a little unbalanced. You might start imagining things, saying things that are unsettling for others."

What is all this verbal fencing? I am used to more direct exchanges. "Was it you who had my last report altered?"

Again, he pauses and studies me. It is a very human gesture but presumably he does it to give himself time to think. I long to grab him, to get inside with him and lay bare whatever he is thinking. This talking through human voices is no way for two Colonists to interact. It lends itself to misunderstanding, even to deliberate deceit.

"What is it you wish to tell the Vaticinatrix?" he says. At least we are getting to the point.

"What I have to say is for Her alone. I will not discuss important matters affecting Colony security with an administrator. So stand aside or be pushed aside. Either way is fine by me."

"You are being rash, Arramar." He raises a hand and two men dressed as security guards step out of wherever they had been watching from and come to stand beside him. "There is no need for any unpleasantness. Be sensible and tell me what you think you have discovered."

"You talk like a human," I say, angry that he is prepared for my resistance, alarmed that the Colony I know has become so changed. I feel I have become a stranger in my own family. I glare at this usurper, wanting to tear him to pieces.

"What right have you to deny me access?" I demand, but the two security guards are clearly my answer. "If you have harmed Her in any way..." I let the threat trail off. The very thought of such a thing fills me with dread. Without a Vaticinatrix, a Colony is nothing, a collection of purposeless individuals.

I turn to leave. There is no point arguing. I need to find another way to see Her.

"Stop him," Celedorn says, softly, and I hear the two guards coming after me.

Defend yourself, I tell Frank and let him go just as the first guard grabs me. I swarm through the guard's field and into his mind. He is prepared for resistance but not such a ferocious attack. I beat him down, driving him back into his ride's unconscious. He retreats to a place where exaggerated, exotic weapons are waiting and he lunges desperately towards them. Even as he grabs a massive, ridiculously ornate scimitar, I snatch up a mace, swinging the spiked iron ball into him with all my strength. He goes down, the scimitar clattering to the ground, and I strike him again. Hurt and barely alive, he tries to crawl away from me. I raise the weapon again but stop in mid-stroke.

I know this man, of course. He is a soldier like me. A comrade.

"Barralan, it is Arramar," I say, to remind him.

"Don't kill me," he says.

The sight of a comrade pleading for his life sickens me. In disgust, I throw the mace aside.

"What is going on here?" I ask. "Why are you doing Celedorn's bidding? Where is the Vaticinatrix? Is She safe?"

Barralan is badly wounded. He may die anyway if he does not receive medical attention. "I don't know. No one has seen Her. Celedorn is in charge. If we don't do as he says... He has the army working for him. No one dare disobey."

"You moron! You are the army. All you have to do is to stop scaring each other and he has no power at all. Surely you can see that?"

Barralan shakes his head. "No one wants to stand alone. No one dares. It would be suicide."

I turn and leave him. "We'll see about that. I will send a medic as soon as I can."

I take charge of Barralan's ride to find Frank is doing all right. He has beaten the second guard to the ground and has his gun drawn, holding off two more, who are slowly advancing on him. I hear footsteps from behind me and turn in time to see four more people rush in.

I face the newcomers. "You idiots!" I shout. "You should be fighting to save the Vaticinatrix. Celedorn is a usurper. He will destroy us all."

I move closer to Frank, who is confused by absolutely everything and just as likely to shoot me as anybody else. He holds his wallet up in front of him as if it still held his police shield. He seems to be trying to bluff his attackers with it, like a modern van Helsing holding up a crucifix to ward off vampires in a very bad movie. The newcomers have guns too and it is clear that Frank's pretend badge isn't going to help us.

"Frank," I say, over my shoulder. "I'm on your side. I think we should get out of here."

"You're one of them," he says, a hint of hysteria in his voice.

"It's complicated. You're just going to have to trust me." There is no way I can grab him to swap rides without him freaking out, so I back towards the entrance and yell at him to follow me.

"Where do you think you can go, Arramar?" Celedorn asks. His voice is unpleasantly calm and confident and I wish that I was the one holding Frank's gun. "You can't leave the Colony. What is a soldier all on his own? What would you do?"

"I am going to free the Vaticinatrix! All of you, listen. Join me. Together we can return things to how they were. What you're doing is madness. Without the Vaticinatrix there is no point to anything for any of us."

"You're not seeing the whole picture, soldier," Celedorn says. "I'm not the bad guy here."

"Oh no? Then where is the Vaticinatrix? What have you done with Her?"

Frank looks at me as if he is more worried now about me than about the others, but I have no time to think about Frank. If I have to sacrifice him, I will. To my relief, the weapons in the hands of our pursuers waver and dip a little. I have shaken their resolve. They must know as well as I do that the situation in the Colony is all wrong.

"Free the Vaticinatrix!" I shout, and run for the exit, taking Frank with me.

We get a small lead on the security men and I hear Celedorn bellowing at them to follow us. We pound through the corridors and the great entrance hall and are out into the driveway before a single shot is fired after us. Frank's car is still where we left it. I run to the driver's door and throw it open. Frank comes up behind me and I stuff him into the driver's seat, yelling at him to get away.

As he fumbles for his key and starts up the engine, I stand outside with a hand on Frank's shoulder and face the troops bundling out of the house. "This soldier needs urgent medical attention," I shout at them, then slip into Frank's mind, leaving Barralan's ride to stagger and fall in the wake of our wheel-spinning exit.

Chapter 8

Frank's mind is a maelstrom as he races down country roads towards the freeway and the distant city. He is trembling with the after-effects of our flight from the Colony. The shock of waking from amnesia to a life-and-death struggle among strangers has unhinged him completely. Now he is driving like the madman he is, terrified and out of control, going so fast he is almost surely going to kill us both.

Slow down, Frank, I say, letting him hear my voice in his head. *No one is following us. We're safe now.*

I should have just taken over the driving, I realise, too late. Frank screams and slams on the brakes. The wheels cope for all of two seconds then the rear end swings around and we're travelling sideways for a moment until the car goes into a roll. Without a seatbelt, Frank is thrown around inside the car like a doll in a cardboard box. We turn over two, three times, and land on our wheels, facing the wrong way on the road.

The engine has stalled and there is no other traffic. In the quiet, I can hear crows cawing and a dog barking far away. Frank has taken quite a battering but I can feel no broken bones and he is still conscious. I make him untangle himself from the seats and climb out of the passenger door. The car may be leaking fuel and I would rather he was well away from it until I know it is safe – however much his body protests.

He half-staggers, half-crawls along the road until I judge he is clear of danger, then I let him collapse onto the grass verge. He prostrates himself and lies there moaning to himself while I think.

Even though we were not followed, it is not good that we have stopped. Colony sniffers will find us eventually, and at any moment, Colony personnel might happen by and discover us. As soon as Frank has recovered a little, I will check the car over and get us moving again.

"I guess it had to happen in the end," Frank says, aloud. I wait for more but nothing comes. I'm about to get him on his feet again when he says, "And what was that? Strangers in a mansion, fighting and shouting about freedom and colonies. All hallucinations. Was I even there?" He pushes himself up so he can look around. "And where the hell am I now? Out in the country, running for my life from imaginary dangers, listening to voices in my head, talking to myself!"

He gets up. His right knee is in a lot of pain but he ignores it and limps back to the car. The roof and the hood are badly dented and the lid of the trunk is lying on the road in front of us. Most of the windows are smashed, including the windscreen, which is still in place but starred and fractured into crystal spiderwebs. I can't smell petrol, so I let him get back in and start the engine. It comes to life on the first try.

"I almost killed myself!" he cries out, almost driving into the ditch as he manoeuvres to face the city again. There is a wobble in the steering wheel that must mean the wheels are bent out of shape, and a metallic scrape that suggests the exhaust manifold is dragging on the ground. "And look at my car! Jesus! I can't afford to wreck my car right now. I probably won't have a job soon to pay for a new one."

He drives slowly and the car makes it to the freeway, but not long after that, steam begins pouring out from under the bonnet.

"So now what?" Frank says. "Well? You're the one who got me into this mess with your 'Slow down, Frank'. How about some useful advice for a change?"

It is tempting to answer him, but I worry it will just send him even more crazy. On the other hand, being part of his imaginary psychosis might not be such a bad idea. I've already tried talking to him from someone else's body and it got me nowhere. Same thing with Dr. Nielsen, of course. Perhaps humans are just more willing to believe in their own madness than in a reality they find unacceptable.

It would certainly be nice to have someone to talk to, even if it is only Frank. My loneliness is becoming oppressive, and now that my own Colony has turned against me, there really is no one.

I have seen humans talking to their pet animals, their televisions, their imaginary gods, even the remains of their dead loved ones; would it be any worse for me to talk to Frank? And I must really want to do it, or why do I keep making the attempt?

All right, I tell myself, isolation is making me as feeble-minded as a human, but there is no point fighting it.

Take the next exit, I say in Frank's mind. *We need a garage.*

Frank nearly jumps out of his skin, sending the car swerving across the next carriageway and back to the hard shoulder before he gets it under control again.

"Ohshitohshitohshitohshit!" he wails. He says it several more times before he spots an exit and leaves the freeway.

"Oh shit, I'm crazy," he says as we enter a small town. "Crazy as a loon. Cuckoo. Nutty as a fruitcake."

There is a run-down gas station and he pulls into it. Nobody comes out and Frank sits there looking around.

Where is everybody? I ask, and Frank moans as if I'd just kicked him. Get used to it, Frank. You're going to be hearing a lot from me in future. *I suppose this is what you call a one-horse town.* I actually quite like human idioms.

Frank giggles. "Yeah, and the horse just died of boredom."

A joke. I can't tell if that is a good sign or not. His thoughts are skittering all over the place. He's in some kind of panic.

I suppose they're all at the funeral then, I say, joining in the fun. *Let's get out and see if we can find a mechanic.*

Without hesitation, Frank climbs out the car and shouts for assistance. After a while, a small, round man appears who squints at Frank as if the sun's in his eyes. He is wearing overalls and looks like he's just come from under a car.

"Yeah?" he says.

"I rolled my car," Frank tells him. "The wheels need straightening or something. Will you take a look?"

The round man squints at the car for a few seconds without speaking then goes over to it and squints some more. He gets down and looks underneath, then moves to the other side and looks under there too. "Pop the hood," he says and waits while Frank reaches in and pulls the lever that unlocks the bonnet. The round man lifts it open and squints inside. Finally, he closes the hood and saunters back to Frank.

"The car's a write-off, Mister. Front axle's bent, cracked sump, looks like the whole chassis is twisted. I can't fix that. Cost you more than it's worth anyway."

Frank and I watch him in silence.

"Tell you what I can do. I'll give you a hundred for it. I can always use the spare parts and it'll save you the cost of having it towed all the way to the nearest scrap yard. There's a bus comes through here in about an hour will take you to the city."

Frank doesn't believe him about the car, but he does not have the expertise to refute anything the man has said.

Shake his hand, Frank, I tell him. *Act grateful.*

Again, without demur, Frank reaches out a hand. "That seems like a very generous offer," he says, smiling.

The round man takes his hand and I slip across into him. The man's contempt for Frank fills him like a bad smell. Dumb city folk deserve what they get, it seems, and this one looks like he's been drinking all morning too. He reckons Frank is insured so what the hell? He'll fill in the forms for the insurer, then break up the car and sell the parts. He could probably make two or three thousand easy.

He leads Frank back to the squalid little desk in the back of the shop that he calls his office while I poke around a bit. This is not a nice man. In fact, I can't wait to get out of there. But first...

By the time Frank leaves, he is the new owner of a beautifully-restored 1970 Plymouth Road Runner convertible, a vehicle which had been the round guy's pride and joy, but which he inexplicably sold to Frank in exchange for his rather battered Ford Taurus. Frank can't believe it and neither can Round Guy. When they shake hands, just before Frank sets off, I slip back into Frank. Round Guy's squint is quickly replaced by wide-eyed horror as he looks from the ownership documents he is holding to the car he laboured on for two years being driven out of town.

"OK, that was weird," Frank says aloud as the big muscle car growls towards the freeway.

It was nothing, Frank, I say. This time, although Frank catches his breath and his anxiety spikes, he manages to keep the car on the ground. I guess he must be getting used to me. *I can make all kinds of things happen for you, if you like. Think of me as your very own fairy godmother. I just need your cooperation in return.*

"I don't understand. Look, I've never been nuts before. I don't know how this works. I just wrecked my car, then I'm driving something from a wall poster. Is everything just a dream now?"

No, Frank, it's all very real. It's the same as it always was, except now you have me living inside your brain.

He surprises me by laughing. "Like a tumour," he says, but I can see it is a real fear with him that he has become delusional because of a malignant growth inside his skull.

No, Frank. I won't hurt you. I'm just hitch-hiking in your mind. I steal a bit of your brain's energy so that I can live, but nothing you can't compensate for by eating a little more each day.

"I am kinda hungry."

I don't like his vague, wistful tone. I know this has been a big shock for him but I want him clear-headed and focused. We are both still in danger and I need Frank to do his bit.

We need to get far away from here first. I want you to take me to Dr Nielsen.

"Nielsen? What's she got to do with anything? If I'm going to see a doctor, it should be a shrink."

All kinds of unpleasant thoughts are worrying him now. He remembers his attraction to the doctor. He wonders if he has developed some kind of obsession. He really believes he's crazy and he doesn't like to think he might be a danger to anyone. He'd rather put a bullet in his head than hurt some innocent person. He re-members waking up last night, standing in the street with his gun, not knowing how he got there. It occurs to him that maybe the pizza delivery boy really was just some kid delivering pizzas.

Stop thinking that way, Frank. The pizza kid brought a shot-gun with him, remember? And those guys who grabbed you in the street, they were armed too, and one of them had a syringe. Plenty of people can corroborate this stuff. The only thing they don't know about is me talking to you. You're not going to hurt anybody. It's me that wants to see Nielsen again, not you?

He laughs again. It is an unpleasant, brittle laugh. "Do you know how totally crazy that sounds?"

Just accept that I'm real, Frank, and it will all make perfect sense.

"Sure you're real. I'm a schizo nut-job and I've got a voice in my head telling me to do things, but you're real all right, buddy. I hear you loud and clear."

OK, Frank, I give up – for now. Think what you like. As long as you get me to Nielsen and don't kill us both along the way, that's all I ask.

I leave him to his driving and the miserable wail of self-pity that echoes around and around inside him. He's driving us to the hospital. That's what matters.

I realise there is another reason for me to stick with Frank. It is standard operational procedure for a soldier to ditch his ride after any kind of trouble and find a new one. That is what Celedorn and his people will expect me to do. They almost certainly did not bother to check Frank's identity or even notice his licence plate. There would be no point. I could have changed rides ten times by now – and would have done if not for the Nielsen thing. Probably the last place anyone would look for me is inside Frank.

No, they will have teams of hunters out with sniffers trying to pick up my trail. Hunters like me, trained like me, as skilled as I am. My only advantage is that I know how they operate and how other soldiers are deployed in the city. I know what I should do to avoid them. They'll be heading for the sector I was assigned to, hoping to pick up my scent there. So I won't be going back there for a while.

Chapter 9

We draw a blank at the hospital again. Dr Nielsen has called in sick. This time, I make Frank reach over the counter and grab the nurse on reception by the arm. Within moments, I have Nielsen's home address from the computer and we're off, leaving a group of alarmed nurses and patients behind.

It takes another thirty minutes to cross town to the inner city apartment block where Nielsen lives. Frank parks the grumbling monster he's driving and gets out. He's still half-convinced that the car is an hallucination, but I can see he likes having it. This human interest in possessions is odd. It's like a mindrider caring about which human he's riding in, or collecting up herds of humans and saying they all belong to him. It is a quaint, ridiculous notion, but I have seen the same fetish for possessions in the Treforgans, and it seems to be quite common among the body-bound generally.

It crops up again when we enter the lobby of Nielsen's building. Frank is impressed by it and a little envious. Apparently, it is a very desirable residence.

"You!" Nielsen says through the door to her apartment when we are finally standing outside. "What do you want?"

"I need to talk to you," Frank says. "It's important."

"Call my office and make an appointment, Mr. Taylor. I can't see patients here."

I take over and through Frank's mouth I say. "Let me in Dr. Nielsen. This is not a medical consultation."

Her voice, through the door, sounds nervous, frightened even. "No. Go away. Go away or I'll call the police."

"I am the police, remember? Now please open the door so we can talk."

She is silent for a long time, but eventually there is the rattle of locks and chains and the door opens a bodywidth. She holds it, ready to slam it shut again and watches me warily.

"May I come in?"

Silently, she steps back and I take Frank inside.

"Nice place you've got," I say, remembering Frank's envy. She says nothing, just watches me as I walk across to a group of chairs and stand there, waiting, as is appropriate, to be invited to sit down. After a while, she closes the door and follows me in. She doesn't sit and doesn't invite me to sit either.

"What do you want?"

"I want to continue the conversation we were having at the hospital yesterday."

"The one where you said you were a visiting alien and then had your friends do that little stunt, finishing each others' sentences? That was quite some trick. You really scared me. Congratulations."

"I didn't mean to scare you. I'm sorry. I just wanted you to know the truth about me."

She regards me carefully for a moment. "Why do you want me to hear this, Frank? May I call you Frank? There are other doctors at the hospital better qualified to talk to you about these things. I could arrange for one to see you any time you like."

It takes me a while to realise that she is trying to encourage Frank to see a psychiatrist.

"You need to hear this, doctor, because you are special. Some very strange things have been happening to me lately and meeting you was one of the strangest. It can't be a coincidence. That would be improbable beyond all reason."

"I'm special," she says, sceptically. "Frank, we only met the other day for the first time. You don't know me at all. Are you listening to what you're saying?"

My patience is about gone. Trying to persuade this woman is clearly a waste of time. She needs another demonstration. I put out Frank's hand towards her, palm up. "Please take my hand."

"What? No."

"Please. I won't hurt you or do anything except hold your hand very gently. Just for a very short while. If you do this and, afterwards, do not agree with everything I've said, I will go away and leave you alone."

She is frightened and suspicious. Perhaps she is remembering that first time. "It's another trick. I don't trust you."

I push back Frank's sleeves to reveal bare arms. "I don't do tricks. Please, just take my hand. Just touch my fingers lightly. Then, if you still want me to, I will go away and never come back."

She looks hard into Frank's eyes and I give him as sincere an expression as I can manage. Slowly, slowly, she raises her hand towards Frank's. I can see from her face the struggle going on inside her. Finally, with a great burst of effort, she closes the gap and our fingers meet.

I surge through the fields into her mind, making her take a firm hold of Frank's hand as I go in. As before, she immediately feels me inside her. As before, she recoils in shock and horror, shutting me out, pushing me back, screaming and fighting, her mind a whirlwind. But this time, I stand my ground. The bars and shutters that come down all around me, I force open again. The blasts of fear that hit me like walls of flame, I resist and quench. We struggle inside her for an age before she begins to weaken and I am able to speak.

I'm sorry, Margaret. I know her name now. Everything she is, is there for me to know should I want it. *This is an unforgivable intrusion, but I must know how you can see me. I must understand how a human mind can perceive a mindrider like myself. It shouldn't be possible, and yet you can do it.*

I see her across a broad, well-lit room. She is a child. She sits in the corner, clutching a stuffed animal, watching me with big, frightened eyes. I am... Well, to her I am a monster. By default I appear in the ancient form of my body-bound ancestors. Cursing my stupidity, I make myself into a small version of Frank. I walk across polished floorboards to her and sit down cross-legged, facing her. I put a smile on my face.

Hello, Margaret. I am so sorry to have scared you. I just have to convince you that what I told you is true. I am an alien, and I am able to live in people's minds. And you are special. No other human being I have ever encountered has been able to see me. No other human being should be able to see me. You should all be too primitive. Your self-awareness should be well below the level where that is possible. And it is. I have been in hundreds of human minds. I know them well and they are exactly as they should be, except for yours.

She is still presenting as a child and still clutching her toy for comfort, but the fear in her eyes is lessening.

I can't tell you how sorry I am to have forced my way in here, Margaret. Such a violation is something my people abhor. So I am leaving now. I'm going back into Frank's mind again. When I'm gone, will you talk to me about this? Little Girl Margaret looks at me but says nothing. *Please? Just say you'll talk to me. It is very important. It may be important for your whole world, for every single human being on this planet.*

I wait but she still doesn't speak. *Yes?*

She nods.

Without another word, I leave her and flow back into Frank.

She drops his hand – throws it aside in disgust – and leaps back from him as if he were alight. She stumbles into an armchair and falls to the ground with a yelp of surprise. Desperately, she scrabbles to get clear of Frank – or me – keeping her eyes on us all the time.

Frank watches her in amazement, having no idea what just went on. He takes a step towards her and she shouts, "Get back!" So he stops in confusion.

"How did you do that?" she asks, scrambling to her feet.

"Do what?"

"You were inside my head."

It was me, Frank, I tell him. *I can go into other people's heads too.*

"It wasn't me," Frank tells her. She is four or five paces away but is not retreating any farther. "It was him. The voice in my head. Whatever it was, he did it, not me."

She goggles at him, wild-eyed and dishevelled, and shakes her head. "No. It was some kind of trick. You hypnotised me some-how, used suggestion. What did you do, you bastard?"

The emotional turmoil inside Frank is getting unbearable. If these two don't come to the right answer soon, I'll have to calm him down and take over again. He takes another step towards her and she screams at him to stay away from her. The violence of her reaction hits him like a slap and he starts gasping for air. He wants to run away. He wants to get the hell out of there and hide. He wants to run off a cliff, into a truck, anything but be there, going mad, full of guilt and fear and shame.

I feel tears run down his cheeks. His chest convulses in sobs. His legs give way and he drops to his knees. He puts his head into his hands and begins to wail miserably. It is time to intervene.

But Margaret says, "Frank?"

He doesn't answer her and I can't see her.

"Frank, I'm scared."

He looks up at her and she is blurry and indistinct.

"It can't be true can it, Frank? It's a trick."

"I don't know," he wails. "I don't know what's real any more. Maybe nothing is real."

It's all real, Frank, I say. He clutches his head and howls.

"You're hearing things," Margaret says. "You're hearing voices in your head, and I'm caught up in your madness somehow."

"Didn't you hear him? Didn't he speak to you?"

"I heard something. I saw..."

Hope flares in Frank's mind.

"You heard him too, didn't you! You heard the voice in my head. A voice like..."

"Like an angel," Margaret says. "Yet he looked like you, and before that..."

"You saw him?"

"What?"

"I can only hear him. I can't see him."

Margaret blinks; once, twice, three times. "It's because I'm special," she says, dreamily. "Only I, in all the world, can see him. That's what he told me." She seems to drift off into a reverie. Frank is pondering the peculiar details of his delusions.

It's all so weird you don't think you could have made it all up, do you? I say in Frank's head. *Well you're right. I don't think you could either. She's probably thinking the same thing. Her name's Margaret, by the way. How do you know that, Frank?*

"Your name's Margaret," he says aloud. "He just told me."

She waves it aside. A gnat. "You're a policeman. It's easy for you to know things like that."

At the mention of his job, a wave of bitterness sweeps all Frank's other thoughts away. "I won't be much longer. Fifteen years on the force and they suspend me pending a murder investigation. My boss as good as accused me of doing it."

"Did you?" she asks, quietly.

"I can't go back there now. How can I work with those people again? In the end, all you've got is trust. And when that's gone..."

Margaret breaks the spell she's under by walking out of the room to the kitchen. I hear a cupboard open, glasses rattle, a tap run. She comes back a short while later and sits down in an arm-chair, the one farthest away from where Frank is still kneeling on the floor. She seems a lot more focused.

"Let's say it's real," she says. "Let's say there's an alien who can live inside our thoughts, moving from mind to mind whenever he chooses."

Frank is fascinated by what she's saying. He thinks it is yet another of his delusions.

"He's like a being of pure energy or something. A parasitic energy being that feeds on our emotions, maybe."

What a load of crap, I tell Frank. *She should stick to bone doctoring and steer clear of this theoretical exobiology bullshit.*

Frank laughs and Margaret frowns at him. "He doesn't think much to your description of him," he tells her. "He says it's bullshit."

"What? He's not a parasite?"

Now it's my turn to laugh. *She says it like it's a bad thing! Parasites are clearly the top of the evolutionary ladder. Ask her why she likes being a host so much.*

"He likes being a parasite," Frank says, and a chill runs through his thoughts.

"So, why is he here and what's he want from us? And why is he even talking to you and me?"

At last! I tell Frank I'll be needing his body for a while and take over. I stand up, walk to the sofa and sit down. "Hello Margaret," I say. "Can we talk now? Or would you like more demonstrations?"

Her eyes widen. Frank's changed demeanour and tone have spooked her again, but each time I scare her, she is more in control. Progress is being made. I don't like that this is taking so long, but I've never had to talk to a human before – no one has! – and I'm learning as I go along how to ease my way through the emotional minefield of their mental fragility.

"I want to answer all your questions," I tell her. "I want to lay it all out for you so you will understand. Then, when I explain why you are so important, you will believe me and perhaps you will help me."

So I tell her about my people, how my Colony left Treforga and came here. How we discovered the nightmares and had to fight them to keep our little toe-hold on this world. How we thought they were pests who came with us, mindless animals that followed us down from space.

Then I go over the details of the past few days. The nightmare that spoke to me. The mindrider who tried to kill me. The humans who tried to kill me. My rough reception at Colony headquarters. And her, the human who can see me.

"We're not a lawless people," I explain. "We're colonists, not invaders. Mostly, we're farmers, not fighters. There are rules about what kind of species we can ride, what kind of planet we can settle. Because of the nightmares, whom I now believe are indigenous, because of you, whose awareness of me suggests a strain of human with an almost cognophytic level of development, I don't think we should be here. I don't know why we are. It must be tied up with why I can't speak to the Vaticinatrix. Something to do with Celedorn."

I let Frank hear it all too. I don't know why. I just feel it would make things easier if he knows more about me. It is probably a mistake. The sound of his own voice telling someone else's story only adds to his sense of disconnection. Thoughts of demonic possession flood his mind, along with bizarre images of a young girl vomiting as her head rotates. There is so much that is dark and strange in Frank's mind that it is impossible to predict what new and disturbing turn his thoughts will take.

Margaret seems much calmer, however. I think she is finally accepting what I say. Her eyes do not leave me as I speak. I can see she is ready to run if I were to try to approach her, but she is not mindlessly afraid now. Just cautious.

"Can I get you a drink?" she says, after a long silence. This is good. It is a sign that I am now a guest and no longer an intruder.

"Thank you. Frank could definitely use a drink, and some food. He hasn't eaten all day."

"You care about him." She sounds surprised.

"It is considered cruel to let your ride suffer needlessly."

"Can he hear us?"

"If I let him. At the moment, yes, he can hear us."

"I want to speak to Frank."

"Very well."

I let Frank go. To be honest, I am glad of the rest. I have been in full control of him so often lately, without a proper rest in between. Fatigue is starting to accumulate. When I let go, Frank looks around in surprise as if he is seeing Margaret's apartment for the first time.

"Frank?"

"Yes!"

"Frank, are you all right?"

"I heard him talking to you."

Margaret stands up. "Come on. We'll go find you a restaurant. You look terrible. Do you want to wash up?"

Not much of what she is saying penetrates his awareness, yet somehow her compassion gets through and it makes him feel better. With a nod he stands up and she shows him to a small bathroom.

Chapter 10

While the two of them eat and talk, I sit in a dark corner of Frank's mind and brood. I learned a lot when I was inside Margaret's mind, but very little that helps.

The fact is, she knows nothing about her abilities. She may well be part of a strain of humanity that is evolving towards greater self-awareness, but she has no idea whether her parents or siblings share the trait. Nor does she know if there are others like her.

Yet there were clues.

A mind is something like a computer program that runs on the hardware of a brain. As a mind evolves towards true consciousness, it sees itself with increasing clarity, it becomes so aware of its relationship to the brain it runs on that, in the end, the abstraction of that relationship itself becomes manipulable. At that point, the mind can run on any brain it likes.

It helps if the computational infrastructure – the wiring and capabilities of the brain – is compatible. My people prefer massively interconnected associative networks of a certain size and complexity, because that is the kind of brain we evolved in. There are quite a lot of species on Earth that would suit us. Human brains are quite luxuriously large compared to Treforgans' for instance, and we'd be just as happy in another primate, or cetaceans, even some squids. I managed to squeeze myself into a horse's brain once, but it wasn't particularly comfortable.

Anyway, the point is that, at higher levels of self-awareness, people should start exhibiting symptoms, or differences, let's say. Mental stability correlates directly with self-awareness. Credulity correlates negatively. Intelligence is not strongly correlated, but happiness is. Margaret is a stable, cynical and contented person – by comparison to most humans. She hasn't made unhappy choices in her relationships, and she understands her needs and abilities well enough to have avoided inappropriate ambitions.

None of this is strong evidence but it suggests to me that her ability to detect my presence in her mind is not just an isolated ability, but is part of a general pattern of increased self-awareness. And if she has it, there must be others.

"I need to talk to members of your family," I say, through Frank.

She blinks in surprise, then frowns at me. "I was talking to Frank."

"Yes, I know."

We are in a restaurant. Not the cheap kind of place Frank goes to when he wants a burger and fries, but a more up-market place, where the waitresses don't wear short skirts and the décor isn't dominated by advertising posters. Frank, I see, has ordered a burger and fries, while the doctor has a pasta dish.

"I need to know how widespread your genetic makeup is. I can get a better idea if I visit your parents and siblings, then cousins, aunts, nieces, and so on."

"And you'd like to try to get into each of their heads, to see what reaction you get."

"That's right." I am pleased she is smart enough to catch on quickly. It makes things so much simpler.

"No."

"What?"

"No, I'm not going to let you mess with my family's heads, just to satisfy your curiosity."

Ah well, not so smart after all. "It's not just curiosity, Margaret. If you are a one-off, some kind of freak, it doesn't matter. It means nothing. But if you're part of a genetic strain that is developing within your species, it matters a great deal. It means we have to leave Earth and leave markers so that other cognophytic species can avoid the place too."

She looks at me for a long time and I assume she is working through the logic of what I'd said.

"You don't really understand us very well, do you?"

"No! That's the whole point. I need to perform a study, to marshal my evidence."

"Well find some other way to get your evidence. My family is off-limits. Keep away from them."

I am astonished that she still doesn't get it. "You are being irrational," I tell her.

"No, I'm perfectly rational. My premises are just different from yours. You start from the view that humans are just farm stock, that you can do what you like with us, because your needs are all that matters. I start from the view that my family are precious individuals whom I love. That makes each and every one of them more important than anything you want to do. Get it?"

I make Frank's face do a scowl.

"Good. Find another way. My family is *verboten*. Now, can I have Frank back, please?"

I release Frank and go back to my silent brooding.

It is surprising and a little amusing that she is standing up to me, but I can see her position and I respect it. Unfortunately for her, the prohibition she has placed on me is only effective if I wish her no harm, or if I fear her. Neither of which is the case. In fact, now that I have exhausted her intel, I do not need her – or her permissions – any longer.

So I must find out who her family members are and where they live. Tomorrow, I can begin tracking them down.

I still do not know what is wrong at the Colony, or whether the Vaticinatrix is safe, but at least I now know that Celedorn is behind it. I must go back there and find out more. How I can do that is another question altogether.

Which leaves me with one gigantic hole in my understanding. Why did a human military unit attack me? There are several possibilities but the only two that seem at all likely are that the humans' government has found out about the Colony and is mounting an attack on us – in which case, I just happen to have been an unlucky early victim – or the attack was something to do with whatever is wrong with the Colony.

If the humans know about us, it could be because they have people like Margaret working for them, helping them track us. Perhaps even Margaret herself! Is it possible she informed somebody about me when I first tried to ride her? If that's the case, then maybe I should just eliminate her now. Given the things I have revealed to her, I may have supplied her military with useful intelligence. Yet everything I've ever been taught about not harming emerging cognophytes means that killing Margaret has to be an option of last resort.

If the attack by the humans was tied in to whatever is going on at the Colony, I am completely at a loss to explain it. If I can't explain one, I certainly can't explain the other.

But perhaps none of this matters. The nightmares have threatened the Colony with war. My people don't know. I wasn't allowed to tell them. The truly important thing now is to get that message through, even if it means giving it to Celedorn and not the Vaticinatrix.

I make Frank stand up and leave. There is a public phone outside in the street.

"Frank? Oh for God's sake!" Margaret hurries to pay the bill and follow us out. By the time she catches me up, I am already speaking to the Colony.

"Arramar!" The voice I have been transferred to is the one I recognise as Celedorn's ride. "You wish to come home. How sensible of you." I wince at the tone of triumph in that smooth voice. "Being alone is not our way. The Colony is where we belong. It nurtures and protects us. It is the unity we all crave. Isolation is an abomination. Come back to us Arramar. You will not be judged. You will be welcomed as the loyal and true soldier we know you are."

"I have a message for the Vaticinatrix," I say. His unctuous words only serve to irritate me. How dare he identify himself with the Colony? How dare he speak to me on its behalf? "If you will be silent, I will give it to you. It is important, Celedorn. The welfare of the Colony is at stake, otherwise I would not speak to you at all."

"Are you threatening us, soldier? Would you presume?"

"Shut up and listen, administrator."

He does not respond, so I tell him about my meeting with the nightmares, about what they said to me, about their threats against us. When I am finished, I add, "Will you pass this to the Vaticinatrix?"

"The Vaticinatrix is indisposed," he says. It sounds like a reflex response. His tone is distant. He seems distracted. I hope it is because he is thinking about what I just told him.

"You should come back now, Arramar. Do not repeat to anyone else what you just told me."

"Who are you to give me orders, administrator?"

"Would you like me to put your commanding officer on the line to repeat what I just said? It is very easily done."

"In that case, no. Until I speak to the Vaticinatrix, I know I can trust nobody."

The awful truth of this strikes me as I say it and I am filled with loneliness and despair. "Just tell me what you have done to Her! Tell me what kind of insurrection you have engineered. If She has been harmed, there is nowhere on this planet that will be safe for you."

Celedorn's voice sounds weary. "Your loyalty does you credit, soldier. You should come back to us. It is not safe for you out there, alone."

"Goodbye, Celedorn. I hope we will meet again, soon."

I hang up and find Margaret standing there, glaring at me.

"You can't just use Frank's body like that whenever you feel like it," she says.

What a ridiculous notion. Of course I can. Ignoring her, I make Frank step out into the street and grab the arm of a passer-by, a young woman in a long coat. I flow into this new ride and she walks quickly away, unaware of me, glancing nervously over her shoulder at Frank. I see Frank looking around in confusion and Margaret rushes over to him.

Then I leave them behind. They have each served their purpose.

Chapter 11

The next day I take my new ride to the city's FBI Headquarters, where I move from host to host until I find someone who has the knowledge and authority to run the computer searches I need, to compile a list of Margaret Nielsen's relatives. I am pleased to discover that most of her family live in or near to the city.

My ride is a senior analyst who specialises in domestic fraud cases. She has all the expertise I need for me to begin another investigation.

I have never seen him, but it is common knowledge within the Colony that the Vaticinatrix rides the body of a very rich man called Sterling. Many of Her staff ride the bodies of Sterling's lieutenants. Sterling has many business interests, mostly in the fields of communications and media. It occurs to me that, if there is a connection between what Celedorn is doing and the military, the connection might be through one of Sterling's companies. The only connection I can imagine is that Celedorn might have put his own people into the minds of military leaders to pursue some plan of his own. It seems far-fetched, since it is hard to imagine what possible use he could have for them at such an early stage of our colonisation, yet it is a lead I need to follow.

I end up with a list of just five Sterling companies that have major military contracts. It doesn't seem hopeful but it is a start.

My next ride is Special Agent Martin Wu and I take him off to visit Nielsen's family. He drives a huge, black SUV, which makes him feel strong and powerful. He is a man who likes having power over his fellows. It helps him manage his fear of being unloved. A fear that is well-founded, from what I see inside him.

Wu is such a pathetic specimen of his species that I find myself feeling nostalgic for Frank and Margaret. Frank has his problems, of course, lots of them, but he is basically a good man. His fears and his anger are turned inwards. In his ignorance of his own psyche, he hurts himself. His character is such that he never thinks of finding relief in making others suffer. For all the darkness in his soul, he is a less grating ride than Wu – or many, many others I have ridden. And as for Margaret... In my exile from the Colony, Margaret is the nearest thing on this planet to someone of my own kind.

Except the nightmares, of course.

I leave my sniffers in the city when I drive out to the suburbs. I don't want them to spook Margaret's parents, who might just be able to sense their presence.

Jack and Mary Nielsen are both at home when I arrive, unannounced, at their little town-house in Bleasdale. Their place is smart and well kept, in a tidy, affluent neighbourhood. Jack is a self-employed commercial artist who works from home. His wife, Mary, is a Web developer, also freelance.

I slip into Jack with no difficulty at all as he shakes my hand on the doorstep. I stay only moments, long enough to glance through a few memories and to get a feel for his life. Dull, ordinary, but brilliantly lit by his love for his wife and his two daughters.

Mary is just coming out of her office as Jack leads me into the house. Looking past her, I see a graduation photo of Margaret on her desk.

"It's the FBI, Mare. They want to talk to us about Maggie."

I take the opportunity of Jack's introduction to step forward and shake Mary's hand. At the first sign of her defences coming up, I pull back into the FBI agent. Mary has barely had time to register the intrusion. She jerks her hand out of mine with a shudder.

"Oh my goodness," she says, embarrassed at her inexplicable reaction. "I just had the queerest feeling." For a moment, she looks me in the eyes, as if half-suspecting it was something to do with me. She shakes her head and leads me to the sitting room where we settle into comfortable chairs.

"So what's this all about, Special Agent Wu?" Jack asks. "I hope Margaret isn't in any kind of trouble."

"Nothing like that, sir. It's just a background check for a new post your daughter is being consider for." I have no real idea whether this excuse is plausible but the Nielsen's seemed to accept it. "Mostly, I just wanted to meet you folks and ask you one or two simple questions."

"Fire away," Jack says.

I turn to him. "Firstly, can I confirm that you and Mrs. Nielsen are Margaret's natural parents."

"Yes, we are. Married thirty years in October. Maggie is our firstborn."

"What kind of post is this she's applied for?" Mary asks.

I turn back to her with a regretful smile. "I'm sorry, Ma'am. I can't discuss that. I'm sure your daughter will give you all the details in due course." I could just imagine *that* conversation. It would probably take Margaret about two seconds to work out what was really going on.

"And you have one other child, I believe?"

"Yes, indeed," says Jack. "Two beautiful girls."

"I don't mean to be rude, Mr. Wu," says Mary. "But do you think I could just see your ID?"

Damn the woman. What was it about me that has her so spooked? "Of course," I say and hand her Wu's badge. She examines it closely and it seems to satisfy her, at least long enough for me to get some information about her own parents and siblings. I take notes in Wu's book, although my memory is extremely accurate.

"I'm sorry," she says, interrupting a rambling exposition by Jack on his own family history. "I'm not really comfortable with all these questions. Why didn't Maggie tell us anything about this?"

"Now, Mary, Special Agent Wu is only doing his job. And it is to help Maggie, after all."

"That's quite all right, sir," I say. "I've imposed on you good people long enough." I put away the notebook and stand up. The Nielsens stand up too. "You've both been very helpful." We head for the door. "There is just one more thing, though. I'll need to get in touch with Margaret's sister, Rachel."

Jack starts speaking but Mary cuts him off. "I'll ask her to give you a call," she says, "if you'd like to leave your number."

"Our records show this house as her current address," I say, with a smile. Humans like you to smile. It makes them feel comfortable, which is strange when you think how easy a smile is to fake. "Is she in?"

"No, she's out."

I see that Jack has finally got the message and is letting his wife do all the talking. I'm just thinking I might have to slip into him and find out where Rachel is, when a vehicle pulls into the drive. We all look out through the window to see a small car stop outside. The driver is a woman who looks a lot like Margaret but young enough to be her sister.

"Perhaps that's her now?" I say and step outside.

The young woman climbs out of her car and looks quizzically as the three of us approach. She is dressed in black with black-painted nails and lips, heavy eye makeup and heavy boots.

"Rachel Nielsen?" I ask, holding out a hand. "I'm Martin Wu. I'm with the FBI."

She holds out a hand to shake mine, looking past me to her parents for an explanation. As with her mother, I peek cautiously into her mind as soon as our hands meet, ready to pull back at once. And that is probably what saves me.

A nightmare comes roaring out of Rachel and into Wu's body like an express train out of a tunnel. It is irresistible. I fall back in confusion as its claws and fangs rip the fabric of Wu's mind. It is all I can do to stay out of its reach. I scramble for cover, diving into the man's unconscious, running like a rabbit.

This is a bad situation. I hardly know Wu's mind. I haven't laid up defences. I have no weapons. Facing a nightmare unprepared is suicide. Many comrades have died in situations just like this. At my back, the beast is slavering and howling. I can feel its hatred, feel how much it wants to destroy me. I shout out to it as I flee. "Wait! We don't have to fight. Just stop and listen to me. What I'm doing here can help your kind. It's in our mutual interest for you to listen to me."

Meanwhile I'm searching. Wu is an inadequate, insecure man. He likes his big car. He likes his FBI status. Does he like guns, too? Is he into military hardware? Does he have fantasies of power and domination? There must be something in here I can use.

The great ugly monster at my heels is saying nothing. I can almost feel its hot breath on my neck. Any moment now I must turn and fight or else it will take me from behind. The fact that it doesn't speak may mean it is not one of the nightmares I spoke to, not the kind that is intelligent and might be reasoned with. Perhaps it is the ordinary kind. The kind they called the muliebri. That's bad news as far as trying to talk my way out of this. But not all bad news. The sentient ones are a lot bigger and fiercer than the standard nightmare. If it is one of the muliebri, I stand some chance as long as I can find a weapon.

I am deep in Wu's mind now. I should be finding his stash of ground-to-air missiles or whatever gets him off. Instead I hurtle into a large, empty room. It looks like a gymnasium but on the ground is a thick, padded mat.

Dojo.

The word means nothing to me until I see the white suit on a hanger. I dodge towards it. It is made of thick, coarse cotton, with three-quarter legs and sleeves. The jacket has no fastenings except a belt at the waist. A black belt.

I grab the suit as I race past, morphing into a semblance of Wu so that I can wear the magical garment. Then, with a dive and a roll, I come to a dead stop, facing my enemy, naked feet planted, hands raised, eyes steady and calm.

The nightmare doesn't pause for a moment, but now I need not fear it. I step lightly aside, batting away a clawed arm with a sweeping block from my own. The monster careens past and staggers to a halt. Bellowing with rage, it charges back at me, fangs bared.

I'd rather Wu imagined himself with a large bazooka but a karate master will just have to do. As the beast approaches, I shift my weight, narrowly dodge its slashing jaws, and slam a superhuman punch into its scaly ribcage. I think I hear bones cracking. Disconcertingly, the blow jars my arm and shoulder. The creature's tail lashes at my legs and I barely manage to leap over it.

I come down off-balance and have to throw myself into a roll to avoid a kick from a hind leg. This should be going a lot better than it is. Trust Wu to have such miserably low self-esteem that he's inadequate even in his own fantasies.

I block another swipe from those taloned fingers and deliver a good solid kick to the nightmare's chest. It rocks back on its haunches and tail but doesn't seem injured. It glares at me with baleful eyes and tilts its massive head, reassessing its prey. It drops to all fours, and crouches, ready to spring.

Not wanting to let it use its great bulk to overwhelm me, I strike first, leaping forward and shooting a kick straight into its muzzle. It is a good kick, with all my weight behind it, and it hits the nightmare square in the face. Yet, apart from a bit of roaring and shrieking, I still don't seem to have hurt it. A kind of bloody snot drips from its snout, but I can see it is more surprised than damaged.

Landing on my feet, and cursing Wu for a spineless jellyfish, I let my momentum carry me into another leap, over the night-mare's shoulder and into a roll across the padded mat. I come up running, the creature screeching at my back as it takes off after me.

Perhaps the blow to its ribs did injure it, because I seem to be better able now to keep ahead of it, to gain a little even. I scrabble my way back up to the surface of Wu's mind. Cursing him for a useless jerkoff.

I hit the top and flow out of Wu into Margaret's sister Rachel as fast as I can go. She and Wu are still standing in the drive, still shaking hands, neither of them able to let go. Mary and Jack are fussing around them, alarmed that they are just standing there mutely, hand in hand, like mannequins.

With a signal that overrides everything in Rachel's whole body, I make her snatch her hand away from Wu. She almost falls over with the force of it, and I almost lose my ass, as the connection between me and Wu breaks.

Without giving her a moment to think, I make Rachel stumble, then run to get the car between herself and Wu. He's an FBI agent and is armed. If the nightmare is the smart kind and not just a dumb beast, I'm still in serious trouble.

But Wu just stands there is a daze, looking around as if a tornado had just dropped him in Oz.

Chapter 12

After all the confusion and amazement has settled down at the Nielsen household, and Special Agent Wu has blustered and shouted and, finally, got back into his big, black car and driven away, I put the idea into Rachel's head to go at once to see her sister and ask her what is going on.

Her parents plan to call the FBI and demand an explanation as soon as I'm gone and I can't help thinking that Wu deserves whatever his bosses do to him for nearly getting me killed.

I have plenty of time to take a look at Rachel on the drive back. Fortunately for me, she isn't a sensitive like her mother and sister. I'd guessed as much when the nightmare appeared, but, who knows, maybe nightmares have a way of slipping into people like Margaret unnoticed. They've had plenty of years to co-evolve with humans and develop survival tricks like that. So I definitely put that aspect of my escape down to blind luck.

Rachel Nielsen is younger than her sister and definitely not such a high achiever. She once started a degree in psychology but dropped out after a year. Since then, she has lived with her parents, earning a little money doing bar work and waitressing. She's thinking of going back to school one day to qualify as a counsellor and dreams of having her own practice. Meanwhile, she has a social life that involves hanging out with a lot of losers she doesn't like much, an on-and-off boyfriend who's a musician, recreational drugs, and her little car, which she loves.

She thinks Margaret got all the brains in the family and all the breaks. It doesn't bother her at all. She doesn't care much what happens to herself, something I am beginning to suspect is a side-effect of hosting a nightmare. In fact, she admires and respects her older sister and is looking forward to seeing her again, despite all the weirdness that is going on with the FBI.

I try to use what knowledge I have of human genetics to fit my four datapoints from Margaret's family but it doesn't narrow down the possibilities much. All I can really say is that it is much more likely now than before that Margaret's abilities are inherited.

I riffle through the junk in Rachel's unconscious, looking for weapons. I was lax earlier when I rode Wu. I should have been better prepared. There is nothing that is very helpful in Rachel's mind. She's a depressive, somewhat nihilistic young woman, but she has no particular bogeymen in her attic. Sure, there are scenes from films and images of horror from the TV news that have disturbed her. Like many people, she fears terrorists and muggers, spiders and large dogs, but there is little that is tangible and powerful that I can use. I just have to hope that I am able to leave her before too long.

She arrives at Margaret's apartment building, having called ahead. Now would be the time to go, find a new ride, and get on with my hunt, but a sentimental urge makes me hang on. I want to know how Margaret and Frank are doing.

Rachel hugs her sister and hurries into the apartment, bursting to tell her the news. She tosses her bag into a chair and manages to say, "You would not believe..." before she sees Frank standing in the kitchen doorway. Her reaction is massive curiosity mixed with embarrassment and surprise. Could this be Margaret's boyfriend? She has never met any of Margaret's men since her sister left home. She has always suspected that there were none.

She sees a tall, wiry man, slim, but strong. He's got a craggy, out-doorsy kind of attractiveness, like a cowboy, she thinks. He looks at her carefully. His steady gaze seems to take her all in and weigh her up, as if he's seen so much and knows so much that each new person he meets is just another example of a familiar type.

He's about Maggie's age, which surprises her, as he seemed rather older at first glance. His hair is damp and he looks freshly scrubbed. He's just had a shower, she realises, confirming, in her mind, her first assumption about Frank's presence. Altogether, she decides her sister has snagged herself a bit of a hunk.

I look at Frank through Rachel's eyes, but all I see is the tired and harried man I have been riding.

"Oh," Margaret says, a little flustered. "Raich, this is Frank. Frank, my sister Rachel."

Frank steps forward to shake her hand but I stay where I am, inside Rachel. She is impressed by his big hands and his smile. Human sexuality is a complete mystery to me. I can understand that their bodies and mannerisms trigger sexual responses in one another, but the subtle nuances of it all are puzzling. I can understand that they are constantly on the lookout for a mate – even when they are pair-bonded – but I find it hard to sympathise with their endlessly distracted state.

"Frank Taylor," he says. "I'm a friend of your sister's. She's very kindly putting me up for a few days."

"Frank." Rachel mulls the word. "Maggie never mentioned she had a friend staying." She looks meaningfully at Margaret who, out of Frank's sight, pulls a face, which Rachel interprets as telling her to shut up and stop fishing.

"What's the big news?" Margaret asks. She walks out to put the kettle on and has to shout from the kitchen. "You sounded quite excited on the phone." Rachel and Frank follow her out there.

Rachel doesn't know whether to say anything with Frank there. "It's sort of a family thing..."

"Are they all right?"

Again Rachel hesitates.

Finally, Frank takes the hint. "Look, I should probably go out and, er, see to a couple of things. I'll leave you two alone."

He starts to leave but Margaret stops him. "No, don't go yet. Raich, what's going on? Don't worry about Frank."

Rachel doesn't like the idea of having a stranger there. At a deeper level, she doesn't like the fact that her sister seems willing to bring this stranger into their family's affairs. Nevertheless, she supposes that Margaret knows what she's doing.

"The FBI came to see Mom and Dad today. A Special Agent Martin Wu. Mean anything?" Margaret shakes her head and she and Frank exchange glances. "I was out. He questioned them about you. He said it was a background check, that you'd applied for a Government job or something. Then he started asking about whether they were your real parents, and who your grandparents were. He asked about me and Mom's brothers and sisters. Then Mom got upset and said she wasn't going to answer any more questions. Apparently Dad would have sat there all day being interrogated if she hadn't made a fuss."

"Did they check his credentials?"

"A couple of times, Mom said."

"Then what did he do – this Special Agent Wu guy?"

"Well, nothing, really. He just got up to leave. Said he wanted to talk to me next."

Margaret is looking grim. Rachel can see her sister is getting angry. Angrier, perhaps, than the story warrants.

"But you were out."

"Well, I got back just as he was leaving. He walked right up to me and introduced himself. Mom looked furious."

"He shook hands," Margaret said.

"Yes, he did. Funny you should say that, but Mom and Dad said that he and I just stood there holding hands for maybe a minute or more. I don't remember it at all, but how creepy is that? Then they said I suddenly jerked my hand back like he'd electrocuted me." She rubbed her arm. "That sounds right because my arm aches like I spent the morning arm wrestling."

"And the agent," Margaret presses her. "What did he do then?"

Rachel considers how to describe it. "He just went nuts, really. He was sort of confused and scared, like he'd just woken up and didn't know where he was. We were all, like, whoa!" She mimed a gesture of warding off the crazy guy. "Then he got in his car and drove way. Mom's going to call the FBI to ask them what they think they're playing at. And I came here to tell you. So *did* you?"

"What?"

"Apply for a secret Government job or something?"

"No. Look, Raich, this is important. Did you touch anybody – anybody at all – since you touched Wu?"

"Touch?" Alarms go off in Rachel's head, her adrenaline surges. "Oh God, it's a medical thing, right? Like some kind of plague or something?"

"No, no. It's nothing like that, but, listen, did you touch anyone since you touched Wu? Mom? Dad? Did you stop for gas?"

"No." She tries to remember if she touched her parents, but the panic she's feeling keeps growing. "No, I don't think so. Jesus, Maggie, what's going on?"

Margaret glares straight at me through her sister's eyes and shouts, "Get out of there you bastard!"

I put Rachel aside for a moment and take over. "Hello, Margaret. I'm sorry about this, I really didn't mean to ride your sister but things got complicated."

Frank is staring at me as if he's seen a ghost. "It's you!" he cries and stumbles back a step.

"I'll leave Rachel soon." I try to sound reassuring but Margaret isn't interested.

"I told you not to go near my family. I told you to stay the hell away from them." She steps forward as if she is about to strike me but stops dead, probably realising who she would really be hurting. The shock on her face shows how close she came.

"I need to know, Margaret. Your concern for your family is misplaced. What I'm doing might save them. It might save your whole species. I won't stop just because it makes you unhappy. Besides, I saved your sister from something much worse than me."

"What could be worse than you?" Frank says. His face is set and angry. At a guess, I'd say Margaret had been explaining a few things to him. "You burrowed into my brain like some kind of

damned maggot and squatted there while I nearly got killed –
twice!" He is speechless with outrage for a moment. "I thought I
was going mad! What right do you have to use people like that?"

He seems to expect an answer, so I say, "Frank, I just did what
was necessary at the time. There is a lot at stake and we need to
stay focused on the important issues. You asked what could be
worse than me, well let me tell you."

I try to explain about the nightmare inside Rachel, but Margaret won't listen.

"Get out of my sister! I can't stand here and watch her like
this. Get out you disgusting... thing. Get out!"

I'm about to ask her where she thinks I should go, when Frank
steps up and takes Rachel's hand.

"No, Frank," Margaret says.

"It's all right, Margaret. It's better me than your sister. At least
this time it's my choice.

"When you're inside," he says to me, "I want to hear what's
going on. You can do that, can't you?"

I nod Rachel's head, and flow into him.

As soon as I am gone, Margaret rushes forward and grabs her
sister, hugging her tightly and pulling her free of Frank's hand.
She leads her away from us, glaring at me over her shoulder.

Rachel pulls away from her, confused and alarmed. "What are
you doing? What's going on?"

She notices Margaret's glare and turns to look at Frank. "Did I... Did I miss something? Maggie?"

"It's all right, darling, I'll explain everything later. Frank was just going out and I need to go with him for a while. I want you to stay here. Don't let anybody in while we're gone. And don't leave the apartment. Not for anything."

"Maggie? You're scaring me. What's going on? Is this something to do with the FBI? Are Mom and Dad all right?"

"They're fine." Margaret looks at me for confirmation and I nod Frank's head. "Frank and I just need to talk something over. In private. OK?"

Rachel shakes her head. "No. Definitely no."

It takes Margaret several more minutes to persuade Rachel to stay put so that we can leave. Frank's mind is jittery with fear and disgust, knowing I'm inside him, but he can't actually feel me and he is torturing himself over nothing.

We go down in the lift and out through the lobby in tense silence. In the street she rounds on me and says, "Don't you ever infest my sister again, you bastard, or any of my family."

"Ride."

"What?"

"We say ride, not infest."

"Well, you would. I want your word you won't do it again. Promise me."

"I didn't plan to do it. I was fighting for my life. Your sister had a nightmare inside her. Do you have any idea what that means?"

"What are you talking about?"

We are standing in the street arguing like a couple of human lovers, and people are watching. "Come on," I tell her, flicking Frank's eyes towards the gawpers. "We need to find somewhere more private."

We find a coffee shop and sit in a quiet corner.

"I want your word," she says again when we have ordered.

"Well you can't have it. I'm not going to promise you anything that might endanger me, or my mission." I suppose I could have lied to her, but lying is not in my nature, and giving one's word is a serious commitment, perhaps more serious than a human can understand.

She purses her lips and tries to get up but I put a hand on her arm and hold her. "You should listen to this. Mine is not the only species that lives in human minds."

She looks at me in astonishment, hearing me at last. She stops struggling to stand up. "You mean there are other aliens here too?"

"Not aliens. An indigenous life-form. We call them night-mares."

It finally dawns on her what I had been saying about her sister. "A nightmare was inside Rachel!" Then she remembers some more. "You fought with it. Is it dead?"

"No, not dead, but gone. I left it inside the FBI guy. It's probably still there."

"But..." She seems overwhelmed by the implications of what I've told her.

"Listen. Not long after we got here, we lost a number of our people to these creatures. They are very strong and very vicious. It took us a while to learn how to fight them, to train our sniffers to recognise them. We lost lots more people. We call them nightmares partly because they are just that for us, but partly because of the dark influence they have on their human hosts; bad dreams, depression, mood changes... They are mindless animals, not self-aware, not intelligent, and very, very aggressive.

"The Vaticinatrix told us we had picked up the creatures on our journey to Earth. Like the cognophyte equivalent of finding rats in our bilge. We were ordered to hunt them down and exterminate them. For our own safety, but also for the health of our livest – Of our human hosts."

Except, now that I look back, the Vaticinatrix had not appeared even then to speak to us. Her administrators had passed on the news and the orders. Just how long had the Vaticinatrix been missing?

"So, as if you're not bad enough, you brought these other bastards with you, too. No, hang on, you said they were indigenous."

"Bear with me. Some days ago, one of them found me. Even though I was ready for it, it took me everything I had to kill it. With its dying breath it accused my people of invading Earth and killing its own people. It told me they were from here, from Earth. It called us murderers."

Margaret frowns. "You said they were mindless animals. Like rats. How could it tell you anything?"

"That's the point. It shouldn't have been able to, but it did. It wasn't like the others I'd seen before. It was bigger and stronger, but it was intelligent too. Others of its kind spoke to me later. They told me the same thing."

"So now you've got some kind of war on your hands and we're just – what? – the battlefield?"

I can feel Frank sharing Margaret's indignation. Neither of them seems to be seeing the bigger picture. Maybe because I haven't told them everything. As far as they're concerned, an in-digenous life-form wiping out an invader probably looks like a good result.

I should tell them the rest, except, first I need to understand my own motives. I rode Rachel back into their lives for sentimental reasons, I told myself. So what am I doing here trying to explain the situation to these two hostile humans? I take a moment to consider it and came to a conclusion.

"There is a problem with my Colony. The Vaticinatrix has been usurped somehow. Ordinary administrators are running the Colony."

"There's that word again."

"Vaticinatrix? It's a real, English word. I assumed you'd know it. A literal translation is 'prophetess' but to us it just means a female leader. The head of every Colony is a female. The only female. The rest of us are males."

"She Who Must Be Obeyed," Margaret says. A reference I don't get.

"My Vaticinatrix has gone missing. The wrong people are in charge, doing the wrong things. The Colony should pack up now and leave as soon as it can. Colonising this planet is immoral and dangerous. The people running the Colony now don't seem to see that. They mean to stay and fight it out."

"Won't they lose? There must be lots of these nightmare things if they're supposed to live here. Won't they just overrun you?" She didn't sound unhappy at the prospect.

"You don't want a war fought between cognophytes. Humanity isn't just the battlefield, to use your analogy, it's also an endless supply of war-horses. There could be large numbers of casualties. Even the skirmishing that has happened so far has claimed many human victims. If you wanted to kill me now, probably the only way you could do it would be to kill Frank. If his brain dies with me in it, I die too. It's like smashing up a computer to stop a program running."

I note that Frank is still putting together the pieces of the last few days, realising just why people have been trying to kill him. For a moment he regrets his chivalry in offering to take me from

Rachel, but I know that he would do it again, even now that he knows the danger – especially now that he knows the danger.

I want to make Margaret understand the peril her species is in. "The nightmares do not seem technically sophisticated. They seem to live a life that is quite independent of their hosts'. Most of them seem to be just what we thought they were, simple animals. There may be more than one species. But even the sentient ones don't seem to be taking an interest in human technologies." It was only an impression. I could easily be wrong. There could even be other varieties of nightmare, or just different cultures, as there are among humans. Some of them might be quite technically sophisticated.

"The point is, the Colony is not simple or backward. We are aware of and make use of technologies that are well in advance of yours. Imagine a fully-equipped army of two thousand US Marines fighting a war with a planetful of Australian Aborigines, or Kalahari bushmen. I think it is quite possible that the Marines might eventually subjugate, even exterminate their more primitive enemy, don't you?"

Margaret was looking at me with horror. Frank was full of gung-ho nonsense about how the human race wouldn't just stand by while other species used them like that. They still hadn't got the point.

"Look, I don't want a war. I want to get my people safely away from here and never come back. You don't want a war either. Trust me, Frank, you don't! But there's going to be one unless I stop it. And, for that, I am going to need your help. Both of you. And Rachel. And anyone else we can recruit."

That's why I came back. Not just because I needed these humans to help me save their species, certainly not because they have any special skills, training or aptitude for what I need them to do, but because these are the only two humans I have come across, in all the hundreds I've ridden, that I believe I can trust.

Now I just need them to trust me.

And there is another reason, one I don't like to admit to myself. I need others. I can't be alone. Celedorn was right. A mindrider alone can't function. We are, above all else, social beings. Of course, a soldier gets used to periods of isolation, but he knows the Colony is always there, just a call away, a short trip. If it weren't for my military training and experience, I think I'd be going mad by now, or running back to the Colony on any terms Celedorn cared to name.

Perhaps I have gone mad. Look at me, sitting here talking to a couple of humans as if they were equals. Almost as far gone as humans I've seen who talk to their cats, or to their gods, all contact with reality lost. Is this me now?

Chapter 13

"This is insane." Frank looks across the dark, wet streets and all he sees are shadows and menace. When I look, although it is through the same eyes, I see cover and the security of invisibility. Frank is frightened and he complains in a pathetic attempt to persuade me not to go on. It is as if he really believes I do not understand the risks.

Keep going, Frank. Everything is exactly the way we planned it.

With a groan of protest, he pushes himself out of his hiding place and runs across the street to a group of dumpsters beside a brick wall. The wall is old, with crumbling mortar and worn bricks. There are high windows, barred and dark.

OK. This is the spot.

Frank pulls a coal chisel out of his jacket and starts working it into the mortar. Chunks crumble away and drop to the ground in falls of grey dust. The grinding and scraping is almost no sound at all, but Frank winces with every thrust of the chisel. It takes nearly five minutes to get the first brick out of the wall. After that, they come out quickly and with very little effort. Within fifteen minutes, there is a hole big enough to crawl through, and a neat pile of bricks standing beside it.

Inside the wall is a framework of wooden batons onto which sheets of drywall are fixed. We have been lucky in that none of the batons block our way. Only the grey cement board stands between us and the interior.

Frank is sweating, not from his labours but from his fears. I adjust his brain chemistry a little to calm him down. I don't want him making any mistakes.

With a hand drill, he bores two holes in the drywall and pushes expanding bolts through. The material is as soft and crumbly as the old mortar and the drill goes in easily. Next, he drills four holes in a big square, wide enough apart for his shoulders, with the two bolts at the centre. With a hand-held keyhole saw, he slowly and quietly connects the four holes with four straight cuts. Finally, he takes hold of the bolts and pulls out the square of board, setting it down gently beside the bricks.

He has seen this done before. He has a memory of it from a crime scene. At the time, he admired its ingenuity. This whole approach was Frank's idea. Now I congratulate him on its success. It has taken us almost thirty minutes to gain access to the Barstowe

Street Barracks, but we have triggered no alarms and the night is still young.

Frank climbs through the hole he has made into the darkness beyond. He takes a folded sheet of blackout cloth and a reel of sticky tape from his pocket. He unfolds the cloth and tapes it to the wall over the hole. This is so no light can escape into the street to give us away. The unrolling of the duct tape is by far the loudest sound we have made so far.

With the hole covered, it is as black as space inside. Frank risks a quick flash of his torch to show us the room. We are in a disused storeroom with empty shelving and a painted concrete floor. There is a single door with no glass in it. A fluorescent strip is in the ceiling above us.

Through the door, turn right and look for an exit on the left.

I have been in the barracks before, just a quick visit earlier in the week, riding a young corporal who got a sudden urge to walk around the site and look at the many buildings. I didn't dare take him into any of them at the time, unsure as to who or what might be inside. The young man's knowledge of his own barracks was hardly encyclopedic, but he knew enough to show me where a certain special ops colonel was billeted.

The corridor is not so dark, being lit by low-wattage bulbs at long intervals. Frank puts his head out and looks for security cameras but can see none. For a long time, he listens to the silent disused building before I nudge him into action.

He runs along the corridor at a crouch, as if it might hide him from the nonexistent observers. I don't bother to talk him out of it. In his head the refrain, "This is such a bad idea. I must be crazy. What the hell am I doing here?" is playing over and over, but I reckon anything that makes him feel better is fine by me. He didn't want to come. He didn't want me riding him. He is here on sufferance. Only Margaret's urgings persuaded him at all. He has a soft spot for our lady doctor, even though he doesn't admit it to himself.

When we find the exit, it is locked. Frank has a small pair of bolt cutters and a hacksaw with him in case we need them, but we don't. While the rest of the building is being allowed to decay, the doors are strong, freshly-painted, and protected by electronic locks. The locks are operated by entering an alphanumeric code. We are in luck.

I place Frank's hand on the lock, letting his body's slight electromagnetic field surround and interpenetrate the mechanism. Interfacing with simple electronic devices is part of a mindrider's basic training. It is a fast and efficient way of operating equipment. In effect, the device becomes an extension of your mind and, with a thought, you can make it obey you. Without needing to know any security codes at all, I tell the logic chips in the lock to open the door, and they do.

Frank is impressed by this too. He has no idea what I've just done. All he sees is that by touching the lock, I have made it open. But electronic chips are like brains, just another computing device, and a cognophyte of my species is as comfortable riding one as the other. There are computers, elsewhere in the Galaxy, with sufficient size and complexity that a colonist could live within one quite happily. Humankind has a long way to go before it reaches that level of technology. At the moment, every computing device on the whole planet, along with the Internet and its millions of routers, all added together, are still computationally simpler than a single human brain.

We peer out into the streets and squares of the barracks. It is a large site, mostly low buildings, widely spread, and almost free of cars. An oasis of space and peace in the midst of the crowded city. Frank and I have both studied maps of the barracks. Despite its name, not many soldiers are billeted there. There are sheds for armoured personnel carriers, a small armoury, and a heliport with three large helicopters standing in the rain like forlorn insects. Most of the site is office buildings, some as old as the wall we came through, some newer and yet more dilapidated. In one corner is a double row of soldiers' quarters, near them a terrace of officers' houses, and beyond that, the base commander's house.

Colonel David Sturtz lives there. As well as running this little empire, Sturtz has his own private army-within-an-army, a black ops unit reporting directly to him. As I know from being inside the head of one of them, the unit takes its orders only from Sturtz and was set up about two years ago – not long after the Colony arrived. It has its own quarters and training facilities and its duties have been extremely odd, mostly involving domestic kidnappings and assassinations.

Come on Frank. You know the way.

I have to keep prodding him because he is so frightened of be-ing caught. I have reassured him again and again that, whatever trouble he gets into, I can easily extricate him. Now I begin to see that his fears are not entirely rational. The image of his fearsome, powerful father is stirring beneath the surface of his mind.

Your father was in the military, I say, making the connection at last. A swirl of mental imagery blows through his mind like a winter squall.

"So?" he whispers, but the reminder is enough to get him moving out of pure agitation. As arranged, he strolls casually across the base, as if he has every right to be there. There is no one around to challenge him, but, if there were, all they would see is a man who obviously belongs, heading home for the night.

I wish I could have brought my sniffers. I wish I had another mindrider as backup. I wish I didn't have to rely on the reluctant Frank.

Stay calm, there are two soldiers approaching.

Frank's autonomic nervous system does back-flips but he man-ages to stay in character as the two guards wander over to him. It is nearly two in the morning and Frank has no ID and no excuse for being there. The soldiers are military policemen, armed and curious. One of them stops a few paces away while the other ap-proaches.

"A bit late for a stroll," he says. He pulls out a torch and shines it in Frank's face.

"Couldn't sleep," Frank tells him. His tone is amiable. He is acting a little drunk. Nothing excessive, just enough to give the MP a reason not to be suspicious. "I suppose you want to see some ID."

Frank reaches into his back pocket for his wallet. The heavy tools hidden in his jacket make it sag and sway the way an inno-cent jacket should not. Frank's heartbeat kicks up a few beats faster.

Steady. Just give him the wallet like we planned.

Frank holds out the wallet and the MP reaches to take it. When the soldier's fingers are holding it, I take Frank's hand and grab the MP by the wrist, flowing into him even before he has regis-tered what has happened. It takes me just a moment to get my bearings and to start tweaking the man's perceptions. A moment later and I'm flowing back into Frank, by which time the MP is shaking Frank's hand and slapping him on the shoulder.

"Hey, Greg," he calls to his worried-looking companion. "This is my old buddy Jerry! We served in the forty-second together in Iraq."

OK Frank, I'm back. His name's Pete.

"Look, Pete, we should get together for a drink, yeah? Like old times." I have to admit, Frank picks up on the fiction quickly. "Only I've got to go now. I'll look you up in the morning, OK?"

"Sure, buddy. That'll be great." They shake hands again and Frank walks on. Behind him, I hear the other MP, Greg, asking

WTF? and Pete reassuring him that Jerry's OK, Jerry's a great guy.

Frank's heart is still racing but he's beginning to think maybe he might just get through this without being arrested on terrorism charges. He doesn't know that I would have made Pete kill Greg and then himself before I would have let them arrest Frank, but it is probably better that Frank doesn't think about such things.

We reach the Colonel's house without further incident and I make Frank check out the alarm system. I disable it easily and we go in through a pair of French doors at the back. Frank stops in the hallway.

"You see that?" he whispers.

I see. There is a woman's coat on the coat rack along with children's shoes below it.

A wife, maybe two kids, both girls, I say.

"We can't do this," he says and starts to retrace his steps. I stop him. "Let me go!" he hisses. I've told him he doesn't need to speak out loud. I can hear it if he just thinks it. I might have to gag him too to get us through this.

Frank, this is not a problem. It is an opportunity.

"Let me go!"

I clamp down on his speech centres. *No one is going to get hurt. Just calm down.* But Frank is convinced the kids are going to be caught in the cross-fire of some ridiculous gun-fight. He can see the images clearly, probably left over from some TV cop show. There is lots of blood and screaming. I don't have time to argue him out of it, so I take over.

I'm sorry, Frank, but you're being ridiculous. I head up the stairs to where I expect to find the bedrooms. There are several doors off the landing and one of them is ajar, with a weak light coming from inside. I peep through and see two single beds, each with a human child in it. The girls are both quite small but I pick the larger one in the hope that she will be the better coordinated of the two.

I move quietly to her bedside and rest my hand on her shoulder. She stirs slightly but does not wake up.

OK Frank. I'm leaving you now and moving into this child. I'm going to wake her up and make her go to her father. She's going to touch him, and I'll get inside him that way. No guns. No bloodbath. No screaming.

I give him a while to think about it. *When I leave you, I want you to go downstairs and wait for me in the kitchen. I'll come down in the colonel. You got that?*

I can see that he does, although he still doesn't like it. The idea of me riding the little girl, even for such a short while fills him with anger and revulsion. But I have no time to worry about Frank's sensibilities.

I give the girl a shake and, as she wakes, I slip into her. I make her get out of bed. She is barefoot and I feel the deep furriness of a bedside rug between her toes. Frank is standing there in the darkness, staring at her. I make her do a shooing movement with her hand. Frank glares but turns and leaves. I give him a moment to get off the landing and down the stairs before I take the child to her father's bedroom.

She has to use both hands to turn the knob but it opens and she steps into the room. It is darker in there than on the landing and we stand for a while to let her eyes adjust to the darkness. He sleeps alone. His wife has the room next door. I can see from the child's mind that she is unhappy about this. Mummy and Daddy used to sleep together before they started shouting at each other all the time.

I move her forward and she stumbles over a pair of shoes set down at the side of the bed. Before she can regain her balance, I hear the colonel snort as he wakes up. There is a clatter, he is do-ing something I can't make out. I make the child say, "Daddy," just as the bedside light comes on to reveal her father swinging a large handgun out from under his pillow and pointing it at her head.

She squeals with fright and I let her. My best chance is to leave her to behave naturally and trust that this man will not shoot his own child.

"Angela?" The gun wavers but he doesn't lower it. "What are you doing here, sweetheart? We talked about not sneaking up on Daddy, didn't we?"

"Are you going to kill me?" Her words, not mine. In her mind is genuine fear. Daddy has been acting strange and aggressive towards her lately. Mummy says to stay away from him. It's his work making him cranky.

"Of course not, sweetheart!" Yet even the child notices that he still does not lower the gun.

Little Angela wants to run, to get to Mummy and safety, but I want to know what is going on. I make her take a step towards him.

"Stop!" He almost shouts it. He's even more frightened than the child is. The gun is steady and threatening. I almost believe he might shoot. "Don't come any closer. Just go back to bed. There's a good girl. You probably just had a bad dream. Everything will be fine in the morning."

"David? Oh my God!" A woman bursts into the room and grabs up the child, I feel her envelope me, sheltering me with her body. I leave the child and flow into her. It is Sturtz's wife. "What the hell are you doing, pointing that thing at Angie? Are you completely mad?" She thinks maybe he is. His behaviour lately has been irrational and paranoid. She thinks he needs professional help. Now she's sure of it. What kind of a monster points a gun at his own child?

Sturtz is looking shocked, abashed. He stammers out an excuse. The child startled him. He was having a bad dream.

His wife is growing angry, now that the first shock has passed. "What, and you sleep with a gun by your bed now? What is wrong with you? You could have shot her. Will you put that damned thing down?" Despite everything, he still has the gun aimed at his wife and child.

He looks desperate, torn. His voice is unsteady. "Sharon, I need you to take Angela and leave my room."

"What?"

"I – I have an important meeting tomorrow. I need to sleep. I can't have you all running in and out of here all night."

Sharon is dumbfounded. "Are you completely out of your mind? Put that gun away right now. Do you hear me?"

"Sharon, I can't. I can't risk it. Just go. Leave the room." He is growing angry too now. He raises his voice, no longer appeasing. "Just get out of the damned room woman and take the child with you!"

Sharon stands up. She is beginning to be frightened now, but she is still angry. She straightens herself, hands still protectively holding her daughter. "All right, if that's what you want, we're leaving."

And she means it. She slams the door on the way out and marches straight to her bedroom. She gets herself dressed and then starts dressing Angela. She is making a lot of noise, slamming drawers and talking loudly. Pretty soon the second child teeters into her room, rubbing her eyes. Sharon sweeps her into the maelstrom, finding her an outfit to put on, sending her for her coat, her favourite toy, her toothbrush. The plan is to drive to Sharon's mother's house and get the kids somewhere safe, away from David.

Chapter 14

None of this is according to plan. None of it is the least bit helpful. I wonder what Frank, hiding in the kitchen, is making of all the commotion. He is probably trying to stuff himself in the broom closet right at that moment.

There can only be one explanation for the Colonel's behaviour; he has learned from his unit's attempt to kill Frank, just how easily a mindrider can pass from one ride to another. Now he dare not let anyone, even his own family, come close to him. No wonder Sharon and the children think he has gone mad.

I need a new plan and quick.

I have Sharon run down the stairs to the kitchen. It is dark and she turns on the lights. "Frank?" I make her whisper. "Come out, it's me."

There are few places you could hide a full-grown human in that room. None, I realise, once I check Sharon's memories of how full various cupboards are. So Frank must be somewhere else in the house, or outside. The back door is unlocked when Sharon tries it, so she steps out onto the patio and scans the shrubbery. I make her call again, and this time Frank appears from behind a bush and waves me over to him.

"What the hell is going on?" he wants to know, as soon as Sharon is within hissing distance.

"Complications. Sturtz knows I'm after him. He pulled a gun on his daughter and wouldn't let her near."

"What? Is she safe?" Frank's reaction is gratifying. Procreation for my people is very different than it is for humans, but we all love and protect our young with a fierceness that would make the idea of threatening them absolutely unthinkable. I had thought humans felt roughly the same, but they are a species that often surprises me. Individual attitudes to most things seem to vary across a very wide spectrum.

"This one is Sharon, the mother. She's taking the kids away. Frank will be alone soon. We need to act before she leaves."

I tell him the plan and, as I suspected, he doesn't like it.

"Can't you just keep the wife at home and wait for an opportunity?"

"Do you want to risk him shooting the children?" Even for me, the idea of the little ones being killed by their own father is revolting. I am hoping Frank will be even more revolted.

"But it's all right if I get shot, is that it?"

I make the woman shrug. "Pretty much."

Frank looks like he might grind his own teeth to dust. But even he can see it is the lesser of two evils. "All right. Let's do it."

I take Sharon back into the kitchen and let go of her mind. She is shocked to find herself there, of course, and looks around for some explanation. With a jolt, she remembers the children and turns to hurry back up the stairs. But before she has gone two paces towards the door, she hears a plant pot fall over in the garden. She turns quickly in alarm and sees Frank run across the patio and hide in the shadows.

Now she really is scared. She stumbles and hurts her wrist as she races up the stairs, taking them almost on all fours. She shouts for her husband, apparently forgetting his crazy behaviour, thinking only that he needs to save them all from the intruder outside. She bursts into his room with his name on her lips and stops dead. The bed is empty.

"Stay where you are."

He is standing to the side of the door, well out of reach, with the gun in his hand. He too is dressed now and he is looking more desperate and confused than ever. "What the hell is going on? What are you shouting about?"

"Th – there's a man in the garden. I – I saw him." The sight of her husband holding a gun on her is somehow worse this time. Now he can offer no excuses for her to half-believe. Now there is just naked, indisputable paranoia. Just David, threatening her, as scary as anything outside.

"A man? A soldier?"

"What? No. Just a man. A big man. A prowler. Hiding."

"Is this some kind of trick?"

"What? For God's sake, David." The conflicting fears, the outrage, are bad, but the emotion that is overwhelming all of them is
resentment at this man's betrayal. This is the man she had loved,
the father of her children, her husband. He is supposed to be
strong for her when she needs him, not going crazy up and waving a gun at her and the girls. Tears fill her eyes so that she can
barely see him. "Oh God," she sobs. Her legs feel weak, and she
would fall to the ground if I don't keep her upright. "Oh God, oh
God."

Sturtz is silent for a long time as she sobs in front of him. "Get
over there," he says at last. His voice is harsh but I can hear the
uncertainty in it. "Over there, by the bed."

"David!" It is a plea. A plea for him to stop being crazy. To be
his old self again. But she stumbles across the room, away from
the door as he told her to.

He immediately dashes through the door onto the landing and
Sharon goes after him. When she gets to the girls' bedroom, he is
standing outside with his back to her, the two girls are in front of
him, frightened and open-mouthed.

"Get back!" he shouts. He whirls on Sharon, waving the gun.
"You too. Stay where you are." To the children, he says, "Get
back into your room and shut the door. Right now!"

Angela looks past him at her mother and says, "Mommy?"

Summoning reserves that surprise her, Sharon manages a smile for her daughters. "Go on now," she says. "You go to your room. I'll be with you in a minute."

They still do not move until Sturtz takes a step towards them and they both turn and flee. I could jump him now. Two paces and a lunge and I'd be on his back, but in the heartbeat that it takes for the girls to scuttle around the corner and out of harm's way, Sturtz turns back to me.

"Don't move. Don't follow me."

"What's going on, David? Who is it outside? Why are you behaving like this?" I know what to say because I can hear the words in Sharon's mind.

"I " Self-doubt is written all over him, in his face, his tense, hesitant movements, his eyes that can't hold hers. "I'm sorry. One day, I'll explain it all, I promise."

He turns and hurries down the stairs. Quietly, I follow behind. I catch up with him at the kitchen door. He is peering in and has a phone against his ear.

"I tell you there's one of them in my fucking garden," he says. Good old Frank is still doing his inept prowler routine, still knocking over pots and flitting from bush to bush. "I want that weapon over here now."

Weapon?

"I know it hasn't been fucking tested. I run the program, you moron. Just get it over here and you can test it all you like."

They're testing a weapon? Against us?

"No, that's too long. I want you here in ten minutes. Don't give me that crap, Bernstein. Just fucking do it! I'm going out to capture the SOB and I want you here for the interrogation – or execution. Now move it!"

He kills the call and stabs another button. "Captain?" I assume he has called his own unit. "Get the men out of bed and get them over to my house, stat. I want a perimeter around it. I've got an intruder and I don't want the bastard leaving until I've had a chance to talk to him. Alert the gate and base security. And, Captain, use the new protocols. Nobody gets within arm's length. If he gets too close, shoot to kill."

I have two minutes, maybe three to get myself and Frank out of there before we're surrounded and cut off. The idea of an experimental weapon on its way chills me. I don't want to be around to be their guinea pig.

Sturtz has his back to the wall and the gun in his hand. He is breathing heavily and sweat stands out on his brow. There is no way he is going to let his wife near him. The man is scared out of his wits. I abandon all my plans for riding the man and focus on escaping.

Normally, I would just hang around in the wife until an opportunity arose to move on. But that seems like a risky option now. If Sturtz suspects her – and the kids – he might have them all arrested and put in isolation. I've also got Frank to think of. I promised him I'd get him out safely. No, I need another way out.

"Are you just going to stand there while there is a man creeping round our house?" I make Sharon say. The Colonel looks up sharply. "Our little girls are up there, or have you forgotten all about them? What kind of coward hides in the hallway while his own children are in danger?"

As she harangues him, she moves around him into the hall and, as soon as she has a clear path to the front door, I get her to sprint to it and through to the garden. Sturtz is bellowing at her to come back. I can't tell if his voice is shaking with anger or concern, and no longer care. All I want to do now is get to Frank and get out of there before the troops arrive.

I make for the back of the house, shouting Frank's name. After a moment, he appears at the side of a small shed and I run to him.

"We've got to get out of here," I say, grabbing his arm with Sharon's hand. As I pass into him, the kitchen window explodes outward and a gunshot destroys the quiet of the barracks. I hear the bullet zipping through the leaves of a nearby bush.

"Don't move. Either of you."

Sturtz is running through the kitchen, trying to keep his gun trained on us as he dodges furniture. I finish the transfer and tell Frank to go. He doesn't need telling twice. He pulls free of Sharon's grip and ducks low. Another wild shot comes from the kitchen. Frank springs into a run and sprints across the garden. Behind us, I hear Sharon cry out and a howl of anguish from Sturtz. Frank hears it too and risks a glance over his shoulder.

In the light from the kitchen, I see Sharon lying on the wet patio with Sturtz standing over her, gun in hand. He looks up at Frank, his features wrecked with emotion, and raises his gun. Frank clears the garden fence in a single bound as bullets come smashing through the shrubbery all around us.

As we race through the dimly-lit streets to the old storehouse and freedom, the barracks comes alive. Lights come on. People emerge from buildings. A few start running towards the Colonel's house, to see what the shooting is about. Frank and I slip unnoticed into the storehouse and out through the wall into the street. We cross to an alley and along it, down a block, around a corner, and there is Frank's Plymouth, just where we left it.

Chapter 15

"It was a damned cock-up, that's what it was."

Frank is pacing up and down in Margaret's apartment. Margaret and Rachel are there and I'm riding Frank. However angry he is with me, he is still nobly taking on the burden of letting me ride him, "So that no other poor bastard has to put up with you," as he puts it. As if he has a choice.

"We got useful intel," I say, aloud, so the others can hear me. They seem quite capable of telling when it is me talking.

"Like what? That Sturtz is a maniac and he's out to get you? We knew most of that before."

"That they know what I can do and how to protect themselves against me. That they are developing a weapon they think can harm me. That the man Sturtz phoned, Bernstein, is probably their head of research. This is all useful."

"Do you think his wife is dead?" It is the first thing Margaret has said for ages.

Frank shakes his head, not in denial, but in hopeless acceptance that it is probably true. "The man was deranged."

"No, he was perfectly rational, but he was scared witless. Me and my kind fill him with revulsion. His worst fear is that one of us gets inside his head."

"Well, I can understand that." Rachel is surly and resentful. Her sister has told her everything she knows and made her agree to keep it a secret, but Rachel is deeply upset by it all. She not only resents the fact that I rode her – she refers to it as a "violation" – and that she had been ridden by a nightmare before that, but also that she does not have her sister's or mother's ability to detect me. This last seems to be the cause of most of her bitterness.

"So what now?" Margaret asks.

Frank is glum. He has just started to believe the need for helping me, just begun to believe that I want my people to leave as much as he does, and now we seem to have hit a dead end. Yet even Frank must know there are still options.

"Frank's the detective," I say, through Frank. "Ask him."

"This is too damned weird," Rachel says. She stands up and goes into her bedroom.

"I should talk to her," Margaret says, staring at the closed door.

"What do you mean, ask me?"

"I mean, use your head and stop wallowing in self-pity. You're a detective. I'm a soldier. You should be the one analysing the case, finding the options, investigating the possibilities."

"What possibilities? You can't go to the Colony. I can't go to the FBI, or whoever you tell about an alien invasion. They'd laugh me out of the room."

"Rachel's right, watching you talking to yourself is weird." Margaret walks away to look out of the window.

Frank goes on. "We know the Army is involved somehow. They're taking it seriously at least. They're building weapons, developing tactics for dealing with you. Maybe we should just leave it to them."

"You mean leave it to the people who have now tried to kill you twice?"

"To kill you, you mean?"

"So you're all right with being collateral damage?"

The argument is a silly one, but it does the trick. It gets Frank out of his depression and thinking again.

"Bernstein!"

"At last!" I say.

Margaret turns to us. "The Army scientist who's building the weapon?"

Frank nods. "We can trace him. I can trace him. Hell, he might even be in the phone book. For sure, he drives a car. We know he lives, or works, within ten minutes of the barracks. How many research establishments can there be in that area? How many Bernsteins?"

"But you can't use police resources," I say, seeing the intention forming in Frank's mind.

"Isn't that a bit paranoid?" Margaret asks.

"No, he's right," says Frank. "Sturtz's men knew when and where to ambush me. We've always assumed it was because they got their information from the Colony, but maybe someone inside the force let them know where to find me."

Margaret doesn't like it. "This is just one conspiracy theory on top of another."

"No," I say. "We need to be cautious. Once my people have infiltrated a population, there is no one you can trust any more."

Margaret pulled a wry face. "Except me."

"That's right. And Frank, when I'm with him."

Bizarrely, Frank feels insulted by this. I have no time to puzzle it out though. We have to get moving before Sturtz realises he has given us a way in and does what he can to block it.

"OK," I say, ready to assign everyone their roles. At that very moment, Frank's phone rings.

He fetches it from his pocket and answers it.

"Arramar? Are you there?"

"Ekkri!" I had almost forgotten I'd left my friend Frank's phone number. "Are you all right? Do you need help?" I take over Frank's body and head for the door.

"It's all right, Arramar. Don't worry. It's just that I am in the city and we could meet."

I reach the hallway, heading for the stairs. "Of course! Tell me where you are and I'll come straight away."

He describes a location I know. A downtown restaurant. "We can fodder our rides and talk at the same time," he says. "I don't have much time to myself."

Passing through the lobby, I head for the street. "I'll be there in fifteen minutes. Can you wait that long?"

"Yes, yes, but hurry."

We hang up as I leave the building.

Frank, I've got to go, I tell him. He comes out from under my control with the usual moment of confusion, then a moment of anger.

"Damn, I wish you wouldn't do that."

I'm in a hurry. I want you and Margaret to get after Bernstein. Just find him. Don't go near him without me. I've got to go and meet someone. Someone from the Colony. I'll probably be back in an hour or two.

I grab the first person who comes within reach. It is a young woman in a business suit. It is early morning and people are heading to work. That's fine. The bigger the crowds, the better. Once I'm inside her, I take control. She has a phone in her purse and I tell Frank the number. He starts typing it into his own phone but I don't wait to watch him finish.

I ride my new host down to the nearest crossing. Cars are roaring by until the lights change, then they all stop. I go to the first car that has its window open and stand beside it. The large, overweight driver looks at me nervously. "Excuse me," I say, leaning in and grab his shoulder. By the time the lights have changed, I'm comfortably settled in my new ride and happy to note that he is going to drive right past where I want to go.

-oOo-

The restaurant is mostly empty. There is a queue at the counter for coffee and doughnuts but I am scanning the few that are seated. Ekkri is in the corner farthest from the entrance, riding a middle-aged woman in a pink blouse. I know it is him because his ride has a hand resting on the table-top, forming the sign by which we can spot one another. The woman is looking my way, so I make the sign too and go to sit at the same table. I have changed rides since the fat guy in the car and now I'm in a young man who studies art history at the nearby university.

Ekkri reaches out to me with the woman's hand, and I take it with the young man's. Our fields join and we meet at last.

"Arramar! It is so good to see you again!"

"And you, my friend. You would not believe how lonely I have been. I feel like I'm going crazy. I have started talking to the humans, I'm so desperate for any kind of contact."

I expect him to laugh. I wish he would. It is a sound I need very much. But Ekkri is grim and full of purpose. "I am sorry to hear it," he says. "But you can't come back now. Celedorn has people looking for you. Not many. Just a handful. He wants you silenced. He calls you a trouble-maker and says you seek to destabilise the Colony."

"Me? Destabilise the Colony? Does no one ask him where the Vaticinatrix is? Does no one ask by what right he gives us orders?"

"You've seen what it is like there. Only it's worse now."

"Worse? Because of me?"

"No, no, although some are saying that you will come back and put things right again. No. A war has started, with the nightmares."

I am silent. There is no point telling him that I warned Celedorn of exactly this. "How bad is it?"

"Very bad indeed. They come at us in hoards, masses, impossible numbers! And their attacks are focused and planned. It's as if their leaders are intelligent and cunning, not simple animals at all."

If I had any blood, it would be boiling. I want to rage and smash things. I want to rush back to the Colony and fight with my comrades. I want to shred Celedorn's mind with something sharp and cold. Instead, I force myself to remain calm. "Are the defences holding?"

"So far. We have fallen back to a tighter perimeter and deployed scramblers and brainworms. We're still holding back the heavy weapons, trying to keep human casualties to a minimum.

Our technology is hugely superior to theirs but there are so many of them."

"How did you get out here to meet me?"

"Life still has to go on. The Colony inhabits key personnel in a major corporation. If we stopped all our corporate activities, it would cause a huge stir among the humans. There would be so many questions, investigations. We can't have that right now. We need to focus on the war. So a few of us are keeping up a front, going to meetings, making decisions. I volunteered for it, hoping I'd get to see you."

"Thank you."

He shrugs it off. "They have us besieged, although our territory is still quite large. But we have routes in and out. The only real danger in coming into the city is if you run into a nightmare by accident."

I glance around. "You must have come with others, with guards, protection."

Ekkri appreciates my concern. It is easy to know such things when I converse with my own kind, so hard when I speak to humans. I can also tell that he feels anxious about his safety. "I gave them the slip," he says. "I told them my ride needed attention. They always need to empty their bladders or something. When I was out of sight, I called you and came here. I will tell them my ride was accosted by a friend and I thought it best to allow them to converse. It is plausible. Since the attacks started, our presence in the wider world has been limited. It makes sense for our rides to be seen out here as much as possible, to avoid questions. I can't stay long, though. A few more minutes."

A waiter comes and takes our order, trying not to stare at the way we are holding hands.

"Ekkri, something strange is going on with the humans. They know we're here. They have tried to kill me." I tell him about last night's visit to the Barstowe Street Barracks and the behaviour of Colonel Sturtz. All I feel in response is incredulity and shock.

"Of course, there are a number of human military personnel who visit the Colony. The corporation has very wide business interests and many military contracts. I suppose it is possible that they found something out. Although I can't see how."

"I need you to find out if the man Sturtz ever visited the Colony. Can you do that for me?"

"Of course. But, Arramar, this weapon...."

"That's why we never colonise a species that is so technically advanced it could detect us or threaten us. That's just one of the many reasons why we shouldn't be on this damned planet at all."

I feel fear from my friend. "You shouldn't speak like that," he says. "Any talk of leaving Earth is treated as treason. It is a dangerous idea, especially now we are at war."

"So there are others who agree with me? Others who want us to go?" The very thought that I might not be alone is a torment of hope.

"Yes, of course. Since you reported that the nightmares are indigenous, even though Celedorn tried to suppress it, word has spread throughout the Colony. Everyone knows. There is a lot of unrest, but no one dares do anything. Some say you are a kind of rebel hero who will restore the proper order," I sense his amusement at the idea, but also a hint of pride in his friend. "But they have seen how you are exiled and hunted. It has made everyone even more cautious about speaking out."

"I need to speak to Celedorn. I need to understand what has happened. I need to draw him out, meet him somewhere safe. Will you help me?"

I sense his fear, his immediate withdrawal, but he says, "I'll do whatever I can, anything to bring you home to us."

"You always were a timid soul," I say with a smile.

"And you always were the reckless one. Remember that day at the Falls of Terrashi?"

I laugh. "I remember waving to you from the bottom and you at the top looking embarrassed."

"That was a look of smug superiority. You almost killed yourself. I am no such fool."

"We had such good times then. I wish..."

He understood, of course. "Nothing has been right since we left Treforga."

"It's this place!"

Food arrives and, for a while, we simply let our rides eat.

"I need to go," Ekkri says aloud, laying down his fork. Our rides take each other's hands again.

"Let me think about how to meet Celedorn," I say. "I'll call you. Get a disposable phone when you leave and send me the number. We will use it to talk. I don't want to put you in danger, but I need your help."

His mind is full of concern, about himself, about me, about the future. There is nothing I can say that will make it go away. He lets go of my hand and stands up. "Of course," he says and leaves, quickly.

Chapter 16

Instead of going straight back to the apartment, I spend a couple of hours making some arrangements in the city. I have my sniffers with me and my mind is full of their yammer. The city has more nightmares in it than at any time since the Colony arrived. I suppose the heightened activity is to do with the war. I can make out no pattern to it, but perhaps they gather here before moving out to the battle lines. All the same, there are not so many that I cannot easily stay out of their way. It makes me nervous though, claustrophobic, and a little paranoid. Each ride I move into could be infested. Each crowd I pass through could contain enemies. Sniffers are good, but they are not infallible.

"Who is it? What do you want?"

Frank's tone is belligerent and challenging. He makes a darkness at the peep-hole as he watches me through the apartment door. I'm riding a realtor from a smart downtown office.

"It's me Frank. Let me in. My ride's name is Toby Johnson."

The sound of locks opening follows immediately. Frank appears with a gun in his hand. He watches Toby Johnson suspiciously.

"We need a password," I say, walking past him. Neither Margaret nor Rachel are there. I make my ride take a seat and put his briefcase on the coffee table. It is heavy and makes a loud clunk. From it, I take a sheaf of documents and two bundles of keys.

"What's that?"

"I got us a new apartment."

"You did what?"

"I need you to sign these papers." I show him where. "It's a much bigger place than this. You won't have to sleep on the sofa any more."

"Why?"

"Because you'll have your own bedroom. It's got plenty of spare rooms too, in case we bring anyone else in. I want Margaret to move there with us, for her safety. Rachel should probably come too."

"Don't you think you should have asked us first?" He changes his mind about the question as soon as he asks it. "Whose apartment is it?"

"Yours. The rent is paid up for two years in advance. At least that's what they think."

"I mean who owns it? Who are you ripping off?"

"It's just some rich guy. Lives overseas. He has properties like this all over the place. Mostly they're empty. Something about investments and tax losses. I could get Toby to explain it all to you."

Franks shakes his head and walks away. His body-language screams "irritated as hell."

"That's not all," I say, pulling more documents out of the case. "You are now a private investigator, fully licensed by the Department of State, Division of Licensing Services. You have various firearm permits too. And these." I pull a couple of semi-automatics out and put them on the table.

"You got me a P.I. license?"

"You were thinking about it anyway, Frank. You know you're going to lose your job with the police. I know how anxious you've been about how you'll get by without it. I also know that you think the only work you're fit for is as a security guard – which you'd hate – and as a P.I. – which you secretly like the sound of." I hold up a hand. "Don't try arguing with me, Frank. I know what you think a lot better than you do."

He looks confused. I imagine he is quite a bit relieved beneath all that surface anger. Being unemployed had been bothering him for days now.

"There are exams and things..." he says, vaguely.

"All taken care of. Your top-marks pass is filed with Licensing Services and your license is right here." I slap it on the table, in a gesture I've seen in movies.

He comes back and picks it up, studying it. "Is that it? No more surprises?"

"Just one. I set up a bank account for your new P.I. business and put some money in it. In fact, money will keep going into your account from your one and only client each month."

"Client?"

I named a very large IT company. "They now have you on a generous retainer, but don't worry, they won't ask you to do anything. Nobody there remembers anything about taking you on, and the CEO's signature is on the authorisation. Besides, you're being paid from a very dodgy secret account that very few people know about.

"Now, will you sign that lease so I can send Toby back to his office?"

For some reason, he just stares at me, without moving.

"Frank?"

Still the staring goes on. Then he wanders off to stare out of the window as if he's forgotten all about our conversation. After a while, he starts speaking.

"Yeah, all right, I get it. It's a war. A goddam alien invasion, no less. And I'm caught up in it, and so are Margaret and Rachel. It could be anybody, but it's us."

I don't bother to correct him.

"So our lives are never going to be the same. We're your guerilla army. Conscripts." He trails off again, watching the traffic in the street below. "Pawns, really. You think you can move us here and there as it suits you. Shit, you probably can. You don't see us as equals. You don't even see us as subordinates. We're more like cattle and sheep." He gave a small, unpleasant laugh. "Maybe Margaret and me are more like pets, yeah? I tell myself you have a kind of affection for us, like we're your dogs or some - thing, that we're not just expendable."

His assessment is pretty good so far, so I let him go on.

"I don't even know why I'm saying all this. You'll be back in my head soon enough and then you'll know every damned thing I think and feel. Right?" At last, he turns to face me. "Well I just want to tell you this, while you're over there and I can look you in the goddam eye. I'm cooperating with this shit because I believe you. Because I trust you – God help me – and I can see what's at stake. And because I don't want millions or billions of you shit-heads infesting the whole goddam world and turning it into a shit-head farm. I want you bastards gone. Honestly, I want you all dead, wiped out, like the parasite scum you are.

"And here's the thing I want you to know. If I didn't think that helping you was in my best interests, if I didn't think that you're trying to save the world, I would fight you with the last breath in my body. I'd throw myself out that window with you inside me, if that was the only way I could kill you. And I bet that goes for ev - ery other human being on this planet. We would never stop until we'd scraped the last damn one of you off our boots."

He walked up to me and pulled a pen from the briefcase. "Now show me where to sign this fucking thing."

Chapter 17

"Holy crap! Look at this place!"

Rachel seems to be the only one who likes the new apartment.

"I can't live here," Frank declares. "There are coffee tables here worth more than I make in a month. The people I bust live like this. Not me." It isn't true. Most of the people he has ever arrested lived in grinding poverty. What is making him so uncomfortable is the memory of someone he never did arrest, a crime boss who has an even more splendid apartment not three blocks from where we are.

"It's not like you have to sell poison to kids to live here," Margaret says. "No one's getting hurt except some Saudi investment corporation that probably never saw the place, only knows it as a line in a ledger, and doesn't care what happens to it."

"Since when were you on his side?"

Margaret walks the length of a sofa as long as her own sitting room, letting her fingertips trail on its soft white leather. Its twin runs parallel to it at the other side of two glass coffee tables, each the size of a double bed.

"Oh wow!" Rachel shouts from another room. She appears in the connecting doorway. "You've got your own freaking cinema in here."

The size and opulence of his new apartment is making Frank increasingly nervous. I leave them all to their inspection and dive down to look at what is driving his fear. But all I find is the status-related neurosis I see in all humans. They have their place in the pecking order. They learn it and grow comfortable with it. After that, any shift in status makes them uneasy. I stop worrying. Frank will get over it eventually.

"You should take it," Margaret is saying when I pop up again. "You deserve it. You can't use your own place because of him. It's only fair he should recompense you."

"You're not so keen to move in here yourself, though," he says, before he can stop himself. He had been hoping she would. He's developing quite a crush on the lady doctor and he took it personally when she said she wouldn't leave her own place. The reason he's being so childish about it is that he also thinks a beautiful, intelligent, educated woman like Margaret wouldn't dream of a romantic attachment with a man like him. It's that status thing again. He thinks she's too good for him. Yet, if she shows any sign that she might think the same thing, he resents it bitterly. Screwed up is normal for humans, but Frank is in a league of his own.

"I like my apartment," she says. "It's close to work. It's comfortable. Besides..." She looks as if she's trying to say something unpleasant but can't find the words.

Frank helps her out, sad but resigned. "Yeah, I know. It's not like we even know each other that well."

Margaret suddenly smiles. "It's got to be better than sleeping on my couch. Trust me, I'm a doctor. I know what that thing is doing to your spine."

"What do you mean, it's close to work?" I ask, just realising what she said.

Her smile drops when she sees who's talking. "I'm a doctor. It's not just a job. It's a vocation. There are people who need me."

"I thought you'd be dedicating all your time to helping me."

"Oh did you? And what about my patients?"

"You know what's at stake."

"I'll still help. I just have other things I need to do." I start to protest but she interrupts me. "Even in a war people get sick. They still need doctors. I know you don't give a damn about all that but I do. If you want my help, it will be on my terms."

"I had hoped we'd all move in here together and use it as our base of operations."

"Like a little Colony away from home?"

That makes me pause. Is that what I'm trying to do, make these people into my surrogate Colony?

"You may be right. I'm not very good at being alone. None of my people are. It would help me if you would all come together so we can fight this thing, whatever it is."

"I want to stay here, with Frank," Rachel says.

"What?" Both Frank and Margaret express their surprise at the same time.

"With the mindrider?" Margaret asks. Rachel has made no effort to hide her disgust of me. While Margaret may call me a mindrider, her sister's term is usually "brain slug" or "body snatcher".

"Sure. You're not going to violate me again are you Sluggy? Not while you've got Frank to be your bitch."

"Rachel!" Margaret sounds almost as shocked as Frank is. "We owe Frank a big debt for taking this on. Maybe the whole world owes him a debt. Anyway, if you feel like that about it, why are you hanging around at all? I think Mom and Dad would be very relieved to see you back home again."

Rachel treats the idea with a sneer of contempt. "Look at this place. It's a palace. Who wouldn't want to live here? Besides, it's only for a while, until we save the world."

Frank is as confused by her motives as I am. Rachel is an attractive young woman and Frank flatters himself he has seen signs of interest from her. Now he is reeling from the insult of being called my "bitch" – and the fact that she is cute makes that so much worse for him.

"So you want to join the team and save the world now, do you?" Margaret is beginning to sound angry. "What brought that on all of a sudden? I thought you were just hanging around 'cause you had nowhere else to go."

Rachel seems ready to give some smart-aleck comeback but she stops herself. For a moment she looks deflated and unhappy. Then she turns to Frank.

"I'm sorry. I didn't mean to be so rude. I know you took on the slug again mostly for my sake." So she's sorry to Frank, but I'm still "the slug". Ah well. "You don't know what it's like – none of you – to have lived with a nightmare in your head like I did."

She's talking to Margaret now. "You all thought I was an asshole at school, with my Goth makeup and all those jerks I used to hang with. But even then I knew it wasn't the real me. I remembered being happy, you know. I used to sit and look at photos of when I was younger. I was always smiling and messing about. I was a happy kid. Then suddenly I was buying vampire posters and listening to thrash metal bands.

"That thing sucked all the happiness out of me. It drained all the colours and left everything grey. Oh, I can't explain it. But while you were all shaking your heads and saying I was just going through a teenage rebellion phase, I knew. I knew there was this black leech inside me, sucking and sucking at my soul."

"You knew?" Margaret asks.

Rachel shook her head. "Not really. Not like you mean. But I knew something was wrong with me. I knew I shouldn't feel that way, that it wasn't the real me."

Margaret takes a step towards her, but Rachel stops her with a gesture and keeps on speaking. "When the brain slug turned up and chased out the nightmare, I felt it go. Not right away, like a veil had been lifted or something, but slowly, really slowly, like the grey clouds I'd been under for so long were thinning, gradually clearing up. Like Spring was coming. And, you know what? I can see the sun again. I can see patches of blue sky. It's incredible. I feel like I'm drunk all the time. Giddy. I could start singing, or dancing."

She smiled and even though Frank was still feeling resentful, he thought how beautiful her smile was.

"So I want to stay here, in the city, and have some fun, get to know my old self again, without my big sister looking over my shoulder all the time."

Margaret doesn't like the sound of it, I can tell. "What'll you tell Mom and Dad?"

I have no interest in listening to them discuss their domestic problems. "I'm going out," I say. *Do you want to come, Frank?* If he doesn't I'll pick up a new ride in the street.

"Where are we going?"

"To find Bernstein." Frank and Margaret have found an address for him and it is high time I looked up the man who was building weapons to use against me.

Frank says goodbye and Margaret tells him to be careful. He grabs a set of keys from the hall table and we take the elevator down to the ground floor. Our new apartment is on top of a thirty-storey block. It has perks that Frank hasn't noticed yet – a roof garden, and a maid the realtor arranged for us. No doubt that will make him even more uncomfortable.

There is a uniformed man behind a desk in the lobby and Frank almost winces when the man calls out an obsequious greeting. Frank walks three more paces before he stops, turns and walks over to the desk. I leave him to do whatever he wants to do.

"How can I help you, Mr. Taylor?"

"What's your name again?"

"Max, sir."

"Right. Of course." There had been introductions all round when the realtor had brought us over to the building earlier in the day. "Look, Max. I'm going to be straight with you. I'm not used to living in a place like this and the whole thing makes me uncomfortable."

Max was looking pretty uncomfortable himself.

"I don't mean to be unfriendly, but when you call me 'Mr. Taylor' like that, it kind of creeps me out. Now, you can call me Frank, or you can just ignore me. It won't bother me a bit. But I don't like all this formal bullshit. I work for a living. So do you. I got lucky is all. OK?"

Max thinks about it for a moment. "And what about the ladies, sir?"

"See there you go sirring me again. It's up to the ladies how they want to organise things, but me, I like it informal. You got it?"

"Yes, s -" He grins. "Sure, Frank. No problem."

Frank grins back and I feel him relax a little. "Catch you later, Max."

Happy now? I ask as we step outside.

"No, not really." But he is. He's bonded with this stranger and it has shifted his whole attitude towards the new apartment. To mask it, he is suddenly all business.

"Bernstein's just a few blocks away, in the Granger Building. We'll be there in ten minutes. What's your plan?"

Well, if they're ready for me, I'll think of something. If not, I'll just grab a ride and walk right in.

"Sounds pretty dumb to me, but, hey, you're the super-being from a pan-galactic civilisation."

Despite his tone, I know that Frank really is awed by what's happening. It is easy to forget what a big deal it is for people on an isolated planet suddenly to discover they're not alone after all. For Frank and the others, it is doubly shocking because they didn't even know they weren't alone on their own world. And, by one of those strange quirks of coincidence that humans call synchronicity, Frank says, "Tell me about the nightmares. How can we have lived with them for so long without even noticing?"

I think you have noticed. You just haven't put the pieces together yet. How many of your people suffer depressions your doctors can't explain? How many hear voices? How many stories do you have of demonic possession? I think you've been noticing their presence for as long as you've lived together, only you've never had the insight that would have led you to the obvious conclusion.

"And you think they're from here, from Earth?"

That's what they say.

"But that means they must have evolved here, from some sentient species."

That's one of the things I like about Frank, even though he's full of superstitious fears and he's ignorant in so many areas, he's pretty smart and he likes to form his opinions based on evidence, rather than on hearsay. He's a believer in science and would rather have an unpleasant truth than the sweetest of lies. Perhaps it comes from being a cop for so long.

Yes, they must have. They could be another offshoot of your own species. There used to be several different kinds of human once.

"Like Neanderthals or something?"

Yes. Then again, they could be another species altogether, something that evolved intelligence and then became cognophytic millions of years ago, tens of millions even. There's something

*about them that makes me suspect they have a different past from
your own.*

"Like what?"

Well, the way they look for a start.

"They way they look? You mean you can see them?"

*No, not really but, when people like me meet within another
mind, it's like being in a virtual world. You know what that is?*

"Sure. Like a simulation of a world." Frank has seen his share
of sci-fi films and virtual realities are a common theme. More evidence, of course, of some kind of dim awareness of the nightmares. But he's also had his share of dreams, and that's just another kind of VR.

*When we meet, we can choose how we look. It can be any-
thing we like, but normally it's based on racial memories of our
original physical form. My people would seem monstrous to you
– ask Margaret, she's seen me – but that's what we looked like
before we evolved into what we are. The nightmares are monstrous too, but not unlike monsters that appear in your own myths
and history, dragons and dinosaurs, but... worse somehow. Like
all the scariest bits joined together.*

Funnily enough, I have never seen a nightmare change its ap-
pearance. Maybe they're just happy looking ugly.

I've only been in a nightmare's chosen reality once, but it was a
real eye-opener. Everything about it was bleak and dismal. It's no
wonder they have such a depressing effect on humans. It's like
they have a collective unconscious perverted by the most awful

cataclysm you could imagine. Something so dreadful their species will never get over it.

Chapter 18

"This is it."

The Granger Building is a glass tower in a prime location, the corporate headquarters of a global engineering giant. I tell Frank to stop half a block away while we take a look at it.

There is a paved forecourt with giant metal statues. The area is well covered by security cameras. Suited people are moving in and out of its wide foyer in a steady trickle.

OK, this is where I leave you. I'll see you back at the apartment.

Before he can reply, I have grabbed the arm of a passer-by and flowed into her. She is nothing to do with the Granger Corporation, so I just let her walk closer until I can grab the arm of a man in a business suit. This ride is better, he is a Granger customer on his way to a presentation about their farm equipment. I ride him into the lobby and look around for someone he recognises. There is no one.

There are chairs and tables around the lobby and, at one end, a coffee shop. We head to the coffee shop, and I pick out a young man in his shirt-sleeves. My ride, under my direction, walks up to him and introduces himself, shaking hands with the surprised young man. They get into an awkward conversation about mistaken identities and the guy goes off for his presentation feeling confused and embarrassed. By then, I am checking out my new ride. This one is much better. He is a salesman – he thinks of his role as "account manager" – for Granger's domestic appliance division. I let him finish his coffee with two fellow sales people and go through the security doors into the building.

He doesn't know Bernstein, but he knows where the military R&D section is, so I make him take me there. I need to be careful now. No doubt people in Bernstein's group – if not everyone in the whole section – will have been briefed on avoiding contact with other people.

The security guard at the reception desk eyes me carefully as I walk out of the elevator. When I get close, he speaks.

"Good morning Mr. ..." He checks a screen on his desk. "... Shimizu. How can I help you?"

I don't know how he knows my ride's name – perhaps an RFID tag in his security pass – but it doesn't matter, my identity is not a problem. I pull Shimizu's cell phone from his pocket and show it to the guard. "I was just down in the café and I think one of the guys from this floor left their phone."

He watches me for a moment. I can't tell if he is genuinely sus-picious or whether he practises that look in the mirror at home.

"That's very kind of you. Would you place the phone on the counter, please?"

So cautious. I put the phone down but, as I let go, I 'acciden-tally' flick it towards the guard. Instinctively, he reaches out to stop it falling off the edge, and I pretend to be afflicted with the same impulse. Our hands meet over the phone and I keep him there for as long as it takes to transfer myself into him. I make him sit down calmly.

Shimizu is now standing in front of the desk looking confused, no doubt wondering what he's doing there.

"Mr. Shimizu," I say through the guard. "Thank you for com-ing down here. Is this your cell phone?"

He looks at it, feels his pockets, looks at it again. "Yes, I think so."

I place it on the counter and he reaches out and takes it. As he examines the address book, I say, "Well, that's that mystery solved. Thanks for coming to collect it. Someone handed it in on their way back from coffee just now. You have a nice day."

Still holding the phone, he walks slowly to the lifts and leaves. Alone, I wait for the next person to come along. It is a woman, young and smartly dressed with a purse and a briefcase. The screen on the desk flashes up her identity, a mugshot and some personnel details. She gives me a little nod as she walks past.

"Ms Perez," I say, standing up and walking round to intercept her. "I'm afraid we're checking bags today." I can see from the guard's memory that spot checks like this are not uncommon. I also see that the new protocols for bag checks involve keeping people well out of reach while it is done. I hope Ms Perez doesn't pay much attention to security memos.

Without complaint, she walks across to a small table and places her bags on it. I simply place a hand on her shoulder while her back is turned and slip across.

"Shouldn't you be behind the desk?" I ask. The guard almost jumps back when he realises where he is. I know how strictly the man's boss has hammered home the new no contact rules. He hurries back to his desk while I pass through the secure door into the research labs. Perez knows Bernstein and takes me straight to his office.

"Maria," he says, as I pop Perez's head around Bernstein's door. He is a small, slender man in his thirties, balding and flaccid.

"David." I walk into the room and close the door behind me. Perez is one of the lab's project managers. Bernstein is not attached to any of her projects, but Perez knows whose teams he is contributing to and which projects. "Jerry wanted me to talk to you about some of the expenses on the Diablo project."

He looks at me sharply. "That's rather unusual, isn't it?"

"Sure is! But Jerry's taking some personal time and I'm sort of covering for him."

"Stop there," he says. I am still three paces from him. I try to put on a look of innocent surprise. "I'm sorry Maria but you know the new protocols. I need to check this with Jerry."

"Right," I say, nodding. Perez does know the new protocols. Anything out of the ordinary, anybody doing absolutely anything they are not supposed to, could mean a breach. Staff are required to challenge the person – no matter what their rank or status – to validate the activity, and to remain out of physical contact. I move a step closer. "Jerry had to leave the office. I'm not sure when he'll be back."

I consider my chances of jumping him before he has a chance to shout for help, but my ride is wearing high heels and a skirt so tight she can barely walk in it, let alone leap across desks. It occurs to me that Frank was actually right for once, this could have done with a bit more planning.

"I'll call Bob then. I assume your boss is aware of Jerry's issues."

"Please don't. I don't want to get Jerry into any trouble. As I say, I'm sort of covering for him." I manage to move forward another half pace as I say this. I wonder if it would work to act seductive, to offer this woman's body for mating. I've seen it done on so many TV shows. The male victim is typically lulled into doing something careless by such an offer. But I'm not sure I could pull it off. Perez herself is confident that she is an attractive woman. She also thinks of Bernstein as a repressed little creep who probably never had sex in his life. Yet, if I tried something like that and I made mistakes, it would be all the proof Bernstein needed that Perez was being ridden. As it is, he still seems uncertain.

"Maria, you know the rules. By rights I should call security and have you questioned."

I try to look horrified. "What, for just walking into your office? Jesus, David, how are we supposed to work like this? It's crazy. Paranoid."

I scan Perez's mind again, more carefully this time. Bernstein is talking as if she's in the know but I can find no knowledge in her of my people or of any weapons against them.

"I'm sorry, Maria. If you knew what we're up against, you'd understand."

He still doesn't really believe Perez is a threat, but he is being stubbornly cautious all the same. I try another tack.

"Then tell me. The rumour is you're making some kind of super-weapon here." Which is a lie. The rumour is that Bernstein is working on cold fusion. "But half the lab's working on some kind of weapon. Why is yours so special?"

Bernstein shakes his head in agitation. "The damn rumours in this place! What are they saying? This is important, Maria. If any of this gets out, we're in real trouble. Where are the rumours coming from and what are they saying?"

This is much better. I seem to have him off his guard now. Well, at least he isn't threatening to call security. I frantically root around in Perez's memory. Maybe I can push this a little farther.

For example, she knows who's been assigned to Bernstein's project. So what skills do they have? Maybe I can come up with some speculations that Perez couldn't.

"Well, I don't want to name any names," I say, equivocating.

Bernstein waves me to a chair. "This is too important not to, Maria." I take the seat he offers, making Perez act as seductively as I can. Bernstein watches her legs as she crosses them and almost goggles as I open another button on her blouse. Maybe that was going too far. I can only go by what I've seen them do. He swallows and says, "The technical work on this project is classified Top Secret, Eyes Only. There are only half a dozen people in the company who know what it is really about. Probably only another half-dozen in the world. If we have a leak here, we need to plug it. If these rumours spread outside the lab, we're dead."

Interesting choice of words. I try to make Perez look suitably awed by the seriousness of it all. I think I've found a few clues in the project personnel.

"Well, they're saying it's a field generator of some kind."

Bernstein's expression freezes, as if suddenly he's trying to hide his emotions. I reckon I'm sniffing along the right trail, so I keep going. "They say it's small, portable." I'm guessing, watching his face, looking for signs, but he's hard to read. Then I find the memory I have been searching for. Jenny Dubrovski, one of his team members, used to work at Patterson Air Force Base – on EMP-based directional anti-satellite weapons. This is not good.

"Well?"

"They say it's an electro-magnetic pulse weapon."

He slams the desk and my fears are confirmed. A powerful enough EMP weapon is just what it would take to kill one of my kind without killing the host. We are at least as sensitive to it as the microelectronics that humans use. Traditionally, we're safe from EMP because, in this kind of medium-tech society, the only 'natural' sources of it are nuclear weapons and massive solar storms. But if they are developing a portable and directional source, we could be in serious trouble.

"So the rumours are right, then?" I say, trying to sound ingenuous. "But who could you use it against? It's such a crude weapon for battlefields, and easy to defend against." Which is true, the military here have been "hardening" their equipment against EMP for decades. All you have to do is put a wire mesh around what you want to protect. "Even foot-soldiers could fairly easily be protected."

But, of course, wearing a wire mesh around your head would be a bit of a giveaway. And it would stop you moving between rides. If the humans deploy this weapon, my people would lose many of their natural advantages. I need to stop this man and his project.

"How do you know so much about EMP, Maria?"

I force a smile. "Oh, you know, you hear things, read things. I like to take an interest in the scientific side of our work here."

"That doesn't sound like the Maria I know."

Shit. I spring to my feet and lunge across the desk at him. He throws himself backwards and I discover his chair is on casters. By the time we have each scrambled to our feet, he has found a gun from somewhere and is pointing it at me.

I back away from him, trying to look terrified. My Perez cover is clearly blown but he will still respond instinctively to emotional cues. I don't make it as far as the door though.

"Stop! Don't take another step. I'll shoot you, I swear."

He picks up the phone. The barrel of his gun is not steady. It wanders about enough to give me hope that, if I ran for the door, I might make it before he is lucky enough to hit me. I don't like the odds though.

"Wouldn't you like to hear our side of the story?" I ask. His eyes widen as he realises I am addressing him directly.

"Jesus, I hardly believed Sturtz when he told us. But he wasn't kidding was he? You're an alien."

"Perhaps the first visit your planet has ever had. Do you really want to kill us?"

"You're not just here to visit us. You're here to colonise us. That's what Sturtz says."

"And how does he know? What makes him think he understands our motives?" I am stalling, looking for some angle to play to get me out of there, but I am also hoping he will tell me.

"You come in here – like that! – and you expect me to trust you?"

"How else do you expect me to travel? Don't worry about Perez. She's fine. She won't even know I was inside her."

Bernstein shakes his head. He doesn't look as if he's feeling quite rational. I have the feeling he might just shoot me out of pure fear.

"It's you who are trying to kill us, remember? What have any of my people done to you, David?"

He shakes his head again, as if he's trying not to let my words get to him. He punches a button on the phone and says, "I need people up here right now. It's an emergency. In my office." He puts down the phone and looks at me. "Don't try anything. I'll kill you if I have to."

"And Perez?"

"What?"

"If you let me leave, Perez will be fine, I promise. If you shoot, she might die. Whatever lies Sturtz has told you about us, do you really want to kill an innocent woman?"

"I don't think Sturtz is lying. I think he's the only one who appreciates how dangerous you are. What are you doing?"

As he was speaking, I had grabbed Perez's blouse and tore it open, exposing her breasts in her lacy bra. It isn't done for Bernstein's titillation, but he can't help staring at them.

"It won't take a moment," I say and rake her fingers through her hair, mussing it up.

"Stop it. Put your hands down."

"All right," I say. As I lower her hands, I rub the back of one across her mouth, smearing her lipstick. It is something I've seen a few times on the TV with minor variations and I hope it will work. The TV is an unreliable source of information, as far as I can tell, but most of my rides are strangely convinced by it.

With my hands at my sides, Bernstein seems more relaxed. "Good," he says. "All right. What the hell was that about?" He keeps looking at Perez's breasts as if he really can't help himself. Which must be so, since any thoughts of mating her at this moment must be stupendously inappropriate. It is an observation I will need to reflect on. If I get out of there.

"Tell me then," he says. "Tell me why you're here. Tell me your side of it."

Before I can speak, three security guards burst into the room. I spin to face them and I can see their eyes flicking between Perez's torn clothes and Bernstein standing there pointing a gun at her.

"Oh, God, help me!" I cry, and throw myself into their midst.

"No! Don't touch her!" Bernstein is almost hysterical. "It's an alien, for fuck's sake! It isn't human."

I have already flowed into the farthest guard. "I think you'd better put the gun down, Dr. Bernstein," I say. "What's been go-ing on in here?"

At that moment, Perez starts screaming and struggling and the other guards try to hold her and calm her down, saying things like, "It's all right, Miss," and, "No one's going to hurt you now." But Perez's last memory was of entering the reception area. Now she's in Bernstein's office with her clothes torn, being held by two security guards.

"Let her go! Let her go, you idiots!" Bernstein's panic is rising. Intentionally or not, he is waving his gun at us all. "Nobody move. Stay exactly where you are."

I pull the gun my ride is wearing and point it at Bernstein. "Put down the gun, Dr. Bernstein." Another of the security guards pulls his gun too.

"Dammit, you don't understand, you morons. It could be in any of you by now."

"Drop the gun, the other guard says. He sounds nervous and raises his voice. "Right now!" The third guard pushes Perez behind him and draws his gun too. Perez, free at last, makes a run for it.

"No! Stop her!"

Bernstein points at her with his gun. Even I am not sure whether he means to shoot her. Two shots explode as I and one of the other guards fire almost simultaneously at the hapless Bernstein. With a look of complete surprise, the scientist staggers back a pace and crumples into a heap. I rush to him and pretend to feel his pulse. I get a much better indication of his vital signs by sensing his electrical field.

The man is dead. I can't go in and look around. I had fired only to wound him, but the shot from the other guard killed him outright.

Bloody humans!

I step away from the body and others rush in. The guard who fired the lethal shot is standing like a statue but no one seems to have noticed his odd silence. At the office doorway is a crowd of anxious people, peering in and I go out to make them move back, slipping into one then another, then another, as I work my way around the crowd, gathering whatever intel I can. By the time I leave the building I have learned all I need to about Project Diablo and the people who work on it. I have also used the knowledge in the head of one young technician to install a software 'bomb' that will erase everything on the lab's servers ten minutes after I am safely on my way.

Chapter 19

"You killed him?"

Margaret has come to the apartment after work and I have just finished briefing them all.

"Not directly, I wounded him. One of the guards actually killed him. I feel no guilt about it. He was planning to kill my whole colony."

"He was doing weapons research, that's not the same thing."

"Really? Working on a weapon intended to kill my people makes him somehow less culpable than the person who actually presses the button that fires it? It's like saying that the person who manufactured the gun, or sold it, is less culpable than the guard who shot Bernstein. They each had a hand in killing the man. Take any one of them out of the chain of events and Bernstein would still be alive."

"My God, now he's Michael Moore," Rachel says. I have no idea who she's talking about. I can only assume it is an unusually sensible human ethicist.

"Whoever did what," Frank says, "and whoever's to blame in the grand scheme of things, a government research project has been disrupted and its head scientist is dead because of what you did today. Do you think that's likely to stop them? Or do you think maybe it will just show them how dangerous your kind is and make them redouble their efforts?"

"I had to delay them. I need to buy some time. The Colony is in enough trouble with the nightmare war. If the Army pitches in with EMP weapons, it might tip the scales."

"And what about us?" Rachel asks. "Where does it leave us now?"

"What do you mean, Raich?" Margaret asks.

"Well, aren't we all accessories after the fact in a murder case? Or maybe that's small potatoes, because, as of today, we're all traitors against our own country!"

No one spoke for a few, long seconds. Then Margaret looked at me and said, "We've been talking it through while you were out." Immediately, I start scanning Frank's recent memories. "None of us likes the way this is going. We're all out of our depth here and getting deeper all the time."

The curious thing is that, as I replay their conversation in Frank's mind, I find that none of them expresses any doubt that I am honestly trying my best to save their species from my own.

They only doubt that I can actually pull it off. It is too complicated, the players are all too powerful, and they know I still don't even understand what is at the back of it all.

I see something else too, which doesn't make sense yet. After he left me at the Granger Building Frank went straight to police HQ and resigned.

"We need to take this to the Government," Margaret says. "Maybe they already know and that's why the Army is after you. But all this is way bigger than the four of us."

"Well," I say, addressing Margaret, who is clearly the spokesperson. "Someone in the Government knows all right. I saw lots of things in the minds of the people at Granger Corporation. They have a testing range for their EMP weapon at Fort Dix. Last week they put on a demonstration for Colonel Sturtz, his commanding officer, General Hackman, and three other people. One was Chet Granger, CEO of Granger Corporation, one was a CIA Director, and one was a US Senator." I can feel Frank's surprise segue into concern. The same feelings are reflected in Margaret's face.

"I know how your government works as well as you do. I know how much opportunity there is for corruption. I know that when big business and secret agencies are involved, there is always a possibility of cover-ups and underhand power-plays. I'm not saying that's what's going on, just that, if I were you, I wouldn't go running to the FBI – or whoever – because there is a chance they will do more than just laugh at you.

"Someone sanctioned Frank's murder, don't forget. Maybe you thought it was a rogue Army colonel exceeding his authority." I know Frank used to think that. "But we now know Sturtz is connected all the way to the top. The sanction could have come from anywhere."

"Christ." Rachel walks away from the group, and then walks back. She glowers at her sister. "If we'd taken your advice, we might all be dead by now."

Again I check Frank's mind. Turns out Margaret had argued that they should go to the Feds while I was away, so I couldn't stop them.

Thanks for your support, Frank. It had been Frank's insistence that they discuss it with me first that had prevented them.

"Which Senator was it?" Margaret asks. She seems a little shaken by Rachel's outburst. Perhaps she had guessed what the risks were.

"I don't know. My informant didn't recognise him and no one was using names or titles on the day. She only recognised General Hackman because Granger Corp has done work for him in the past."

"It could be perfectly innocent," Frank says. "They wouldn't want it to get out that there was an alien invasion going on. The panic would be catastrophic."

"True," I say, "but remember the attempt to kill you." It is like talking to children, sometimes. "Even if this is all straight up and above board, the people involved think it is worth killing innocent civilians to keep it a secret. What happened to Sturtz's wife?"

"What?"

"He shot her. We saw her go down. She looked dead, or seriously wounded. Why wasn't it in the papers? Why isn't it on the news? They covered it up, that's why. Whoever they are, they believe that a certain level of collateral damage is acceptable. And they have the power to make sure nothing they do reaches the media. They could have all three of you murdered and no one would ever know. Maybe you'd all die in the same 'accident'."

"Or they'd ship us out to some terrorist holding facility where they can do what they like with us." Rachel, at least, seems appropriately scared.

Margaret holds up her hands in surrender. "All right, all right. Maybe it was a bad idea. But if we can't go to our own government about this, what can we do? I tell you, I'm scared. We don't seem to have any options."

She stops on a sob and I feel Frank's urge to go to her and comfort her. He even takes an awkward step forward but Rachel has already put her arm around Margaret's shoulders and neither notices his hesitant gesture.

"I'm tired of being so scared all the time," Margaret says, rallying. "I thought, with you going off to see Bernstein, we were finally taking the initiative, taking the fight to them. But now Bernstein's dead and everything is worse than before."

Frank agrees, I can tell, and Rachel is glaring at me accusingly, as she so often does. Yet I don't see it that way. We have more information now. We know better what we are up against.

Unease is growing in Frank's mind. I think about shutting him up but I let him speak.

"I just realised," he says. The women look at him, Rachel angrily and Margaret with a slight flinch, hearing from his tone, no doubt, that more bad news is coming. "When we went to the Granger Building, we stopped maybe half a block away. It seemed safe enough. I was only worried about being caught on the building's own security cameras, but now that there has been a murder..."

He is right. Even if no one at Granger tells the police what has really happened, someone at the company, or at the FBI more likely, will start looking at CCTV recordings from the streets outside. If they push the search far enough, someone might recognise Frank.

"Don't leave us," says Margaret.

Smart woman. The thought was already in my mind that I should get out of there before Sturtz's men storm the apartment. My ride is potentially compromised. It is the sensible thing to do.

"I can't let them stop me," I say.

"Stop you?" says Rachel. "What are you two...? Oh Christ! They're coming after us."

"You're the only protection we've got," says Margaret – which hurts Frank's feelings. Stupidly, I can't help feeling some responsibility for them. If Sturtz gets hold of them they would be interrogated and locked away at the very least. There is also the possibility that they might be able to give away useful intel about the Colony.

"All right, I'll stay. But you need to listen to me. All of you. Only Frank is on their radar as far as we know." I speak to Margaret. "You and Rachel should get out of here now. Go back to your own home and don't try to contact us. You'll be all right. They have no reason to suspect you. Frank and I will leave too, but we have something else to do."

"You'll take care of Frank, won't you?"

"I'll be all right, Margaret," Frank says. "You should get going."

"Look after him," Margaret insists, obviously to me. "Tell me you will. Promise me."

"I'll do my best."

She looks away, apparently irritated that I won't give her more reassurance.

"Don't worry about me. OK?" Frank smiles his rugged, cowboy smile at her and she relents and gives him a weak smile in return.

"Where are you going?" Rachel wants to know.

"To find some allies," I tell her.

-oOo-

"What allies?" Frank asks when we are alone.

You'll see. You should bring a gun.

"A gun?"

It's just a precaution.

We set off on foot through the city, quickly leaving the smart neighbourhood of Frank's new apartment and entering the dirtier, dingier precincts that fill the spaces between the office blocks and couturier clothing outlets. On a bright, August day, I've seen this city looking clean and friendly. But those days are the exception. Mostly the city is drab. Grey pavements and grey buildings under grey skies. The people here try to ignore one another, mainly because any kind of interaction could start somebody snarling. When I'm in their heads, I can see that they don't like it any more than I do. They wonder how it all got so bad, how this cramped and dismal life crept up on everybody. They feel trapped and resentful. It isn't what they chose for themselves. It isn't how life is supposed to be.

As we head deeper into the cheaper, nastier parts of town, the people look more harried and less healthy. I feel Frank growing nervous. He doesn't like the way three men in a doorway watch him pass. He spots a boy on a corner dealing dope and another boy nearby nudge his companion and nod in our direction. Frank thinks he looks like a cop and it makes him feel vulnerable and exposed.

Don't worry, I say. *I won't let anything happen to you.*

"I don't need your help," he mutters. "Are we nearly there?" Frank doesn't like walking around the streets. He thinks we should have taken a cab.

I don't know. I think so. I have my sniffers scouting ahead and they are getting a strong scent. What's down there?

We cut through an alley and onto a street that runs beside a fly-over. Even the grey sky is blocked from view by the segmented concrete ribbon that winds above us, a monstrous millipede on massive concrete legs. Beneath the elevated road are other roads running on each side. In the wasteland between them, I finally see what I'm looking for, a jumble of makeshift shelters.

I tell Frank he doesn't have to go any farther if he doesn't want to. He shrugs and presses on. There are men and women among the cardboard and plastic tents, in groups and alone. One group has lit a fire and sits around it on decrepit chairs and an old sofa. We walk up to them and they stop talking to stare at us. The ground is a litter of rubbish and empty bottles. The faces that watch us are wary and hostile. For a moment, everyone is silent. The noise of the road above us pervades everything.

"I want to speak with you," I say through Frank.

"You a cop?" one of them asks.

"I'm a mindrider," I say. "I am the one who killed Berreg. Reveal yourself."

One stands up and shambles towards me. "Can you spare a bit of change for an old vet down on his luck?" He has a hand out and he's getting too close for comfort. So I pull Frank's gun and aim it at him. He stops and lowers his hand.

"I'm here to ask a favour. I need your help."

In his head, Frank is raging at me. He thinks I've gone mad. Other vagrants are approaching. There must be about twenty altogether in the little settlement. I wonder if they are all hosts. I will soon be surrounded and Frank's gun carries just fifteen rounds. Perhaps he is right and I have gone mad.

"Do not come any closer or I will shoot," I say. I sound like a character in an old English war movie, Frank thinks. I'd like to ask him what I should have said, but now is not the time. "I don't want to kill anybody, just to talk."

The circle stops closing around me.

"It doesn't want to kill," one of the tramps says, sneering.

"It wants to ask us a favour."

"We should tear it apart."

"Rend it."

"I want to stop the war," I say. "I need you to take me to my people and get me into their stronghold."

"How can it stop the war?" one asks.

"Can it kill them all?"

"Kill them all!"

"Kill them all!"

I raise my voice. "Let me talk! I thought you were an intelligent species, but you're acting like a bunch of idiots. Who speaks for you? Where is your leader?"

They fall silent and watch me. I realise they have begun linking hands. A vagrant from outside the circle, a woman, shapeless and raddled, shuffles forwards until she is inside with me. The two derelicts closest to her put their free hands on her shoulders. She holds out a hand to me, an invitation to join them.

Frank is telling me not to be stupid and I can't help but feel he is right, but I am desperate and my life is not such a big price to pay if I can pull this off.

If you come to and I'm not there any more, I say to Frank, *get out of here and don't come back*. Then I reach out and take the tramp's hand.

Chapter 20

Darkness engulfs me. Black clouds scud across a lowering sky. Smoke and dust fill the air as if the world is on fire. Nothing lives, nothing moves. The jagged remains of burnt trees dot the endless plain of soot and cinders. A nightmare, massive and strong, fills the space in front of me, black on black. Its reptilian eyes narrow as it watches me. The creature raises a clawed hand to its scaly chest and slashes its arm out and up in a gesture of revelation. My gaze follows where those long, cruel talons point and I have to blink and shake my head to make out what I am looking straight at.

What I had thought was a broken hillside, a massive jumble of obsidian boulders, resolves itself into a gigantic structure. A building of sorts, as big as a city, built of shattered rocks, each the size of a house. It is an artificial mountain, half labyrinth, half cathedral. A miracle of architecture. A hideous testament to twisted imagination. I realise now that what I had thought were windblown swirls of ash, whirling around its towers and massifs, are flocks of nightmares, flying through the pall of gloom that surrounds it. Hundreds of them. Thousands.

"My clanholm," the nightmare says. Its voice is a hiss of gas erupting from boiling lava. I tear my gaze from that terrible city of darkness. I try not to dwell on all that it tells me about the enemy my people are fighting. I give my attention to the creature that confronts me.

"Speak, slayer of Berreg. There is no debt owed you. Tell me why I should not destroy you."

I try to gather my thoughts. "My people should not be here," I say. "This is your world. We should go."

"Then go."

"I want to, but there are others of my kind who want us to stay. They keep us here against our own laws and against our own best interests."

"Then die."

"My people are strong. You must have seen that by now. You must understand how many lives will be lost before this war is over."

"We are strong, too. And we are many."

I suspect the nightmares have not yet understood how advanced my people are. They cannot imagine the wars that have been fought between cognophytes – between whole groups of planets – or the kinds of weapons such bitter conflict drives a species to develop.

"I need to speak to my people and convince them to leave. I want you to take me to my Colony and to protect me so that I can persuade them. I want one of you to talk to them too, and a human friend of mine..." Margaret was going to hate me for it but she must show the Colony what she is. "If we can do that, they will listen and I can gather enough support to force them to leave this planet."

The nightmare begins to writhe and hiss, clenching its fists and bending its body. The sound is horrible and the sight unnerving, but for all I know, it is just having a good laugh. I let the performance go on for a while longer.

"Well?"

Slowly the creature quietens down and unknots itself.

"Others wish to speak with you. Come."

At which, it leaps into the air and unfurls its gigantic wings. I am almost knocked over as it surges forward and upward with slow, powerful beats. Cursing its miserable black hide, I morph out of Frank's form into that of a Treforgan male. My double wings are bright and rainbow-hued, my yellow body the one splash of brightness in that blasted mindscape. Within seconds I have caught up with the nightmare. Treforgan males are fast and agile fliers.

We head for the coal-black city of rock, my companion saying nothing as we speed across the plain. "Where are you taking me?" I demand. "Who are we going to see?" But I get no answer. It doesn't matter. That they want to talk to me at all is a major triumph. Besides, the question I really want to ask is, how are we doing this?

There are many nightmares in the air around us. As we reach the rock-jumble outskirts of the city, there are many more. As far as I know, cognophytes need physical contact between hosts to meet inside a mind, or at least close proximity. It is supposed that, with the sensitivity to electromagnetic fields that a sniffer possesses, it would be possible for many minds to connect in the same mindspace without even touching. Yet what I am seeing is orders of magnitude beyond that. This whole city is populated by thousands of nightmares, all seeming to share the same mental world. I can't begin to imagine the abilities required to achieve such a massive joining of minds. It should be impossible, yet here it is.

Perhaps it is all illusion. Yet as we soar above the jagged towers of the black city, hundreds of malevolent eyes turn to watch me pass.

The immensity of the city begins to daunt me. Beneath us, the chaotic mountain of jet streams past endlessly as we press on and on towards the central summit, a massive peak of broken stone riddled with cavernous entrances. We fly higher and farther than seems possible until the central tower is a cliff wall and my companion swoops straight into it, disappearing into the blacker blackness within, through a cave-mouth as big as an aircraft hangar.

I drop to the ground in confusion, unable to see anything inside, afraid I will smash into the walls I imagine narrowing around me.

"Come!" the nightmare shouts angrily from far ahead.

"I cannot see," I shout back.

Ahead I hear grumbling and cursing but I hold my position. It occurs to me to wonder whose mind I am in. Am I still under the flyover with the tramps around their fire? Or have we moved across many minds to some other part of the physical city? How many minds, I wonder, are in harness to create this monstrous place?

And I realise that I have been too caught up in the nightmare's world, that, whatever I see and hear and feel around me, somewhere beneath it all is a human host, with a human mind. And since that must be true...

Summoning my strength, I push through the veil of darkness and ruin around me, into the mind below. It is a struggle. The roots of the illusion are deep. The mind I discover is fractured and steeped in blackness, but it is a human mind, a man, with his memories and dreams, his thwarted desires and suppressed horrors. I feel the nightmare coming after me. I don't have long to explore this wrecked and corrupted place. There is a lot of unused junk, menacing figures, police and street gangs, a girl he once kissed, a dog he once killed and ate. But there is something useful, a torch the man once saw burning in a movie as a child. I snatch it up and return to the nightmare and its Stygian clanholm.

As I emerge, I find it standing over me, snarling in anger. It flinches back from the torch and turns its face away.

Interesting.

"I need the light," I say. Yet there is nothing much to see in the giant cave. The torchlight barely reaches to the walls around me.

The nightmare sneers at what must seem a great weakness and launches itself into the air again. I follow behind, with just enough illumination to keep my worst fears at bay.

We wind through corridors that are broad and high, they branch into other routes and open onto black, cavernous rooms. We pass nightmares and sometimes smaller, scuttling things that turn their heads away from the light and scurry into the shadows. After a minute or so, the corridor narrows and we must fold our wings and walk. I resume Frank's form and feel the cindery floor crunching beneath my shoes.

Abruptly, my guide stops and turns to me. "We have arrived. The Clanlord expects you. Be careful to speak with respect or his wives will tear you to pieces."

We pass through a high arch into a large chamber. The biggest damn nightmare I've ever seen is crouching at the far end of the room, surrounded by smaller nightmares. With a start, I recognise them as muliebri, the mindless beasts I have been fighting and killing since my arrival on Earth. Could these be the clanlord's wives? And does that mean that these nasty, aggressive, brutes are the females of the species? In nature, all things are possible, as the old saying goes, but I have not encountered this particular sexual dimorphism before.

"Beautiful, aren't they?" the clanlord says, seeing me staring at his muliebri. "Is that why your people are here, to steal our women?"

I can't tell if he's joking, and I don't feel like laughing. "I have come to ask for a favour, for an alliance."

He looks away, as if distracted. "I know."

"To be honest, I don't know why my people are here. We should not be. We should go. This planet is yours and we have no right to be here."

"Yes," he says, still not looking at me. "I know."

"My people are divided. Many of us want what I want. There is a small but powerful faction that has seized control and keeps us here." At last, he looks at me. "I want your help to get me into the Colony so that I can organise resistance to this faction and lead my people away from here."

"You now how to get past your colony's defences?"

I don't like the way he puts the question, but I suppress my disquiet and say, "Yes, I do."

"And you would betray your people?"

"No, I've told you. My people have already been betrayed. I want to save them, get them away from this damned planet."

"Why should I help you? Why should I not wipe out your colony and have done with it? The other clanlords might think I am weak if I don't kill them all." At the word "weak" the muliebri begin to hiss and snarl, baring their teeth at me and rolling their eyes. The clanlord silences them with a word and they cower, their pale eyes fixed on me, resenting my very existence.

I am growing tired of this supplication, tired of begging for help from this ignorant savage with his primitive beast-harem and his rock-pile castle. I assume my own, native form. I am a being of dignity and strength, a soldier of a civilised and powerful race. It is galling to depend on the support of such a low creature as this. I step forward and raise my voice. Let his bitches attack, I am in the mood for a fight.

"You should help me because I'm your only chance of surviving this war. My people will destroy you if I do not stop them. We have not shown you a tiny fraction of our power yet. We have weapons that can eradicate your whole clan, every member of your whole species. If I do not stop them, sooner or later they will wipe this planet clean of you and take it for themselves."

The females begin their snarling again. Like a pack of wolves, they spread out from their clanlord and begin to advance on me. I stand my ground.

"If you want the respect of the other clanlords," I shout over the hissing, groaning muliebri, "you will help me end this war. Then you can show them how close they came to extinction. You will be a hero."

I don't have time for more. The closest female is within pouncing distance. I hold the torch ready. It is my only weapon and I am badly outnumbered.

The clanlord barks out another one-word command and his wives become statues, frozen in postures of threat and menace.

"Come back to me, my lovelies," he says and they turn immediately and rejoin him. I watch in amazement as he reaches out a viciously-taloned claw and they simper and purr to his touch.

"Extinction, you say?"

"Complete, and utter."

"How would you prove that we avoided such a fate?"

"I could provide a demonstration."

"What else could you provide?"

"What?"

"Being a hero is a fine thing, but if I also had some of your weapons, that would guarantee me a hero's respect."

Do I care what these beings do to one another after my people have gone? Not much. Perversely, I feel a greater affinity to the humans than to this strange brood of cognophytes. I would be doing the humans a favour to let the nightmares wipe themselves out. Yet if I were to give these creatures the means to destroy themselves, how would that be any different from letting Celedorn destroy them?

"With our weapons," I say, choosing my words carefully, "you could rule your people. Every other clanlord would fear your power." Nothing is promised. Everything is implied.

He looks away again with that distracted air, idly fondling his wives while he considers the opportunity that has just dropped into his lap.

"Very well, killer of Berreg. Tell me your plan."

Chapter 21

I eventually find Frank at Margaret's place. His hair is damp from the shower and his mind is still full of resentment about waking up lying in the dirt where I'd left him with his wallet and his shoes gone.

When I'd left the dark collective mind of the nightmares, it was to find myself in the body of a charity worker ladling soup from the back of a van half-way across town. I pulled the woman's hand free of the tramp that was clutching it and hailed the first cab I could find.

I suppose Margaret and the others are getting used to strangers turning up on their doorstep with me inside. No one bats an eyelid as I swap into Frank, leaving a confused and frightened woman in the hallway to make her way home.

"So was it worth the risk?" Frank asks. His tone is peevish. The resentment at me having ignored his protests is almost as great as his resentment at having been robbed.

"It was. And don't worry, you've got plenty of money now, and it's probably a good thing that you lost your credit cards. They're too easy to trace."

"And my shoes? What's the upside there?"

"Yeah, well, we'll need to get you some more, I guess."

"Would you two stop that and tell us what happened?" Margaret asked.

"I made a deal with the nightmares."

"You did what?"

"I told you," Frank said. Until I got back, it seems Margaret had doubted what he told her.

"They can get me into the Colony if I help them. Once I'm in, I plan to take control."

Margaret throws up her arms. "It'll be like the invasion of Iraq all over again."

I search Frank's memory for the reference and find it. It seems their country invaded another one recently, for very murky reasons, and their government had told them they were liberating the country and would be welcomed by the grateful Iraqis. The reality of their reception and subsequent occupation had been very different.

"Many of my people want to end this. They just need someone to stand up to Celedorn and restore the Vaticinatrix to power."

"You don't know that."

"I know my people. And Ekkri said as much when we met."

"No, I don't think you do know your people. Everything they've done has surprised you. The whole idea that there could have been a coup against your queen is beyond anything you could ever have believed possible. You don't know what you're dealing with at all, do you? If you go back to the Colony they could shoot you on sight for all you really know."

It scares me to admit that Margaret may be right. I try not to dwell on it, but the way Celedorn has taken over the Colony and the way everyone else is letting him, fill me with a persistent, nagging fear. There is a mystery that I cannot penetrate, an inexplicable break with the natural order. Fear scatters my thoughts like startled animals when I try to think about it.

"I have no option, Margaret. It is all I can do. I have to convince the Colony to leave. To do that, I have to go back in there. For that I need protection. Who else could I turn to?"

"Us," she says and it takes me a moment to realise that she doesn't mean the three of them, but her people, the humans.

"We've spoken about this before," I say. "I'm sure you're right that there are some humans who would help us, but how could we know who they are? Who could we trust?"

"How do you know you can trust the nightmares?"

"I know." How could I explain to a human, even Margaret, what it is like when two cognophytes communicate mind to mind? Something deeper than language passes between us. The thoughts we exchange are richly layered with nuance and coloured with emotion. We can disguise our meanings, even lie, but it is almost impossible to do so without a trace. "You'll just have to take my word for it."

"And I suppose you want Frank to go along too."

"Yes, and you."

"Me? Why do you want me? What can I do?"

"You can let any doubters try to enter you. Once they see that humans are not as backward as they think, they will not be able to argue with me."

She shakes her head. "No, you're wrong again. Haven't you thought this through at all? Your people are at war with the night-mares, right? So they must all know by now there is a big popula-tion of indigenous cognophytes. What difference will it make to parade me in front of them too?"

"No, you don't understand. If the Vaticinatrix says the attack-ers are mindless vermin, they will never doubt her. She is..." How can I explain such a thing to a human? "She is our mother."

I can see from the frowns on Margaret's and her sister's faces that they find this unsatisfactory. Even Frank, who knows me bet-ter than all of them, is thinking I have an unsophisticated and naïve attitude. It makes him doubt my judgement, just as Mar-garet clearly doubts it.

What they don't understand is that I am merely describing the way my people are, the absolute faith that we place in the Vatici-natrix. And they can hardly know the comfort and happiness that comes from such trust. They might, some of them, if they were lucky, have known the same feeling as a small child, lost in the warmth of their mother's protective embrace. But for them, the joy of those moments soon passes. Fallibility and weakness are all they see, even in their parents.

It breaks my heart to acknowledge how like them I have become. Alone and separate, exiled and grown different, I can no longer simply accept what I am told, knowing it will be true. I must question everything, make every decision on my own, face every uncertainty, every moral dilemma, without Her guidance, without even the support of my brothers. The Colony has been the medium in which I have moved my whole life, like water to a fish, or air to a human. The gentle sussuration of the cosmic microwave background, always there if I listen for it, could hardly have seemed more pervasive and enveloping than the Colony.

Until now.

"Margaret," I say, wanting at least her to understand. "You should have asked how I could have been such a fool as never to have suspected what was happening. The Colony has been on Earth for two years and it never once occurred to me to ask why the nightmares I hunted and killed were so viciously opposed to my kind. Why should they be, if they were some sort of low, cognophytic vermin we had picked up on our journey from Treforga? Why hadn't they bothered us on the ship? Why didn't they just disperse and disappear when we got to Earth? And why were there so many of them?

"These are all such obvious questions to me now, but I tell you, I didn't ask them, and no one else in the Colony asked them either. Why would we, when the Vaticinatrix Herself had told us about them? And, even though I didn't hear it from Her directly, even though I don't remember speaking to Her in person once since our ship left Treforga, I was just as incapable of believing that one of my brothers would lie to me as that She would.

"You think I don't know my own people, but I do. I know that, whatever Celedorn tells them, they will believe. And they'll go on believing it in the face of mounting evidence to the contrary, not just because that is how we are, but because the possibility that he could lie, or worse, that the Vaticinatrix could be wrong, is too scary even to consider."

Rachel carries on scowling at me, but I think I see a glimmer of understanding in Margaret's expression. Frank is unconvinced. He can't see how anybody can be so naïve. He certainly can't see how a whole race of such trusting fools could survive.

"Yet you dared to think the Vaticinatrix could be wrong," Margaret says.

"I did." I still cannot say it without feeling shame. "And others will too. I'm not that different from my brothers." I wonder if the others can hear the plaintive hope in my tone. "That's why I have to get among them and talk to them, show them you, make them face up to all those doubts that must have been troubling them. If I can do that, I can stop the fighting and get us off this planet."

"But, if you do that, your colony would never be the same," she says, getting it at last. "Everyone would be so traumatised."

I see a flicker of concern in her eyes and I almost make Frank hug her for that moment of empathy. "You see why you have to come?"

"She's not going anywhere with you." Rachel steps forward, as if to physically prevent me taking her sister.

Margaret reaches out and gently touches Rachel's arm. "Raich, it's all right."

But Rachel turns on her. "No, it's not all right. Nothing about any of this is all right. He wants you to go with him into the middle of some alien war? And for what? So you can convince his buddies to pack up and leave? By letting them poke their slimy tentacles into your brain? All this assuming they don't just kill you to shut you up. And then what? It's *hasta la vista* from the brain slugs, leaving us all behind with the other lot, the nightmares. And, speaking from experience, I don't know which I think is worse."

"I won't leave you in any danger," I tell Margaret. "Rachel, you have to understand that if we don't do something, the war is going to get worse. I've seen how many nightmares there are out there. Their numbers are overwhelming. The only way my people can win this war is to take extreme action. Trust me, they have weapons that can cleanse this planet of all cognophytic life. The kind of thing they could use from orbit while remaining safe. But there will be massive collateral damage. Millions of humans could die.

"As for being left with the nightmares, nothing will have changed. They have always been with you. Your species have co-evolved and humanity is thriving. You won't be any worse off than before."

I see in Frank's mind the arguments that must be forming in Rachel's too. Being ridden by nightmares has been a burden on their race. The creatures' malign influence almost certainly accounts for so much of what they feel as depression, mental illness, and all the nebulous, unholy fears they are prey to. There is a vein of sickness in human psychology that manifests itself in their art and literature, that drives them to apathy, drug abuse, nihilism, superstition, and darkness. Without doubt the nightmares are at the root of most of it. When I compare their obsession with death-cult religions, their criminality, and violence, to the open-hearted cheerfulness of the Treforgans, I can't help feeling pity for them.

Frank could almost wish that my people would stay and rid the world of nightmares. Even, in his terms, the substitution of one evil, pernicious parasite for another, less pernicious one, would be an improvement.

"It's not my job to sort out your problems," I say to them both. "I need to get my people out of here and to another planet, one we can colonise without breaking the law. Anything else is up to you."

Besides, what they want from us is genocide. The nightmares aren't the kind of people I'd want to share a beer with, but they are cognophytes all the same, fully developed sentients. To wipe out a race of cognophytes to protect its host species is a bizarre idea. It would be like burning all the vegetation on a planet to stop it sucking nutrients out of the ground.

"He's right," Margaret says. "The nightmares are not his problem. If we want to be rid of them, we need to sort that out ourselves. We should tackle this one problem at a time. First, we get the Colony off our backs. Then we work out what to do next." She speaks to her sister. "We three have been given a chance to do something important, something that no one else can do. The Army is messing about with its secret projects and hit squads and whatever else, but the chances are they can't do anything about the Colony. They certainly can't stop the war in time. But we can — I can if we help him now.

"I'm sorry, Raich, but I'm going to do it. I'm pretty sure Frank feels the same." She gives him a small smile, which he returns. "You know it's the right thing to do. None of us has any option, really."

Rachel glares at her sister without speaking, emotions move across her features that I take to be a mixture of anger and despair. Without a word, she walks away, leaves the apartment, slams the door behind her.

"She'll come round," Frank says. He says it only to comfort Margaret, not from any knowledge of Rachel, but Margaret nods, accepting his kindness. I find the exchange touching and, for a moment, I wish there were some way I could let the two of them open their minds directly to one another. But I can't. They have to communicate in their limited human way and to make the best of it.

"The nightmares are ready whenever I am," I tell them. "The sooner we go the better."

Frank's anxiety level surges but he steels himself for what we have to do. Margaret too seems frightened but resolved. "Thank you," I say, and we set off.

Chapter 22

Day and night, night and day. The rapid switching from light to dark and back again that characterises this world is hard to get used to. On Treforga, the days were twenty times as long. Temperatures varied from minus forty after midnight to plus sixty after noon. This planet, Earth, is a balmy temperate paradise by comparison, but the cost is this endless flickering of day and night.

Evening is darkening towards night as we get into Frank's car and set off. I use Frank's phone to call Ekkri. When he answers, I ask for Mr. Thompson. He tells me I have the wrong number and hangs up. Then he calls me back on a secure phone.

"Are you mad?" he asks, after I explain my plan.

"Is the Colony holding its perimeter?"

"No, we fell back." His voice sounds calm but this is shocking news.

"Where's the perimeter now?"

He names a series of roads that form a rough square around the Colony. The area they contain is small, not much more than the grounds of the estate. The Colony has almost no leeway now. If this perimeter does not hold, they will need to take drastic action to save themselves.

"Arramar, how can you even think of bringing the enemy in here with you? We're at war. People are dying. It will look to everyone as if you have betrayed us."

"If I come in without them, Celedorn will shut me up before I can persuade anybody. Ekkri, the nightmares don't want this war either. They see us as invaders. In their eyes they are merely defending themselves."

Why am I having this conversation? I thought Ekkri understood. I thought he would leap at the chance to help me.

"But if they breach our defences, what is to stop them slaughtering us?"

"Me. You have to trust me. I am coming with one of their leaders. I have made a deal. I believe he will keep his word."

"You are asking a lot."

"There is a lot at stake. This may be our only chance to end this, Ekkri." There is silence on the line. After a moment I can't bear the pain of my friend's indecision. "Ekkri, if you love me, you will do as I ask."

When he finally speaks, his voice is subdued and flat. "Of course. Let me make some preparations. I will call you back in a few minutes with the arrangements." I can't tell if I have shamed him into doing what is right, or if he is helping me reluctantly, despite his fears.

I hang up the phone, aware that Frank and Margaret have heard it all. I ignore them and retreat into Frank to think about what just happened. That Ekkri should doubt me is like a fist around my heart. Ekkri, who has been closer to me than my own thoughts, the one with whom I dreamed one day of making the Transformation and starting our own Colony.

My only consolation is that, when this is over, he will see that I was right.

When he calls back, he is brusque and business-like. He has arranged for a gap to appear in the patrols. Knowing the time and place, I can slip inside the perimeter with my nightmares and my humans. He says he has to go, that there is much still to do. Then he is gone.

I stare out through Frank's eyes as he drives. The night is black now and the roads have become narrow and unlit. Ekkri had not offered me one word of support. He had not even wished me luck. In his reluctance to talk about anything but the arrangements he had made, I felt his resentment. I have forced him to act against his better judgement.

But Ekkri always was more cautious and timid than me. I should have foreseen his fear and reluctance. Ekkri is no hero, but a kind and gentle soul. That he is helping me at all must be, for him, a titanic act of bravery. I must not resent his reluctance. I must acknowledge his timidity and give him credit for the great love he has shown me in doing what I ask.

Frank and Margaret want me to reassure them that everything is still all right. I give them a few platitudes and sink down into Frank's murky unconscious, leaving them to work it out for themselves. We are almost at the rendezvous point and I need some time alone.

-oOo-

"You're committed then?"

Margaret is speaking as I re-emerge. I have only been away for a few minutes but have not been paying any attention. I refrain from announcing myself, curious about how they interact when I'm not there. From Frank's memory, I see that he has just told her about giving up his job.

"I don't know about that," he says. "I went to the office to see what was going on with my case. I saw Al and he said the DA wasn't going to prosecute. Seems there is enough evidence to convince them it was self-defence."

"I'd have thought the shotgun bruises on your back would have been enough!"

"There was that, and the fact that the kid brought a stolen gun with him to my apartment, and I was lying face-down unconscious with powder burns from my gun all over my own ass." He shakes his head, understanding how it all must have looked to his colleagues. "It doesn't make any sense to anybody – not the cops, the labs, or the DA's office – but no one can get past the fact that the kid came in, shot me, and then got hit by a blind, lucky shot as I tried to save myself." A bitter thought flicks through his mind. "They don't know the kid was just some innocent bystander and the real murderers here are up the road ahead of us.

"Same story with the kidnap and murder attempt by Sturtz's men. A crowd of people saw them grab me and then saw one of them turn on the others." He falls silent and Margaret leaves him to it, perhaps sensing that he is momentarily filled with anger at my people. In a while, he goes on.

"Anyway, Al says it's just a matter of getting the forms signed and I can go back to work, but it suddenly came to me that I didn't want to. I don't know why. It wasn't just that my own department had kind of turned on me and had treated me like a criminal. I can understand all that. It was more like... I've seen a bigger picture, you know? I don't want to go through the motions of busting crack-heads and pimps, keeping the crazies off the streets, when for all I know every one of the poor bastards has a nightmare in his head."

Margaret was watching him carefully. "I don't think you can blame all human weakness on the nightmares."

"Yeah, maybe, but I know what it's like. I've heard voices in my head and thought I was going cuckoo. I've had blackouts and woken up in another place, hours later, not knowing what the hell I've been doing. I've felt the strange urges I can't explain, to be somewhere or to see someone. It feels like you're nuts. It makes you desperate. It scares you senseless. And that's just our friend the soldier ant. What must it be like with one of the other lot inside you? You've said yourself how Rachel was, and how she changed. Can you imagine what that was like for her?"

Margaret is silent.

"So I told Al he could keep the badge. I've got my swanky new apartment, a PI license, a small armoury, and a ton of money rolling in every month. I thought, maybe I could make use of all that to do some good, hunt them down somehow, try to make a difference."

He feels like an idiot, saying it out loud, even though he means every word. He imagines Margaret will think he's some kind of fantasist, with childish dreams of his own importance. But Margaret reaches out a hand and rests it on Frank's arm. When he glances her way, he sees only tenderness in her eyes.

When he looks back at the road, we both see the bar where the rendezvous is to take place. Reluctantly, he turns his thoughts away from what he just saw to focus on what we must do next.

-oOo-

A couple of dozen motorbikes are parked outside the bar, along with a few old pickups. "Oh great, a biker bar," Frank grumbles. He tells Margaret to stay in the car and keep the doors locked. We get out and he reaches into his jacket to unhook the holster that holds his gun.

You won't need that, I say, but he doesn't believe me. *When we get inside, I will do all the talking.*

"Yeah, I figured."

People all around turn to stare at Frank as we walk in. There is loud music playing and a hubbub of voices that quietens for a moment. The place reeks of cigarette smoke and beer. Frank is nervous as a kitten. I pick up the thought that this is not the kind of place he'd ever go without calling for backup first.

I hear a voice nearby growl, "Fucking cop." A thick-set man with copious facial hair spits on the floor near Frank's feet. From Frank's reaction, I can see this is meant as a sign of contempt. But he keeps on walking until we are at the centre of the room. Then I take over.

"Clanlord," I say as loudly as I can. "I am here."

A burly man with a scarred face stands up and walks over to me. He stands very close, his face almost touching Frank's. "Why don't you shut the fuck up, you crazy motherfucker, before I push this glass in your face?"

I ignore him. "Clanlord, show yourself!"

The scarred man grabs me by Frank's throat. He is becoming a nuisance. So I flow into him, surprised to find no nightmare inside. I take control of his body and make him let go of Frank. Then I make him do a chicken dance between the tables while making clucking noises. I'd seen this on a TV show and I know the humans find it ridiculous. All around him, people gape in astonishment. Finally, I made him kneel down in front of Frank and say, "Please forgive me, I'm such a total moron," while clutching at Frank's sleeve. I flow back into Frank and, with a final nudge of his brain, make the man smash his glass onto his own head.

The man stumbles as he tries to get up, blood pouring from his scalp. He is watching Frank with horror, not understanding why he is on the floor and bleeding. A woman tries to help him up and he shrugs her off violently.

"Clanlord, I'm waiting," I shout, growing angry. "Do we have a deal or not?"

The scarred man is in Frank's face again, scared and angry. "What did you just do to me you cocksucker?"

I scan the room for signs of the clanlord, but everyone is gawping, open-mouthed, instead of coming up to meet me.

"Hey! Look at me you motherfucking faggot!"

The scarred guy is poking Frank in the chest and I am just about to do something more permanently disabling to him when another man stands up, walks up behind the first and punches him hard in the kidneys. Scarface goes down again and I get a good look at his attacker. He is a big man, older than most of the people in the bar, but dressed in the same dirty leather-and-denim outfit. He is grinning at me. Four others from around the room also stand up and quickly take up positions behind him.

Scarface drags himself to his feet and, with a roar, launches himself at the older guy. But his assault is over before it has properly begun. One of the grinning man's four friends knocks Scarface back to the ground with a vicious blow to the jaw. This time the man lies still and doesn't get up again.

"You're the Clanlord?" I ask.

The man nods in acknowledgement. "Killer of Berreg."

"Are these all the soldiers you have brought?"

"How many does it take to kill a few murdering dogs?"

I hope he's not going to be playing silly buggers all night. "More than that," I say.

He shrugs and another ten bikers stand up around the room.

"Better," I say. "Let's go. I'm parked outside. Follow me when I leave."

Chapter 23

Margaret keeps watching the swarm of motorbike headlights behind us. "Are you sure this is such a good idea?" she asks. Frank reassures her that we're safe, for now. "I just didn't expect them to be so... rough," she says.

"Those are just the hosts," I tell her. "It's what's inside them that is really dangerous."

"Thanks," she says. "I feel so much better now."

We drive on in silence. The big engine of Frank's car gurgles and purrs like a contented panther and, behind us, fifteen motorbikes snarl and growl impatiently, waiting to be unleashed. Eventually, I spot the little dirt road and we turn onto it, our headlights carving a tunnel through the trees ahead of us.

"OK, stop here," I say, and Frank pulls up. The track we are on is narrow. There is nowhere to make a turn. As the motorbikes rumble to a halt behind us, I realise there is no way to make a quick retreat if things go wrong. Frank has the same thought, but neither of us says anything so as not to frighten Margaret. She is holding Frank's hand as we walk, seeking human contact in her moment of fear.

It is a half-mile walk to the place where we can cross the perimeter into the Colony. For a moment I look back at the bikers following us silently towards my people's stronghold and I have my first real doubts about what I am doing. Fifteen nightmares, possibly all of them males, could overwhelm me easily. If they were to time this breach with an external attack, it could be disastrous for the Colony. And I am taking this risk on the word of an alien I have met once and for whom the urge to betray me must be a powerful temptation.

On the other hand, my instincts said to trust this peculiar being, and a soldier learns to trust his own instincts.

"There's someone up ahead," Frank says. His warning is unnecessary. I see everything he sees. Margaret's hand tightens on his.

"It will be Ekkri." I try to sound confident, for their sakes. I need them both to remain calm and functional.

We keep walking until I am face-to-face with my old friend, riding the same body I saw him in the last time I was in the Colony. I reach out a hand to touch and greet, but he steps back. He is staring over my shoulder at the silent bikers.

"You brought so many," he says.

"I brought enough for my purpose." My tone is snappish. I am hurt and angry. Withholding contact is an insult, a sign of mistrust. It is a bitter blow that Ekkri should treat me this way.

"The way to the mansion is clear?" I ask. It goes without saying that Ekkri would keep his word, but I don't care if I hurt him in return. His attitude has made me edgy and peevish. I don't understand it and can't spare the time to think about it. He hesitates, on the edge of saying something, but whatever it might have been – a tart remark, more scolding about how stupid this is – he thinks better of it. With a quick nod he turns and leads us on towards the house.

It is in sight, lit up and stately at the end of the avenue of trees along which we approach. We are coming at it from the side, past the formal gardens. Near us, a row of greenhouses glistens in the starlight. Our route is unlit and the Moon is behind cloud, but soon we will be within the halo of light around the big old house. The clanlord has moved up to walk beside me and I feel his presence as a dark malevolence. When he cries out an alarm, I am as surprised as Frank.

"What's this?" he shouts, turning slowly, scanning the trees that flank our path. His followers draw weapons, shotguns and sub-machine guns. I peer into the darkness and see shapes emerging from the trees on both sides of the road. There are at least twenty, possibly twice that many, and they too are armed.

Frank reaches for his own gun but I stay his hand. Margaret steps closer and holds Frank's arm with both hands. I shrug her off and step away. Frank wants to get Margaret out of there, but I shut him down. All I can think is that Ekkri has betrayed me. Ekkri has set up this ambush. My own, dear, Ekkri, has led me into this trap. I turn to confront him, but he has gone, run off into the darkness.

"Fools!" I cry in anguish to the silent people surrounding us. "I am here to save you, not to betray you. Celedorn is your real enemy. Not me. I have with me all the proof you could want that this planet is not for us. I can show you right now how Celedorn has duped us. I have with me sentient cognophytes, native to this planet. I have with me a human female, whose own mental capacity is advanced enough she can tell when a mindrider enters her."

A figure detaches itself from those surrounding us and walks up to me. I recognise the body that Celedorn rides. "Nobody cares, Arramar," he says. "It's too late for any of that, now."

The clanlord beside me growls. He is still scanning the mindriders around him. "You'd better talk fast, Killer of Berreg. I don't like the way this is going."

"I see you have made friends with the enemy, Arramar. I hope you didn't get too close, I'll be asking them to leave in a moment."

"These creatures are not our enemy." I speak loudly, so everyone can hear. "We have invaded their planet. They are merely defending themselves against us. But we can stop this stupidity and put things right. They will stop their attack as soon as we agree to leave. No one else need die."

Celedorn steps even closer. "I'm afraid I disagree, Arramar. It seems you've had a wasted trip. Now, tell your friends to go home. I'll give them an escort back to their vehicles. You are coming with me."

It is dark and the people surrounding us seem only to have human weapons. We are surrounded and outnumbered at least two to one, but there is still a chance that we can break through this ambush and reach the house. Yet the silence from Celedorn's followers is worrying. I feel the need for some sign that it might be worthwhile to take such a desperate risk.

"I don't care what your opinion is, Celedorn, I want to hear from the others. Does anyone here doubt that what I say is true? Do any of you still think we belong on this planet?"

Celedorn turns to his men. "Well? Speak up, someone. Tell Arramar what you think."

"I think you should never have brought these nightmare vermin into the Colony," one says.

Another calls out, "I say if he sides with the enemy, we should treat him like the enemy."

"Kill them all!" shouts another.

The shock of what I am hearing sends me reeling. How could my own people act like this? "What about the law?" I shout. "Doesn't that mean anything?"

"What about survival?" one shouts back.

"What about the Colony?" says another.

I am stupefied, aghast. "It's not a matter of survival..." I begin, but then the night erupts into violence.

The clanlord, drawing the obvious conclusion that my plan was a non-starter, rushes the cordon of mindriders. His men, acting in complete unison, follow his lead, opening fire with their weapons to clear a path. Everyone is taken by surprise and several of my people fall dead. Then there is a pandemonium of crashing noise and stuttering light as both sides open fire.

I drag Margaret and Frank to the ground moments before bullets begin to zip through the air where we had stood. There is plenty of light now, strobing the motions of shooting, dying, struggling people. It is quickly obvious that, in close, hand-to-hand fighting, the nightmares have the advantage. They seem to share their comprehension of the whole battle, using their superior awareness of the EM fields around them, not just to sense approaching danger, but to communicate between themselves.

They are so fierce and so well-coordinated that it looks like they might easily break free. Except that freedom doesn't seem to be their main objective. With an insane bravery, they change the thrust of their assault to swing around in a pincer movement against the remaining colonists who have foolishly bunched up, expecting, no doubt, to be chasing them through the trees.

Whatever my plans, whatever my intentions, when I see the danger my people are in, I can only leap up and run to their defence. I intercept one of the charging bikers and bring him down with a body block that jars Frank to the core. In a moment, I am rushing into the biker's body and the nightmare is facing me. It's a big one, black and mean. Around us is the bleak volcanic waste-land these creatures inhabit. In the seconds which it takes for my opponent to get over his astonishment and attack, I grab control of the biker's body, turn to Frank and say, "Get yourself and Margaret to safety. I'll be O -"

I can say no more because the beast is upon me. I catch a last glimpse of understanding dawning in Frank's wide eyes and then I have to deal with the claws and fangs of my attacker. The creature is powerful. The force of its attack knocks me down and we roll in a tangle of flailing limbs across the ash and cinders of its dismal world.

Breaking free for a moment, I see others around us. Inside the nightmare's world, nightmares and colonists are locked in combat. Again I am amazed at their ability to link minds, to bring us into their own miserable reality. I dodge a blow and leap on my attacker's back. My own claws rake at its exposed neck, but its hide is tough and I do little damage. With a roar of anger it throws me off. This battle is hopeless. It is too uneven. Fighting out here, in their world, on their terms, the Colonists don't stand a chance.

"Get below!" I shout. "You can't win here. You need weapons." Some of my people look around, hearing me. "You're still in a human mind. Get below and you have the advantage."

I can't wait to see if they understand. The creature is upon me again, its jaws snapping at my face. With all the strength I have, I drag us both down into the biker's subconscious mind.

The nightmare is briefly disoriented and I struggle free and run. I am in a bar, much like the real one I saw earlier in the evening, except, in this bar, most of the patrons are large-breasted young women with very few clothes on. The only men in the room are the bar staff – who, interestingly, also have few clothes on. The women call to me, pleading for sex, and I curse my luck at having fallen into such a useless fantasy. I have only seconds before I must fight the nightmare again.

At my waist, I feel a heavy awkward object and grab at it. It is a revolver. A Colt .45 Magnum. A hugely oversized handgun. My biker has always wanted one. To him it is the ultimate in power. With such a gun, he believes, he would be nobody's bitch. Almost laughing with relief, I pull the gun from my waistband, it is over-long making it awkward and unwieldy. But I don't care. In the biker's mind, his Colt has "stopping power". I turn recklessly, falling backwards as I bring the gun to bear on the charging mon-ster behind me. The enormous barrel almost pokes it in the chest. I see its eyes narrow in fury as I squeeze the trigger, unleashing a mighty explosion that sends a bullet ripping through the beast's body.

I hit the ground with a bone-jarring crash and slide across the wooden floor, smashing through chairs and tables and squealing females. The Colt is knocked from my hand and I try to keep track of where it goes. The nightmare tumbles after me, coming to rest with its great bulk across my legs. Desperately, I struggle to free myself, terrified of being trapped there. But I soon see that the nightmare is not moving. More carefully and effectively, I push the creature off me and rise.

I am cut and damaged, but not badly. I drag the beast onto its back to reveal a fist-sized hole in its chest. It is clearly dead, so I retrieve the gun and head back to the surface of the biker's mind.

The gloom and devastation have gone. Without the nightmare to connect him to their shared reality, his consciousness is just like any other human's. I quickly take his body and look to see how the battle is going.

It is a scene that would seem strange to human eyes. People stand together in pairs or threes, touching one another, but not moving. Within their minds, great battles are being fought, but from the outside, nothing is visible. There is still sporadic gunfire, from within the woods. The standing groups would make easy targets, but no one would shoot them, not knowing whether any particular body contains friend or foe.

Frank and Margaret are nowhere to be seen.

I head for the nearest pair of quiet combatants, meaning to re-enter the fray, but I am caught in the headlights of a group of vehicles approaching from the direction of the house. I make for the trees. A lone human in this situation is a natural target and, if these are reinforcements from the Colony, standing around in a biker's body is suicide.

A blast of machine gun fire tears up the vegetation ahead of me and I skitter to a halt, looking for cover.

"Do not move. Stay where you are." The amplified voice comes from the lead vehicle. It is a voice I recognise.

The vehicles come right up to where we are. The lead vehicle is broad and flat, a human military vehicle. Behind it is a smaller version of the same kind of thing, behind that, an ordinary saloon car. It is the lead vehicle that has my attention, though. On its open back, there is a bulky machine. It seems to be a haphazard pile of black boxes, hastily lashed together in a metal frame. On top of that is a long, fat tube of wire mesh which is turning on a post, as if it is being sighted on a target but the operator cannot decide quite who to pick.

A group of men jump out of the second vehicle. They are dressed in what seem to be thick, grey hazmat suits. They carry machine guns and spread out around the lead vehicle, silhouetted in the bright headlamps behind them, their faces dark holes behind tinted visors. Figures also emerge from the car at the back but I cannot make them out.

It is too late to run now. I am trapped. The shooting in the woods stops and I can only hope that, if my people are the victors there, they will have the sense to stay away from here until they can bring help. I can't believe that the humans have turned up right here, right now. The coincidence is too much to accept. Yet here they are, Colonel Sturtz and his special forces team. And, if I am not mistaken, the contraption they have with them is the prototype EMP weapon that Bernstein's group demonstrated for them.

Chapter 24

From behind the line of Sturtz's soldiers a woman steps forward. I goggle in astonishment at the sight of Rachel. She is with two soldiers who are arguing with her, trying to persuade her to go back to the car. Sturtz climbs down from the cab of the lead vehicle and goes to her. He too is wearing one of the grey coveralls and has a helmet under one arm. They are all just seven or eight meters away from me.

"Well, is he here?" Sturtz asks.

Rachel shakes her head. "No. I can't see them." She points at the EMP weapon. "You can't use that thing until I'm sure they're safe."

"If they're not here, they're safe."

Rachel is angry. "No. You promised me Maggie and Frank would be safe."

"They're not here, you said so yourself. Now get back in the car or I can't answer for your safety either." To the soldiers, he snaps, "Get her into the car and keep her there."

The soldiers lead her away, but someone else comes running up shouting, "Sturtz, you moron, what are you doing here?" Celedorn gets almost to the human colonel before a suited soldier grabs him and pushes the muzzle of a gun in his face.

I watch for a second, then two, waiting for the soldier to fall down in agony or dance off into the bushes, but nothing happens. Celedorn looks as surprised as I feel.

So, not hazmat suits at all, but Faraday suits. The humans have worked out how to keep a mindrider from invading them.

"Back off, Celedorn." Sturtz is pushing his face into the administrator's. "This is my show now. You and your buddies had your chance and you let things get way out of hand. Now we're going to put that right."

He calls to someone in the back of the truck. "Target that couple over there."

The big tube swivels towards a pair of combatants.

"No!" Celedorn bellows, struggling against the soldier who is holding him. He reaches out to grab Sturtz's exposed head and the colonel leaps back in horror as the administrator's hand almost makes contact.

"Fucking E.T. Bastard!" Sturtz yells pulling on his helmet. "I should put you out there in the kill zone for that."

"Kill as many nightmares as you like, you damned savage, but my people are out there too. Harm a single one of them and I'll –"

But Celedorn's threat is cut off by Sturtz yelling "Fire!"

There is a blinding flash of pain. Everything is confusion, a crackling blizzard of memories and sensation. The parts of my mind seem to whirl like stars, like sparks sucked into a swirling flame. I see brilliant colours. I am wracked by explosions of heat and cold. Then there is just a grey fizzing, a massive discharge of energy, fading to static.

I open my ride's eyes to find his face pressed into the earth. With an effort of trembling limbs and weakened muscles, I push him off the ground and to his knees.

Where there had been standing groups of fighting men, there are bodies strewn across the road. Some are moving, struggling to get up, but some are not. The pair at the centre of the weapon's beam are lying still on the ground. As far as I can tell, they are both dead, their human hosts along with them.

I turn back to Sturtz. Even in their Faraday suits, the humans do not seem completely unaffected. Sturtz is leaning against his vehicle, looking dazed. And one of the soldiers has fallen down. Celedorn is down too, moving feebly.

This would probably be a good time to make a run for it, but my host's limbs are weak and trembling and it is all I can do to get him to his feet. Besides, the revelations I have just witnessed – Ekkri's betrayal, Rachel's betrayal, and the astonishing fact that Celedorn has been working with the humans – leave me more stunned and dispirited than the EM pulse, or whatever it was. A simple EMP weapon would not have killed the human hosts.

Sturtz is bellowing at the technicians in the back of the truck. It seems the strength and widespread effect of the weapon had not been expected. A voice from the truck responds with the whining tone in which humans so often justify themselves. I look away to find Celedorn on his feet and approaching Sturtz again. The administrator moves unsteadily and looks as feeble as I feel, but he is animated by a boiling rage.

"You stupid, murderous savage!" he yells and Sturtz turns to face him. "You killed my people. Killed them! And for what? A show of strength? To test your primitive machine? It's pathetic! It's like letting a monkey play with explosives."

Sturtz begins to respond, but Celedorn throws up a hand in a curious open-handed gesture, indicating the EMP weapon. "You see that? You see that ridiculous contraption? Do you think we let you build it so you could threaten us with it? Do you think we permitted you to have it so that you might one day use it on us?" He keeps his hand outstretched towards the machine. All eyes are on him. "You had better remember your place in the order of things, little colonel. You had better remember by whose grace you are permitted even to stand there gaping at me like a drowning fish."

At which, he draws back his hand, clenching it into a fist, an unmistakable gesture of crushing and destroying. He shouts, in

Treforgan, a language very difficult to speak with a human larynx, "Riders! Protect your hosts!"

Not one of my people hesitates for a moment. We all throw ourselves to the ground and curl up, protecting heads and underbellies. If a human soldier heard the cry, "Fire in the hole!" the reaction might be the same.

Sure enough, within moments, the weapon and the truck it is mounted on, erupt into flame. The truck explodes with a stupendous violence. A searing wave of heat passes over me, followed almost instantly by a shock wave that slams me into the ground.

Shrapnel tears through the air like bullets but I am too deafened by the explosion to know if anyone screams and dies. Something fast and hot hits my host's leg and I have to block out the pain or I would be screaming myself. I wait a few seconds more as debris rains down all around me, before I dare look up.

No one is standing. The truck burns and a mushroom of smoke rises above it. Bikers and soldiers alike lie in contorted postures, heads, chests, backs, bloody messes. My own people have not escaped damage, but every one that I can see is still alive, looking around, like me, in bewilderment.

I look past the burning truck and see that the vehicle behind it has been damaged in the blast. Soldiers are emerging from it, some of them cut and bloodied. Beyond that, the saloon has its windscreen starred but is otherwise okay. At least I won't have to tell Margaret her sister is dead.

Celedorn stands and walks over to where Sturtz lies on the ground. The colonel is face down and bleeding from wounds all over his back, but he is still breathing. I get to my feet and try to go over to join them, but the wound in my leg is bad and I fall down with my first step. Celedorn glances at me but says nothing.

Two of Sturtz's soldiers are still fit enough and have enough presence of mind to grab their weapons and hurry over to their commanding officer. When they get there, Celedorn only has to look at them to make them stop, too afraid to come any closer. From my perspective, Celedorn had signalled gunners on the roof of the house, half a kilometre away across the lawns, and they had fired a high-energy laser bolt into the truck. From the perspective of the humans, the alien magician had destroyed their weapon with a single gesture.

"He's still alive," Celedorn tells them. "You may take him away, and the rest of them. And you will take a message back to Senator Keneally. Tell him Sturtz is a fool. Tell Keneally he is a fool too for using such a man. Tell him I want to see him, here, tomorrow morning. Now go. Clear away your dead and wounded."

As he is delivering this message, I get up again and, more carefully this time, limp past them, heading for the car with Rachel in it. Two of my people intercept me. I prepare to force my way past them, but Celedorn calls out, "Let him do whatever he's doing, but stay with him. This is our friend and brother, Arramar. It is you, isn't it?"

I ignore him and keep going. There are four people in the car, three soldiers and Rachel. The two in the front get out and go to join the others loading their fallen comrades into the back of the second vehicle. They sidle past me and my escort, as nervous as kittens, just a couple of scared men without Sturtz to lead them.

"Hello, Rachel," I say, leaning into the car. She stares at my unfamiliar face. She is wide-eyed with fright, tense and breathing fast.

"Who are you?"

"Don't you recognise me?"

She looks into my eyes and I see the moment when it finally dawns on her.

"Are Maggie and Frank–?"

I cut her off. "What did you think you were doing? Do you know how many people you got killed tonight because you led Sturtz here?" I see emotions flicker across her features, but I don't see regret among them. She finally settles on anger.

"All you think about is your damned colony and how to per-suade it to leave. Well some of us don't give a crap about you and your mindriders. Sturtz understands. He knows who the real en-emy is here. You? You haven't got a clue what's been going on. You're just blundering around causing trouble. You're an irrele-vance."

I want to question her further but Celedorn arrives with more of my people. "That's enough for now, Arramar. These people have to be going."

I withdraw from the car window and face him. "I want to talk to you."

"You seem to have misunderstood your situation, Arramar. You are my prisoner. You don't get to choose who you talk to. But don't worry. We will be having a chat soon enough. Take him away. Incapacitate him if he gives you any trouble. I don't need his host intact."

The soldiers, dead and alive, crammed into their two remaining vehicles, slam the last door and start up their engines. We stand in silence and watch them drive away, the flames from the burning truck lighting up the scene. From the smell, there are still bodies among the flames.

"You've got some explaining to do," I say to Celedorn, but he just shakes his head, sadly, and walks off towards the house. My guards prod me with their guns and I set off after him, dragging my injured leg.

Chapter 25

I am left alone in a cellar of the big house. My host is suffering badly from his wound and drifts in and out of consciousness, feverish and weak with blood loss, dragging me with him into darkness and dreams.

I see Ekkri again, not as I last saw him, but as I know him in my heart, a mindrider, beautiful and gentle, funny and kind, my dear friend of so many happy years. We are on the ship, in orbit, leaving Treforga for the last time, excited at the prospect of this great adventure. A new Colony on a new world! So few of us ever have such a chance.

And we mean to make the most of it. We make our plans. We will shine, we will excel in our duties, we will be tireless, unstinting, we will help build the finest Colony our race has known. And, when the time is right, we will step forward, the first to ask the Vaticinatrix's blessing, the first to seek Transformation.

Then back to consciousness, back to the cellar and my host's misery and pain.

I can hardly believe how stupid I have been. Did I really think I could convince anyone to listen to me, to follow me even? I couldn't even persuade Ekkri. My thoughts veer away from him, but they return and flap around him like crows around roadkill. He was the one person who should have been with me no matter what, the one person I would have believed could never betray me. Am I such a fool that even Ekkri cannot stomach my folly?

Fighting the fog in my host's febrile mind, I remember Celedorn standing among the humans. He cursed them and struck at them, but he was with them. They were working together. There is an alliance, that much is clear, between my people and senior levels in this country's government.

"Sturtz understands," Rachel had said. "He knows who the real enemy is."

And now I understand too. It is blindingly obvious to everyone except me, it seems. Ekkri tried to tell me on the phone. "How can you even think of bringing the enemy in here with you?" he said. The enemy. The nightmares. "We're at war. People are dying."

To the humans, the existence of the nightmares must have been a terrible revelation. Why wouldn't they want an alliance with the Colony in the face of such a huge and ubiquitous threat? We must have seemed like saviours to them, not invaders, their only hope of defeating a foe that fills them with unimaginable horror. I remember Rachel's reaction to being ridden, even by me. I should not have underestimated the disgust she felt. I should have realised the overwhelming loathing she would feel for the nightmares, who had ridden her for years. Of course, they were the enemy. Of course she would do anything to help destroy them, even if it meant betraying her own sister. Betraying me would mean nothing to her.

Yet how do I explain Celedorn? Why would he want an alliance with the humans? What could that give the Colony that we could not easily take for ourselves? As we all saw last night, such an unstable and aggressive ally is more of a liability than an asset.

I drift away into unconsciousness, lulled to sleep by the feeble moaning of my ride. Why does no one come to fix this human? Are they leaving him to die slowly – and me with him – as a punishment? Since when were my people so cruel?

The Vaticinatrix comes to see me. I am too weak to stand and I cry like a human at the disrespect I must show Her. She touches my hand and I am brought into Her shining presence. I try to apologise for my foolishness and incompetence, but She silences me with a gesture.

"You have served me well, Arramar," She says.

It must be true, although it seems wrong. "But I have not saved you. I need to find you and set you free."

"You will, my brave soldier. I know you will."

I close my eyes and bask in the warmth of Her approbation. To please Her is all I could ever want. But I need to know more. "Tell me where to find you. I don't know where you are."

She smiles, pleased with me. "You will find me, Arramar. I trust you completely. Of all my children, only you have not deserted me."

My joy is like a bird, soaring on the wind, yet still something mars my perfect bliss. "But my ride is injured. They will not send a doctor. They plan to let me die down here. How can I help you if I cannot even keep this host conscious?" There is a human poem I read once, something about how I feel. "The centre cannot hold," I say, trying to remember it for Her. "What rough beast..."

"What's that, old friend?"

I force my eyes open at the sound of this new voice.

A medic is working on my ride, cleaning the wound and examining the leg. I look around. The cellar is the same. My visit from the Vaticinatrix just another dream.

"Who are you?" I ask.

"Orovon. You remember?"

"Of course." We had struck up a friendship way back on Treforga when we were both in training. Orovon was an astute, sensible man, and I learned to value his opinions. "Why did they leave me so long?"

"Sorry about that. Straight after they brought you down here, there was another attack. Seems you pissed off the enemy with your antics last night, stirred up a rage we hadn't seen before. They got through the outer perimeter and almost breached the inner defences before Celedorn ordered the use of screamers. That did the trick, only we've now got a lot of bodies to clear up.

"Anyway, I knew you'd live and I had plenty to do elsewhere, so I'm afraid you had to wait in line. We lost a lot of people last night. Some are saying it's all your fault."

"My fault? But that's ridiculous. I tried to stop all this. What poison has Celedorn been spreading? Can't you hurry this up? I need to get out of here." I try to get up, realising for the first time that I am strapped to the bed.

Orovon shoots me the briefest of glances. "Celedorn is afraid that if you are allowed to touch anyone, you will attack them and escape." I notice he is wearing insulated gloves as he works on my leg.

A wave of tiredness takes me and my head flops back onto the pillow. "I would never harm you, Orovon. I would never harm any of my people. How could Celedorn think so?"

"There," he says, standing up. He has finished and already my ride feels better, more clear-headed.

"Thank you. This body's fever dreams were driving me nuts."

"I'll call in again in a couple of hours to check that the healing is proceeding correctly. I'm getting a lot of practice on human bodies lately. You're lucky you didn't get blown up two years ago."

"No, wait. I have a lot of questions I need to ask you. You must know some of the answers."

"Can't help you, I'm afraid. Orders. You'll just have to wait until Celedorn gets here. Meanwhile, give that body a bit of rest and it'll mend nicely."

He moves away. "No, Orovon. You must tell me something. Just one thing. Please. Tell me what happened to the Vaticinatrix. Tell me where She is."

He stops and looks at me in silence for some seconds before he says, "She is gone, Arramar. We're alone here."

I am senseless with shock. Gone? How can She be gone? The Vaticinatrix doesn't just go. It is unthinkable. Impossible. Or could he mean...? No, She can't be dead. My people are immortal. She could only die if some enemy killed Her. And no enemy could ever reach her. The whole Colony would have sacrificed itself before that happened, every last one of us.

I open my mouth to tell him so, but he has gone.

Chapter 26

By the time I have another visitor, my ride is well again. Orovon's treatments have stimulated rapid repairs. New blood has grown to replace what was lost. New flesh has knitted up the holes left by the shrapnel.

My ride is still suffering, but now it is from hunger and thirst, not a leg wound.

"Welcome home, Arramar." It is Celedorn, smiling sadly at me, backed by two armed soldiers. The soldiers wear insulated body armour and they carry scramblers.

"I don't feel very welcome." I yank at my restraints to make the point.

Celedorn stands nearby. The soldiers stand farther back. "The last time you were in this house, you behaved rather badly. I thought it best not to risk it again."

"I hear we were attacked. Are we secure?"

"Perfectly. Your friends are just as susceptible to screamers as we are. Since we used them, they have fallen back. No doubt they are re-evaluating their strategy of throwing themselves at our lines like rabid dogs." The man's insouciance infuriates me. Screamers are low-yield field shapers. They twist and distort the substrate of a cognophyte's mind, tearing the victim apart in a moment of horrible pain. A single screamer can take out an area half a kilometre in diameter, killing everything within that region – cognophyte, human, and animal. The carnage must be immense.

"No one needs to die any more, Celedorn, or are you too crazy to see that?"

He rolls his eyes, perhaps showing off his mastery of human gestures. "Please, Arramar, change the record. You haven't the least idea what you're talking about. Besides, it was only night-mares and humans that died."

"You bastard! When I get free of this damned bed, I'm going to shred you with my bare hands."

He looks at me in silence for a long time. Then he walks across the room, picks up a chair, brings it over to my bedside, and sits.

"I'm going to tell you a story," he says. "You won't like it be-cause it has a very bad ending. Worst of all, it is a true story." His presence at my bedside, just out of reach, and the way he softly utters the traditional formula for opening a children's story, make everything strange and unreal, as if I am back in my fever dreams. But he has my attention. All of it.

"When two mindriders are in love, they may choose to Transform. The happy couple approaches the Vaticinatrix and asks for Her blessing. Being wise beyond the reckoning of mere Colonists, the Vaticinatrix weighs the many political, practical, and personal factors that apply, and comes to a decision. More often than not, the application is rejected and the couple must wait, but sometimes..."

Sometimes She says yes, and the Transformation can proceed. Bitterly, I recall how close Ekkri and I came to making our application. Now, all I see when I think of him, is his ride's back as he runs off into the night, leaving me to the consequences of his betrayal.

"The ceremony is long and beautiful," Celedorn continues, his voice dreamy and soft, as if he is seeing the scene unfolding in his mind. "It takes several days, perhaps a week, but, at the end, the two lovers have merged their minds, submerged their personalities, and become One. A new Vaticinatrix has been born, a female, wise and fecund, a creature made of love, a mind so far above the two that went into its making, that we rightly revere and honour it above all others."

The Transformation is the deep mystery at the heart of our species' success and expansion. All mindriders dream of finding their soul mate and making that marvellous union that will change them from a sterile male into a new Vaticinatrix, a female, able to create new life, to seed a whole new Colony of Her own, to raise it and lead it and, one day, to oversee the Transformations that will lead to more females and more colonies.

"The mind of a Vaticinatrix is not like yours or mine, Arramar. Two quite ordinary minds go into the Transformation, true, but what comes out is more than the sum of those two parts. A Vaticinatrix is intelligent beyond our capacity to understand, wise beyond the adding of two lifetimes of experience, just and caring to a degree we can only marvel at and never hope to achieve. From the dross of our minds, the Transformation gives us something exquisite and beautiful, a being to love us and lead us, to give our lives meaning and purpose."

He is no longer looking at me as he recites the familiar litany. He is staring into the middle distance. It worries me that, instead of the rapture that should be in his voice, I hear sadness, an aching pain that makes me close my eyes and harden my mind against his words.

"I have never heard, in all the tales we tell, of a Transformation going wrong. I have even searched the archives – the collected knowledge of our race that stretches back twenty thousand years – and have found no mention of such a thing. Yet it happened. Our Vaticinatrix was the malformed product of such an impossible Transformation."

"No!" How could he utter such hideous nonsense? The Vaticinatrix is perfect, beautiful, infallible. I strain at the restraints, trying to reach him and shut his filthy mouth.

He lets me rage for a while and says, "I understand how you feel. I do, really. It takes a long time to come to terms with what happened to us. I had lots of time myself to observe and absorb the terrible truth about our leader.

"I was woken from stasis while we were still en route from Treforga. The ship was fine, but we were dangerously low on fuel. I went to alert the Vaticinatrix and found Her in Her quarters, already awake. She–" He struggles to say the words. "She told me to go away and to prepare myself for death.

"I begged Her for an explanation, a reason. A few other administrators had been woken by the ship's alarms too and they gathered with me to receive our orders from the Vaticinatrix. But She would say no more at that point. She held a small globe of Treforga in Her hand and turned it obsessively. 'If you want to know why we're dying, ask them,' She said, and crushed the sphere in her fist. Blood ran between her fingers and several rushed to Her aid, but She pushed them away, screaming at us to get out and leave Her alone.

"In confusion, we retreated to the bridge and I got everyone working on where we were and how we might survive. The news was not good. Instead of the hundred light year journey we had planned to our designated colony world, we had travelled five thousand light years, deep into uncharted space. Our fuel was dangerously low. Soon enough we would have no life support and, long before that, not enough fuel to slow the ship and make planetfall.

"I returned to the Vaticinatrix to report on behalf of the others. She was still in Her rooms, talking to Herself as if I were not even there. She babbled all kinds of nonsense, hideous, paranoid nonsense about how the other Vaticinatrices had conspired against Her. She said they had doomed Her and all Her children. I stammered out my report, but She appeared not to hear me. 'They couldn't just kill me,' She said. 'It was an unthinkable crime. But they could send me and all my twisted progeny out here to take our chances in the deserts of space, hoping we would die.' I told Her I did not understand, I was blubbering like a child, and, for a while, She seemed to see me again.

"'I am an abomination,' She said, but She said it sweetly, the way She always used to speak to us. 'Don't cry, little one, the end will soon be here.' 'But, why?' I wailed, and She took my hand and pulled me close, opened up Her mind to me, and let me see Her life."

Again Celedorn fell silent, leaving me out there in that doomed ship, five thousand light years from civilisation, lost and exhausted and full of tortured, frightened people.

"No one had realised that She was ill-made, not at first. She had seemed perfect. She and a retinue donated by her former Colony took possession of her territory and She began to create Her children.

"It was many years later, when we were almost grown, that the first signs began to show. Her sisters began to see signs of instability in Her, of waning powers. Her mind was not as sharp as it should be, Her judgement not so fine. She was brought before a Council of the Metacolony and judged by Her peers. In Her mind, their judgement was grossly biased, the first open show of the conspiracy against Her. Yet even I could see that Her sisters judged Her fairly and that their conclusions were just.

"Our Vaticinatrix was fatally flawed. The mental degeneration that was evident would grow worse. In the end, She would become a danger to Herself and to others. Something had to be done, but there was no precedent and no prescriptions in the Law. In the end, this was the solution. They gave Her – and us – the chance to build a new Colony, away from the rest of them, away from all the known worlds." He gives me a quirky smile. "Of course that's only how She saw it. She believed at the time that the Council had given Her the freedom and honour She deserved. It was obvious to me that the Council planned our deaths all along."

"What happened?" I ask, caught up in the tale.

"I went back to the others and told them what I have just told you. There was panic and fear, as you can imagine, but I got them working on the job of finding an inhabited planet and getting us safely down. I had to push and bully them, but I eventually got them focused and busy. Of course, the Vaticinatrix's great mind would have been a huge help to us, but She was hopelessly lost to us, sinking farther each day into Her own mire of paranoia and distress.

"Then a miracle happened. We found a planet, within range of our meagre reserves, inhabited by a sentient race compatible with our needs. This place. Earth. There was no time for the usual due diligence. I ordered the course correction and the braking manoeuvre and then we must all return to stasis to conserve power. I hurried to the Vaticinatrix to tell Her the good news.

"I had not seen Her for a few days. To be honest, we were all avoiding Her. I supposed we each hoped in secret that Her malady would pass, that the beautiful and caring Mother we all loved so dearly would come back to us. Well, hope is the thief of wit, as the Treforgans say.

"She did not answer when I entered Her rooms and called. Her quarters were a mess. It was shocking. Furniture was upended or smashed, the walls were cut with claw-marks and smeared with mess, some of it blood and some of it excrement.

"Without a thought for protocols, I raced through the rooms, until I found Her in the nest. She was still alive, but bleeding from several self-inflicted wounds, and so close to death I knew we would never have time to save Her. Without hesitation, I offered Her my own host, not caring that I would have to take Her dying body. You can imagine, I suppose, all I could think was that She must live, no matter what.

"I managed to bring Her to consciousness, so that we could swap, but She fought me off. Even in Her feeble state I was no match for Her. If She would not leave voluntarily, there was no way I could force Her, even to save Her life."

Again Celedorn falls silent. His head hangs down as if he no longer has the strength to animate his host. But I can not let him stop there. I have to know. "Did you save Her? Is She alive?"

He shakes his head, a human gesture, but eloquent.

I close my eyes and let the grief wash through me. I have feared it, prepared for it, yet, now I know at last, it still hits me like a death-blow. It takes me a while to realise Celedorn has begun speaking again.

"...me and a few others. We believed we could keep it from the rest of you, at least long enough to get to Earth and establish some kind of Colony. There was no time to work out any sort of strategy. We got the ship on course, then we cleared up the mess in the Vaticinatrix's quarters, ejecting the host into space. After that, we got ourselves into stasis and I, for one, tried not to think about the future."

"Better by far if you'd driven the ship into the nearest star and put an end to it."

"There were several who thought so. For myself, all I could think of was keeping the Colony alive."

"At any cost?"

"Yes. At any cost." He considers me for a moment, as if I were part of that cost. "You know the rest. We arrived. We dropped tethers and sent down explorers to capture humans. Eventually, I brought the colony down."

"Tell me about Senator Keneally, and Sturtz, and the other humans you are doing deals with."

He looks away. "That was unfortunate. We were discovered while still in orbit. That's when we first realised their technology might be a problem.

"When we did not respond to any of their attempts at communication, they sent up a spacecraft to take a look at us. It was an amazingly primitive thing, barely more than an airtight box with a rocket engine on the back. I had it brought aboard so we could make a full inspection. There were four astronauts inside and, in the mind of one of them, we found a nightmare."

Celedorn stands and walks about the room, agitated and silent. I can imagine the crisis he is remembering. Problems with human technology are one thing, but such difficulties can be overcome if the technology is not too advanced. But to find an indigenous cognophyte is a problem of an entirely different magnitude, especially if, as I suppose, the nightmare they found was aggressive and strong.

"You have to understand," he says, at last. "You were all still in stasis. It was just me and a few others. The Vaticinatrix was gone and we had to do what we could to keep the Colony safe. We couldn't fly on. We had no more fuel, nor any way of fabricating any until we had pushed Earth technology considerably farther. There was a planet full of prime hosts below us, perfect for colonisation. Only the natives stood between us and the chance to survive, but they were hostile, implacable, almost mindless, a degenerate breed of cognophyte such as we had never seen before, or even imagined. What could it possibly matter if we eliminated them? Our laws were framed with intelligent, civilized species in mind."

"You didn't look closely enough."

"What?"

"Every nightmare we have encountered until recently has been a female. The males are rather different. But you knew that, even before you got my report, didn't you? Just how long have you known, Celedorn?"

"We didn't know at the time, that's all that matters. We had to decide what to do. The ship had enough power for a landing and that was it. We could have stayed in orbit for a year or two more, but long before then, the humans would have found a way to drive us off, or shoot us down.

"We realised that the humans did not know about the nightmares. Why would they? I reasoned that, faced with the much greater threat, they could be convinced that we were potential friends and allies." I start to object but he silences me with a gesture. "All I wanted was some time, a breathing space in which to fuel the ship and get us away from here. I thought if I could educate the humans about the nightmares, help them with a few, simple technologies, in return we could have their protection and the scientific and industrial base we need to refuel.

"It was only later that I realised there was a much better way forward."

I have been feeling almost sympathetic. His decisions were wrong, but I can see that he has done what he felt was necessary to save the Colony in the most appalling circumstances. Yet the way he looks at me as he says there is a better way, brings back all my suspicion and distrust.

He takes a mobile phone from his pocket and makes a call. "We're ready," he says into the device, then returns to my bedside. "I want you to keep an open mind, Arramar. I want you to think about your people, all of them, your brothers. Think about what is best for them. And remember how far we are from home. Remember our status as exiles and castaways. The Metacolony has abandoned us. The Law itself does not apply out here in this wilderness of unknown stars. Do what is right for the Colony."

I watch him leave, his bodyguard with him. I am miserably unhappy with everything he has said, glad that I can at last be alone with my grief. The Vaticinatrix is dead, but the Colony lives on. It is an unthinkable, unnatural situation. No mindrider should outlive his own mother, not least because none of us is equipped to deal with such a monumental loss.

And perhaps in that simple truth lies the explanation for Celedorn's behaviour. Perhaps the madness that is invading my soul has long since lodged in Celedorn's. Yet where I can think only of embracing death and defeat, Celedorn could think only of saving the Colony, no matter what. As wild as his behaviour seems, I can see it for what it is, a twisted perversion of the loyalty we all feel towards our brethren. Every one of us who knows the truth must be going out of his mind with grief and anguish. Every one of us must be going crazy in his own way. There just isn't a sane response to what has happened. Whatever our minds and our instincts tell us, we are now, all of us, living lives that make no sense at all. And whatever we do now will be ridiculous.

The humans have a comic expression that fits well. We are running around like headless chickens.

Chapter 27

Ekkri walks in unaccompanied and stands over me. For a moment, I want to laugh.

He comes close and, after a moment's hesitation, unfastens the straps that hold me down. I sit up, suppressing the pain from my ride's leg, and Ekkri takes a step backwards.

"Are you not afraid that I might attack you?" I ask.

He shakes his head.

"I should. I should tear you apart for such a betrayal. Does your honour mean nothing to you? Do you know what contempt I hold you in, now?"

He says nothing. I reach out to touch him and, although he stiffens, he does not move. As soon as our fields merge, I can feel his shame, just as he must feel my anger and bitterness.

"We must all learn to live without honour in this terrible place," he says.

"You were always a quick study."

"I thought you might understand. I thought you might forgive me, now that you know."

"All I know is that Celedorn is a fool and he has condemned us all to participating in his illegal schemes."

I feel Ekkri flinch at that. He knows something that he has not yet told me, and he is afraid of my disapproval. "What new madness is this?"

He shies away from an answer. For a moment I consider going in and wrenching it out of him. The alarm he feels at my temptation is enough to make me remember myself. This place will brutalise me as it has the rest of them.

"Celedorn believes that if we can create a new Vaticinatrix, She can take us all under Her wing and lead us."

"That's impossible," I say. Even if there were two people willing to Transform under these circumstances, the ritual requires the Vaticinatrix's participation. To proceed without Her would be to risk catastrophe for the participants.

"It's worth the risk."

"Is that what you think, or is that more craziness from Celedorn? Besides, who does he think would be stupid enough to try it?" Even as I ask, the answer comes to me. There are only two people in the whole Colony who are ready to Transform. Only two who have declared their bond.

"So that's why Celedorn has kept me alive. That's why you're allowed visiting privileges." I feel the pain in Ekkri's mind as he recognises my disgust at the idea. In an instant, my heart softens.

This is Ekkri, after all, my dear, sweet Ekkri, and I don't have it in me to hurt him despite what he has done.

"Ekkri, you must realise it is impossible now. You betrayed me. You dishonoured yourself. How could I ever feel the same about you? How could I ever trust you again the way I once did? You will always be dear to me, but we will never be close again. Not after this."

He steps away from me, no doubt to hide his feelings. Yet his misery leaks out onto his ride's face and is plain enough to see. We stand in silence for some time before he speaks again.

"Without our ..." He could not say the word and my heart went out to him. "Celedorn wants you to lead us. Wants us to. Without that, he has no use for you. I don't know what he might do. He has led us for so long because no one knew what had become of the Vaticinatrix. Since you started to stir up trouble, the story has started to come out. Most of us know what happened now."

"And most of us have clung to Celedorn's leadership because it's the only option."

He nods. "His control of the Colony is fragile. He has some devoted followers, but most of us just do what he says because there's no one else to tell us what to do."

"So he can't let me stay here, giving people an option."

"No."

"And keeping me in exile didn't work out too well, did it? There really is only one thing he can do with me now, isn't there?"

Again, Ekkri nods.

"Then you need to get me out of here."

"What?"

"You heard me. I need to escape. It's your fault I'm here. If I die, it will be on your conscience. Can you live with that?"

He looks at me in fear. "I can't just get you out. You're guarded. Celedorn is watching me. How could I possibly? Even if I could, where would you go? What would you do? You're alone out there."

"If remaining with my family means dying, I choose to live alone among strangers." I cannot help sounding bitter and a bit melodramatic. News of the Vaticinatrix's death has filled me with despair and all that I love has turned to betrayal and disillusion- ment. All the same, I feel a defiance stirring in me. I won't just lay down and let them kill me. I am a soldier and I will fight to my last thought, even though there is nothing left to fight for.

"Besides," I say, "I'm less alone than you think. I have friends among the humans." A gross exaggeration, of course. "And even the nightmares are better company than none." Also dubious, and I doubt they will be extending any olive branches after my recent débâcle. "And I have grown used to exile. After a while, com- muning with other minds begins to feel overly intimate. You learn to prefer the barriers and the silences."

I don't know who I think I am kidding, or even why I'm saying all this. I seem to want to impress on Ekkri that leaving the Colony is not just an act of desperation, even though I know it is.

"Out there, I can find another way to reach out to the others and change their minds about the path Celedorn is taking them down. In here, I have no chance to make this right."

Ekkri regards me with a look that says everything about how wild my ramblings must sound to him. "You've changed, Arramar," is all he says.

His passivity makes me angry. "Everything has changed! Everything is out of kilter. Everything is wrong. We need to make this right, Ekkri. We need to stop all this craziness."

He goes to the chair and sits down, as if suddenly too tired to stand up. "I wish we were back on Treforga."

I go to stand near him but I do not touch him, respecting his privacy. "So do I. I wish I had been awake when the Vaticinatrix ..."

If it had been me and not Celedorn, I would have destroyed us all. It would have been the only proper course. The Metacolony was right to send us all to our doom. It is unforgivable hubris to want to go on beyond your own Vaticinatrix. If I could destroy the Colony now, I would. It is the only dignified course left to us.

My own destruction calls to me like a rescuer to a drowning man. It would be so easy to let Celedorn put an end to me now, but I cannot. I must go on and stop this travesty of a life he has created for us all.

I nod towards the door. "How many are out there?"

"Two. It's all Celedorn could spare from the defences." His tone is guarded. He doesn't want to help me.

"There are two of us."

"You think I want to go on the run too? I am no rebel, Arramar. I am not you."

His words fill me with bitterness. I might have Transformed with this man. The one good thing in this whole catastrophe is that it has revealed him as less than I once thought. "All right then, give me a diversion. Make it look like an accident, then Celedorn won't punish you."

He turns away in shame. At least I hope it is shame. After a while, he says, "What should I do?"

"Just come here and make your ride stand still for a moment. When I tell you to, run to the door and call for help. When the guards come in, cling to one like you're terrified of me. OK?"

He nods and stands still. I begin shouting, railing at Ekkri for betraying me, for being a coward, telling him I mean to kill him. I throw over the bed, then smash the wooden chair against the wall. With one of the legs, I strike Ekkri's ride across the forehead, causing a deep gash. It causes Ekkri to stagger a little before he gets his ride under control. As I had hoped, blood pours profusely from the cut, covering his face and dribbling onto his clothes. "Now the door," I say. "Shout a bit."

He runs to the door, screaming for help. The guards are already standing outside, trying to spot me. I am standing calmly behind Ekkri.

"He's trying to kill me! Save me! He's gone mad."

I give the guards a shrug and try to look confused. One pushes past Ekkri into the room, but the other cannot come in because Ekkri is hanging onto him, begging for protection.

"What's going on here?" The guard in the room marches up to me, drawing a handgun. It is a scrambler, but he doesn't point it at me. I am clearly calm and not threatening. It is Ekkri who is making all the fuss and shouting like a madman. As soon as the guard is within a couple of paces, I swing up the chair leg, which has been hidden behind my leg, and hit the guard with it across the temples. I hit him as hard as my ride is able and he drops to the floor instantly, unconscious or dead.

"Get off me you bloody fool!" The second guard fights his way past Ekkri, drawing his scrambler and tries to shoot me, but I have already retrieved the gun from where the first guard dropped it and I fire first. I am a good shot and Ekkri is in no danger. The guard goes into convulsions as the tightly-focused beam scrambles his mind and disintegrates his personality. He will probably recover, but it is not guaranteed.

Ekkri is looking shocked and scared, as if I am going to scramble him next. "Lie down," I tell him. "Wait for one of these two to try to wake you. If they don't wake up in an hour, go and fetch medical help. Give me an hour, that's all I ask."

"Arramar." He reaches out and catches my sleeve. "Don't hate me."

My thoughts are as hard as steel. For a moment, I want to strike him down, but I relent as quickly as the idea forms. "I'm angry now, but I won't always be. Our ..." It is hard to say, but I force myself. "Our love was a mistake. We didn't really know each other. One day, that's all I'll think about what happened. One day. But don't ask me to be so reasonable today."

He holds my arm a little while longer and I feel the sadness he feels. Then he lets me go and I leave, possibly never to see him again.

Chapter 28

The basement of the mansion is enormous in its own right, with corridors and rooms and people working. I need to ditch my ride as soon as possible, not just because he can barely walk on his injured leg, but also because he stands out like a beacon in his filthy denims and leather jacket.

I find a woman quietly working in a room full of computing equipment and comms racks, a young technician, keeping the Colony's computers running. I place the scrambler on a small table by the door. The room smells of plastics and ozone.

"Excuse me, I seem to be lost."

She looks up at me in alarm and I make the sign that identifies us to one another. She gets up from her chair and reaches out to touch me, completely trusting. I remember Ekkri saying we must all learn to live without honour in this place. I offer her my hand.

As soon as we touch, I swarm into her. The rider I find inside is so shocked, he offers no resistance. I attack without giving him a moment to recover and chase him out and into the biker. He is unharmed but disoriented. Taking control of the woman's body, I pull free and kick him savagely on his wounded leg. The biker is bigger and stronger than this woman, so I need to act fast. The man topples over, too surprised to deal with the sudden pain that must be filling his ride's mind. I sprint to the table by the door, grab the scrambler and fire.

My ride finds it hard going, dragging the beefy biker out of sight behind a cabinet and she is sweating and panting by the time we leave the computer room. By then, I have scanned her memories and know that no one will come to relieve her for several more hours. Unfortunately, the ride's memories are not the rider's memories, or I would know a lot more about the security measures in place around the mansion.

She, of course, is completely unaware of the Colony. She knows nothing of the rider who has been living inside her, or of the war that is raging around her. All she knows is she is a computer technician in the employ of the Sterling Corporation and her awareness of the security of the mansion is limited to the codes for a couple of doors and the card she carries to get her through the main gate. Even I know more about it than she does.

I grab her lunch as a cover for wandering about in the grounds and make my way up to ground level. I have no trouble getting to the main entrance hall, crossing it, and leaving the building. The guards on the door do not even challenge me, just give me a friendly hello as I pass.

There is a large limo parked outside, with government plates and a big, black SUV behind it. I remember Celedorn telling the humans to send their Senator Keneally to see him in the morning. Obviously, when Celedorn makes such a demand, the Senator drops what he's doing and obeys. Given how prideful and status-driven the humans are, I am surprised at the Senator's obeisance. The soldiers that were killed and injured last night, the weapon that was destroyed, must represent something of a crisis in human-Colony relations. The Senator's presence is a sign of just how important the humans consider that relationship to be.

I am still pondering this interesting new fact as I stroll round the building and set off along a side-road towards the perimeter. I know from my own experience that the humans find cognophytes disgusting. The very idea of being ridden terrifies them. So it is almost certainly fear that has brought the Senator calling. Not fear of the Colony, which they could mostly wipe out with a single air strike, but fear of a worse enemy, the nightmares. "Sturtz understands who the real enemy is," Rachel had said. And the Colony represents their enemy's enemy.

Ahead, I see the charred remains of the army truck. There is no one around and the bodies have been cleared away. I suppose everyone has been too busy with the second nightmare attack Celedorn mentioned to do more than was immediately necessary to remove any evidence of death a passing aircraft might notice.

I carry on down the road and there is Frank's car, with a group of motorbikes beyond it. Some of the bikes have been pushed to the side of the road and toppled into the bushes. I stand for a moment and study the scene, wondering why anyone would move the bikes but not finish the job, and why they would just abandon them so untidily when they could have been driven back to the house and hidden safely.

Human senses are not great, a narrow spectrum of visible light, so-so hearing, and couple of other, less significant ones. However, their sight is fine-tuned for noticing movement and, as I stand motionless, letting the road, the trees, and the shrubs fill my mind, I see a small shift, a tiny incongruous movement, something pale behind the dark leaves. There is someone hiding near the bikes.

I am standing in the road, exposed. Casually, I move towards the roadside, reaching for the scrambler I have concealed in the woman's purse. I make sure the lunch box I am carrying is visible. I am an office worker, looking for a quiet spot to have a snack. All the while, I am getting nearer to the car and the bikes, and to whoever is waiting in the bushes.

As soon as I am close enough, I draw the weapon and take shelter behind the car, tossing the lunch box aside. "Come out of there." I don't have to shout because the person is barely ten metres away. "Come out now, or I will shoot you."

The bushes rustle and then part and a tall, lean man emerges with his hands out to the side so I can see he isn't armed.

"Frank?" I stand up and move closer. "Frank. What in all the high heavens are you doing here?"

He stops walking and stares at me quizzically.

I lower the gun. "Yes, it's me. Who else would know your name?"

"Holy shit!" His hands drop to his sides and he hurries forward. "I thought I was a dead man. We really do need that password." He stops when we are an arm's length apart. He is grinning with relief and, perhaps, the pleasure of meeting me again. "I thought you must be dead too. Pretty cute ride you picked up, by the way."

The idea that the woman might be "cute" had never occurred to me, but humans think about such things all the time, no matter what the circumstances.

"Her name is Lena. I'll introduce you later. Meanwhile, I need to do this." I reach out quickly and grab him, not to ride him, but to check he is not already being ridden. He is empty.

He stiffens at my touch and steps back when I let him go. "Where are you now?" he asks.

"I'm still here, don't worry. It will be best if there are two of us. We should take a couple of these motorbikes and leave now."

"I –" He seems embarrassed. "I came back for my Plymouth. I was just shifting the bikes out of the way."

Frank is always surprising me. I had no idea he liked the car so much. "The car is no use to you. Anyone could have seen the plates. They could find it any time they wanted to. You too, for that matter."

He grins again. "I've been using false plates almost since I got it. I know a guy who can get me what I need. Also, I used to have access to the police computers, remember. All the false IDs I've got for this car point to other Plymouths, same model, same colour. In there ..." He points to a bag on the back seat of the car. "... I've got a whole new set of plates."

It still makes no sense wasting time clearing a path for the car when we could just take a couple of bikes and be gone, but I set to and help Frank move the abandoned motorbikes out of the way. It only takes us a couple of minutes before Frank is behind the wheel and the engine is rumbling.

"Is Margaret safe?"

Frank looks at me sharply. "You actually care?"

"Sure."

"She's fine. We got out together. I suppose I need to thank you for that."

"How did you get back in here, Frank?"

"I snuck through the perimeter, across the fields. I didn't see anybody though. I reckon I could have just walked up the road. Don't you guys have any security at all?"

"There was a big fight last night – after the little skirmish we caused. Security will be tighter than ever. But they don't need to post people at every point on the perimeter. They'll have sniffers out patrolling for nightmares. You walked right through them because you're just a human."

We are already approaching the turning to the main road. Soon we'll be outside the perimeter. "And I'm going to pass straight out of here because I'm a mindrider and the sniffers think I'm one of the good guys."

At least, that's the theory. It is possible the handlers have trained the sniffers on my "scent" and that the alarm will go off as soon as they notice me, but it seems like a safe bet that no one has had the time to take that kind of precaution yet.

Almost immediately, I feel a sniffer probing at my mind. I glance around, looking for a bird or a dog, something small and mobile that the sniffer could be riding. If the cry goes up, I want a target to shoot at. But I see nothing. The sniffer is still there, in my mind, poking and insinuating itself. I fight the urge to slap it away and, instead, I touch it back, I greet it, I welcome it. Good doggy. I feel its response, a lick of pleasure and the sniffer is gone.

Frank turns onto the main road and the car speeds up. I am suddenly dead tired. The effort of controlling Lena for so long on top of the events of the past twelve hours have drained me more than I had realised. Now I need to let go and recharge.

"Frank, I'm going to get some rest. You're going to have to deal with Lena for a while, OK?"

"Isn't she going to freak?"

"Just do what you can. Tell her everything if it helps. If she gets too much to handle, I'll dump her and ride you. We'll soon be far enough away that it won't matter."

I let the woman go and drop back, glad to be free of the burden. I still watch and listen but, otherwise, she is on her own.

Considering her last memory was of being attacked by a strange man in the computer room, she handles coming round in a car being driven by another strange man very well.

Frank appears to be coping well too. Perhaps being a cop for so many years has given him the skills needed to keep a terrified woman from tearing the dash off the car while she listens to insane tales about aliens that hijack your brain without you knowing. Whatever the reason, he is pretty good at it, and Lena barely shouts or screams at all.

When it is clear that Frank has the situation under control, I stop listening. I am exhausted, not just physically drained, but emotionally too. Grief, shock, betrayal, and horror at what has become of us, have taken their toll. I am disoriented and lost and I have no idea what to do next. All I want is oblivion. Without the Vaticinatrix, my life is futile.

I marvel at the ridiculous antics of Celedorn and his followers. What do they hope to achieve by surviving? What is the point? Only the Colony makes sense of an individual's existence, and only the Vaticinatrix can give purpose to the Colony. Without Her, we might as well be humans, or Treforgans, living our tiny, body-bound lives like insapient animals.

Someone needs to put a stop to the farce our existence has become. Yet I am the only one who seems to care. Everyone else, even Ekkri, seems willing to go along with Celedorn. Knowing the Vaticinatrix is dead has only made them more willing to accept his leadership. As if one of us could possibly lead without Transformation. Celedorn must be mad.

A disturbing thought strikes me. I have never heard of an ordinary mindrider wanting to lead a Colony, let alone doing it. More disturbing still is the notion that someone like me would stand against such a person, especially if the rest of the Colony accepts him. I am just an ordinary soldier. I am not special. Why should I have the idea that I am right and all my brothers are wrong? In my way, I am just as unnatural as Celedorn. Could it be that living among humans has deranged us both?

The idea is appealing. The humans are themselves so deranged, it is hard not to be influenced. There is also the pernicious effect of the nightmares on humanity to consider. Such extreme levels of madness and depression must seem normal to the humans, yet I have seen other worlds where there was no such infestation, where sanity and stability are the norm.

But the truth is obvious, and more mundane. Celedorn and I are defective simply because our mother was defective. The madness that destroyed Her is inside us too. However much I want to believe I am a good Colonist and the same as all my brothers, the fact is I am not. Like my mother, I am the product of a failed Transformation. My odd ways of thinking and acting are not borne on me by necessity, but born in me by corruption.

My thoughts run along these dismal lines for endless ages. Slowly, I come to accept the disgrace of my innate difference. Painfully, the fact of my broken nature seeps into me and I begin to forge it into my identity. I am reworked and reconfigured by it, twisted out of shape, ugly and ill-made, but, in the end, I am what I am, and I begin to own my true nature.

Chapter 29

My sniffers are waiting for me when we arrive at Frank's apartment. They mob me, needing reassurance, glad to see me again. I pet them and call them by names that only I know. In the end, they are satisfied and gladly move out to resume their posts, ready to alert me to any and all comers.

Lena looks around at Frank's luxurious quarters and I feel suspicion flood her mind. "I thought you were a cop," she says.

"Used to be. I work for myself now."

"Doing well."

She is still hostile. She doesn't want to believe anything Frank tells her and wants to find a reason to distrust or discredit him.

"I provide a unique service," he says. "I'm part chauffeur, part bodyguard, part dogsbody."

"Sounds crap."

"It pays well, and I get to save the world from brain sucking parasites."

Despite the hostility, I can see that Lena is starting to like Frank. She thinks he has a nice smile and she likes his sense of humour. She also sees him as a kind of kidnapper.

"Ever had one in you?"

"Yes, I have."

"How do you know you haven't got one in there right now?"

"I was checked out just before we set out on our drive. Do you want a coffee?"

"Sure. Checked out by who?"

"By one of the Colonists. He's sort of a friend of ours. He's not like the others, anyway. He wants to help."

"How do you know I haven't got one inside me? You said I've had one in me ever since I started working at the mansion. Maybe it's still there." She is teasing him, but she is nervous too. She already half-believes his story.

"That one's gone," he says, turning on the espresso machine and spooning grounds into the filter. "There's another one riding you now. That sort-of friend I was telling you about."

She doesn't like this at all. Fear and anger flare inside her. "Yeah, right. Up yours, Frank." Hers is a typical reaction. So many humans counter uncertainty with aggression. "I've had enough of this crap. I've heard you out and all you've got is some 'Invasion of the Body Snatchers' bullshit. Well I like sci-fi as much as the next guy, so thanks for the entertainment, but I've got a job to get back to out there in the real world."

She makes for the door, but Frank calmly says, "I can prove it to you," and she stops and waits.

She half wants him to do it, and half dreads that he can. She stands there frozen, her back to Frank. Inside her head, I say, *Frank is telling the truth, Lena. I've been inside you ever since that man attacked you in the computer room.*

For a moment there is panic, blind, terrified panic. I hold her rigid so she won't scream or run about, and that makes her even more frightened. It doesn't last long and, by the time it is over, she has no more doubts in her mind. I let her go and she falls to the deeply-carpeted floor with a sob.

Frank helps her up. He takes her to a sofa and settles her. Then he fetches the cappuccino he has been making and she holds it in shaky hands.

"I really do," she says. Her voice is small and her thoughts are skittering over the surface of this new knowledge.

"Do what?" asks Frank.

"Like science fiction. I'm a big fan, really. A bit of a geek. You know, with the computers and all. I still visit comic book conventions, even though I'm starting to feel a hundred years older than most of the other people there. But I never thought..."

She never thought any of it was real. Not until now. Briefly, she loses her grip on the horror she is repressing. She grabs at her own hair and pulls, shouting, "Oh God! Get it out. Get it out!" I quickly tweak her brain chemistry, flooding her with endorphins.

She calms down immediately, vaguely aware that she is terrified I can do that to her.

"What's Lena doing here?" Frank asks.

I take control and answer him. "I thought you might like a break. She can go now. I can ride you again, or go find another one."

He stands up, agitated and restless. "You've frightened her half to death, you've trashed her job at the Colony, you've let me tell her every scary, disturbing thing about mindriders and night-mares, and you didn't even have a good reason for bringing her here?"

"She's my ride. I'm not responsible for her whole life. She just got caught up in something for a while. Most of it was unavoid-able. Besides, I'm coming to think you all deserve the truth. It would simplify things."

He looks at me as if I've gone mad. "You are joking, right? You did see Sturtz and his guys last night, didn't you? You saw Lena trying to pull her own head open just now?" He waits, as if expecting me to answer his rhetorical questions. "Well that's what happens when people know the truth. I wish to God I'd never learned what's going on either."

"Frank, you were a miserable, lonely man. You're a damaged and deeply unhappy individual. You had a miserable childhood, a miserable adolescence, and you've been miserable ever since. You joined the police as a psychic prop to save yourself from going right over the edge. Even so, your drinking was getting worse, you'd alienated your own partner, and you were slipping into a major depression.

"Since you met me and Margaret, your life has changed completely. You're happier, better adjusted, you've got purpose and energy for maybe the first time in your life. You feel important, useful, needed. You haven't had a drink in days and you are looking forward to a life outside the police with real optimism. Frank, the truth about all this is the best thing that ever happened to you."

He glares at me with undisguised fury for several seconds, on the verge of arguing, but obviously aware that everything I said came straight from inside him.

"You are a complete and total shit," he says. He turns away, grabs his jacket from a chair and heads for the door.

"Where are you going?"

"Out. You can stay here and play with your new toy. I hope you find her a bit less screwed up."

"What's making you so mad?" I really don't understand. Everything I told him was something he knew already.

"Screw you!"

-oOo-

Frank still isn't back an hour or so later when Lena hears movement out in the apartment. She has been in the bed, sleeping, a suggestion I put into her mind after Frank left. Whatever the situation, I find that sleep helps humans cope better and I couldn't be bothered to go out and find a new ride.

I get Lena up and go to the bedroom door to take a look. There is someone moving around in the sitting room. By the sounds they are making, I can tell there is no stealth involved, so I go out to greet them and find Margaret taking off her coat. She starts when she sees me, or when she sees Lena, I suppose, and says, "Oh, I'm sorry. I didn't know... Frank gave me a key, you see. I'm..." She looks towards the bedroom, then back at Lena. The way her eyes move up and down, examining my ride, makes me look down too. I realise Lena has only her underwear on. It is quite a taboo for humans not to be fully dressed except in certain, well-proscribed circumstances. I assume Margaret's embarrassment is something to do with that. "Can you tell Frank I'm here. No. Wait. Look. I'll just go. You don't even have to say I..." She stops in confusion, then hurries to leave.

"Margaret? Are you all right? Is it the underwear?"

She goggles at me. "You?" For a moment she seems even more confused. She looks again at the bedroom. "You and Frank?" Her cheeks and neck turn pink and quickly darken to a deep red. I watch in fascination. In all my time here, I have never seen someone blush with embarrassment.

"Frank isn't here," I say, finally realising what she is thinking. "I was giving my ride a rest." It is always sex with these people. I had forgotten what symbolic significance bedrooms have for them. It is appalling that she knows me so little that she thinks I would actively participate in a human mating session.

"Of course," she says, as if that had been the last thing on her mind. "I came to see if Frank was OK. He said he was going back to the Colony for his car."

"He did. That's where we met."

"Look, do you mind putting some clothes on? It's just..."

"That's all right." I go to the bedroom and dress. I dress Lena quickly. There are subtleties in how clothing is worn and I find it easy to make silly mistakes, but it won't matter since it is just for Margaret's benefit.

When I get back, Margaret is watching the news on the TV. She mutes the sound. "So where is he?" she asks. "And who is this?"

"This is Lena. I'll introduce you in a minute. She was working at the mansion as a computer technician. I took her when I escaped. Then I met Frank trying to get his car back. And that's it, really. Lena knows everything. Frank explained it all to her. Then he and I had a bit of an upset, and he went out to cool off."

She frowns at me in silence, as if struggling to understand what I'd said. She doesn't say anything so I go on.

"I need to talk to you – and Frank – about what I learned while I was captive. It changes everything."

Again, she just stares at me. Eventually, she says, "And what about my sister? Is she safe?"

"Rachel? I don't know. I suppose so. She wasn't hurt when Celedorn blew up Sturtz's weapon. I spoke with her afterwards."

"I know, Frank and I saw everything. We were hiding in the trees, hoping we could get you away. What did she say? Why were Sturtz's men holding her? It looked like the Army and the Colony were working together."

Cross-talk. Half of what humans say to one another is confused and at cross-purposes. If I could just enter Margaret's mind for a moment, everything would be so easy.

"Margaret, Rachel was with Sturtz because she had betrayed me to him. She was helping him. She believes that only the night-mares are worth considering as a threat and only the military can save you from them. She's probably still with the Army. They probably think they're keeping her safe."

Margaret is wide-eyed with amazement. She puts a hand to her mouth in a gesture of worry and self-reproach. She is about to speak when I grab the TV remote out of her hand and turn on the sound.

Above a "Breaking News" banner, are images of a city street with crashed cars and dead bodies. The scene shifts to another street, with more crashed cars and a burning building. Police cars and ambulances are at the scene and fire tenders are arriving.

A half-shouted voice-over is saying, "One survivor I spoke to said a strange, silver rain began falling about an hour ago. People went outside to see it. Then people began behaving oddly before what can only be described as an outbreak of madness occurred."

The image switches to a dishevelled and frightened woman who recounts the same thing in broken, barely-coherent phrases.

"It's one of their weapons, isn't it?" Margaret says, barely audible.

"Yes. Not a bad one. They're still showing restraint."

The scene changes to a studio shot. Two men are pointing at a map of the city. Out on one edge, a graphic overlay shows the area of the destruction. The two men are agitatedly discussing the extent of this boundary, mentioning new reports as they come in.

"It's a catastrophe, Mike," one of them says.

"We're lucky it was way out there on the edge of the most populated areas, Doug. If this had happened fifteen miles to the East it would have been right over the city centre. We could be looking at thousands dead."

"As it is, the death toll stands at eighty-five, Mike, but emergency services are telling us we could be looking at a figure as high as four hundred, maybe more."

Another shift of image, this time to another studio where a woman is speaking to the image of another woman on a huge screen. The screen woman looks harassed and nervous. The caption below her says, "Mayor Angela Thompson".

"Four hundred dead?" Margaret says. "You call that restraint?"

"You saw the map. All they have done is clear a two-kilometre radius around the mansion."

"Four hundred dead!"

"Margaret, they could have destroyed the whole planet, if they'd wanted to."

She got up and paced across the room. I switched off the TV. Celedorn is behaving better than I had expected. The weapon he used is a simple biomechanical agent. Nano-scale robots in a solvent aerosol that enter the host through their lungs or their skin and build transmitters in the brain to fry any cognophyte that might be there.

Unfortunately a large percentage of the hosts would have their minds disrupted too. Some would die outright. Others would be driven temporarily insane with random thoughts, feelings and hallucinations. By the time the city's forensic teams could analyse the brains of the victims, the nano-machines would have decayed to their harmless, constituent chemicals, undetectable by human technologies.

The attack was obviously meant to clear the nightmares away from the perimeter of the Colony – and to serve as a warning not to come too close in future.

"So what are we going to do about it?" Margaret demanded.

"Do? There is nothing to do."

"We can't let them do this again. Or something worse. You must know how to stop them."

"Well I don't. I've taken my shot and I failed. You don't know what's going on in there. We're well past the point where I could talk them out of it. The only thing that would work now is a military strike, and your people just don't have the sense to do it."

"But you know the place, the layout, you could sneak in, destroy their weapons, or something. Don't just stand there shaking your head. These are your people and they're killing mine. You have to stop them."

"Well I can't. I'm just one man. I've got no support, no friends, and one handgun to my name. The Colony is an army, well armed, well trained, and dedicated to preserving itself. There's nothing I can do. There's nothing anyone can do. They're fighting a war with the nightmares and humans just don't matter to them."

I suddenly remember Jen, the woman I had to kill the night I met Frank. She used to hate watching Western movies, where the cavalry would fight the Indians. She couldn't bear to see all the horses being killed and injured. It's all she could think about when Dave insisted on watching a film like that. Dave told her she was being silly and sentimental, and she always thought he was a typical, heartless man. It strikes me that my own feelings, watching the news images earlier, were something like Jen's. The big tragedy, of course, was the murder of so many nightmares, but I couldn't help being upset that the humans were dying too. Silly and sentimental.

"Well?"

What can I tell her. I'm too depressed to console her. I'm too exhausted to think straight. I'm too sick of this whole mess to care about anything, even my own safety.

"Margaret, I've told you. I can't help. If you want to stop the Colony, you think of some way to do it. I'm too tired. I'm leaving you with Lena now. Goodbye."

"Goodbye?" She is furious in her impotence. "Goodbye, you little shit? Get out here and talk to me! Do you hear me?"

I let her rage and threaten. I tune out of Lena's sensorium and sink down into the blissful peace of her fondest memories.

Chapter 30

When I re-emerge, I find Lena in conversation with Frank and Margaret.

"I say we go to the FBI," Margaret is saying. "I've said so all along."

"We should give him another chance," says Frank. "He's upset about something. It's making him act funny, but he's the only one in all of this who wants to get the Colony off the Earth."

"You didn't hear him," says Margaret. "He's given up. He's not going to help us any more." She sounds bitter and miserable, as well she might. "We're on our own now, Frank, even Rachel..."

Frank puts an arm around her. "We can all understand why she feels that way. The nightmares stole a big chunk of her life. And she's not the only one. God knows how many millions of people are infected with those things."

"She could have talked to me, Frank. She could have let me help. She didn't have to go running off to Sturtz like that."

As they talk, I rummage around in Lena's memories for the bits I've missed. There isn't much. The death toll around the Colony is close to five hundred now. No one has a clue as to what caused it but Homeland Security is treating it as a terrorist attack and the country is on red alert. Al Qaeda has claimed responsibility, along with dozens of other terrorist organisations and individuals.

Margaret has spoken to Rachel on the phone. Sturtz is critically injured, in a medically induced coma, leaving his team and his investigation in some disarray. Everyone is happy about that, but I can't see that it matters much in the long run. The Army and the CIA are still solidly behind the Colony, despite what happened to Sturtz and his unit. The military and intelligence benefits of such an alliance far outweigh anything the Colony might do.

I wonder how Senator Keneally is feeling about the silver rain attack and the five hundred dead. Perhaps, as long as the truth is not revealed, the government will be content to go on treating it as a terrorist attack. They could then use it to enact some more anti-terror legislation, giving their agencies yet more powers and even bigger budgets.

Again, I ask myself why I should care.

"Er..." It is Lena, trying to interrupt. Frank and Margaret turn to look at her. "I'm kinda new here, and I'm still trying to get my head around all this, but..." I can see what she is about to say and the deference she feels. To her, Frank and Margaret are battle-hardened freedom fighters in humanity's war against the alien invaders. She feels like a child among grown-ups.

"I'm sorry, Lena," Margaret says, with a smile. "You're so quiet. I keep forgetting you're there."

Lena smiles back. She likes being a mouse. She likes being small and unnoticed. She is a timid, reclusive creature, but her thoughts are fierce.

"Why do we need this mindrider guy?" she says. "If he's crawled off somewhere in my head to lick his wounds, why don't we just leave him to it? This is our fight, isn't it? We don't need him, and we don't dare go to the government because they'd just try to stop us. They want the Colony on their side. If we're going to strike back, it seems to me it's up to us. Just us."

Frank is looking at her with approval, I think, but Margaret is shaking her head. "We're not striking back. No way. You saw what they did today. Frank and I saw what they did last night."

No one seems to have noticed the earlier screamer attack. Perhaps the government hushed it up, or maybe the silver rain came so close on its heels that it masked the carnage.

"Even apart from being able to enter your mind and control you, they've got weapons – death rays and poison rain and all kinds of stuff we haven't even seen yet. The three of us sneaking back to the mansion with backpacks full of Semtex, or whatever you have in mind, would just get us all killed. This is so much bigger and worse than any of us can deal with."

In fact, backpacks full of Semtex was almost exactly what Lena had in mind, although, at the mention of death rays, her mental image shifted to racing down corridors with elaborate rifles spitting red beams, a scene from one of her favourite video games.

"Margaret's probably right," Frank says. "There's nothing I'd like more than to blow those bastards to pieces, but we just don't have the skills or the resources for that kind of thing. There's also a bit of a moral issue nobody's mentioning. The only way we know to kill one of them is to kill the person it's inside. To wipe out the Colony, we'd have to wipe out nearly two thousand people."

"There's the EMP weapon the Army was building," Lena says. It can't have been the only one in existence, can it?"

Margaret shakes her head again. "No, there's a few of them. Some of them are even portable and directional – although not like the prototype we saw. That was something special. It seemed to affect even human brains." She notices Frank's surprised expression. "What? I can't look it up on Wikipedia?" They exchange grins.

"Besides," Frank says, "if the government wanted to wipe them out, they could always explode a small nuke high in the atmosphere. There'd be fallout and a load of electrical systems and power lines would be fried in a wide area, but no people would be hurt directly." He glances at Margaret. "Yeah, I've got a Web browser too."

"So that's it then," Margaret says. "We go to the government and we persuade them to do an EMP strike on the place. What else can we do?"

Nobody answers her. Lena is thinking that, after all she's heard, persuading the government to nuke their new best friends would be about as likely as talking them into nuking the White-house.

A silence falls on the little group, into which I say, "I think I know how it can be done."

-oOo-

We talk into the night. I let Lena join in, the way I used to with Frank. Unlike Frank, she is neither reluctant nor revolted. After her initial shock, she has become excited by my presence. She has begun to think of herself as The Vessel. Choosing her to be my ride seems to her a sign of her own specialness, not blind chance, as it really was. Even though she is "cute" and really quite bright, she suffers from a crushing lack of self-esteem, a problem created by unkind parents that is at the root of all her social awkward-ness. It has made her a fantasist and her life is all about escaping and avoiding a world that she doesn't like very much.

Browsing around inside her mind as we all talk, it occurs to me that my kind could be of immense help to humans, if they would let us in and let us augment the self-awareness they lack so badly. We would make the perfect therapists.

It is a disturbing thought. Again I remember Jen and her horses. Some humans spend their whole lives tending to horses, or other animals, lavishing more care on these dimly sentient creatures than on their own species. Could I make humanity my mission? Could I set up the equivalent of a donkey refuge for them, caring for the emotionally lame and abandoned?

I almost laugh out loud at the idea. My own desperate need for purpose is leading me well beyond the bounds of reason. Yet it is an interesting diversion. The humans live their lives in an isolated and purposeless state. Perhaps I should look to them for lessons in how to survive it? I should observe them more carefully and try to understand the tricks they use to keep themselves going.

In the end, everyone is tired and goes to bed. Frank's apartment has plenty of room for all of them. They each sleep separately, of course, even though they might prefer not to. Lena takes the bedroom that Rachel has been using. It still contains Rachel's belongings and Lena examines them, trying to get an impression of Margaret's younger sister. The one who betrayed her. She wonders if Rachel's clothes will fit her. They might. But Rachel's clothes, it seems, are hideous, the kind of thing you see those aggressive post-punk girls wearing, hanging around in sullen groups in the street, trying to catch your eye so they can shout, "What you fucking looking at, bitch?"

No, she thinks, it would be better to wear today's outfit again, the blue cotton blouse, the straight skirt. Her work clothes. But she could collect some more tomorrow. Or could she? Could she go home again? Would the Colony be watching for her? Would the police? She makes a mental note to ask me about it, unaware that her every thought is open to me if I choose to listen.

She has opened two buttons on her blouse before she realises what she is doing. "Oh my God!" she says aloud. It has just occurred to her that I am a male and I might be watching her undress. She isn't aware that I have already undressed her and dressed her again earlier that day.

She rushes out of the room and across to where Margaret is sleeping. She taps, timidly, and puts her lips close to the wooden door to call in a whisper, "Margaret!"

Margaret opens the door in a T-shirt and satin shorts. Lena is overwhelmed with shock and guilt. She closes her eyes tight shut, so that I can't see Margaret in her nightclothes.

"Lena? What's wrong?"

"Oh God," she says. "I'm sorry. I don't know what to do." She still has her eyes squeezed shut, although now she is starting to feel just a little silly.

"Is there something wrong with your eyes?"

I feel Margaret's fingers on Lena's face, automatically reaching to examine her.

Lena pulls back and opens her eyes, then looks away quickly. "No, no. It's not that. I – I suppose I never thought this through."

I decide to intervene. "Lena thinks I'm going to leer at her luscious young body if she undresses for bed."

I can hear the frown in Margaret's voice. "Now don't tease her. Don't you think the poor girl has been through enough today? Lena?"

"Yes?"

Margaret takes a gentle hold of Lena's chin and turns her head to face her. "You don't know quite how alien he is yet, honey. Human sexuality means absolutely -"

The sound of a door being pulled open nearby makes them both look around in surprise. They see Frank, naked except for a towel around his waist. He is soaking wet and carries a gun in a two-handed grip. "Shit!" he says. "I heard voices."

Margaret chuckles. Lena gapes at the gun and then at Frank's torso. She stares for quite a while, letting her eyes drift from his abdomen to his chest and back before she is overcome with embarrassment again and looks away.

"Everything's fine, Frank. Come on, Lena." Margaret leads her into her bedroom and shuts the door behind them. They sit on the end of the bed. When Lena can look Margaret in the face again, she sees her new friend is highly amused. It brings on another fit of embarrassment.

"Margaret's right, you know," I say. "My species doesn't actually have sex in any sense that you would recognise it. And, even if we did, flesh is not what stimulates us."

"So how do you reproduce?" Margaret asks, her professional interest piqued, apparently.

"It's... complicated." I think about Ekkri and the pain squeezes out from under the lid I have put on it. "The thing is, I'm male only in the sense that I can't produce offspring. To do that I would need to join with another male and Transform into a female." It sounds so clinical to describe such a joyous whirl of love and fulfilment as a mere biological process. The knowledge of what I have lost threatens to crush me. Nevertheless, I keep talking.

"You should think of us as asexual beings. Your bodies – especially when you are mating – are actually quite unpleasant."

"Maybe you could stay with Frank tonight," Margaret says to me, but Lena thinks for a moment that Margaret's words were spoken to her and blushes hotly. I suppress the urge to make her run to the mirror so I can see it.

"I meant –" Margaret says.

"Right. Yes, of course. I mean, no. No, that's all right. I'm just being silly."

Lena doesn't want to hand me over. She is The Vessel. She is special. She stands up and goes to the door. "I – I'm just not used to this yet." She tells herself she can cope with the embarrassment. She tells herself that she has to be strong, that the fate of the world is at stake.

"Thank you," she says, and she hurries us away from any risk of further embarrassing herself.

Chapter 31

After a night with Lena and her paranoid fantasies of alien lust and trans-species fetishism – especially after the anguish she endures taking her morning shower – I am ready to ditch her and go back to riding Frank. But there is a lot to do if I am going to attempt an assault on the Colony and it will go faster if Frank is free to run errands while I ride Lena to get done what I need to.

Frank is already making breakfast when we emerge from Lena's room. He takes his duties as host seriously. It is quaint and endearing. Margaret is already up and she and Frank are chatting about the plan I proposed.

"I used to think being a doctor was stressful," Margaret is saying. "But I think breaking into an armed compound to fight ruthless aliens probably has it beat."

"Yeah, it makes patrolling the Bones look like a walk in the park." He is referring to a particularly rough section of the city. One I haven't seen yet. It's a big city.

"Breaking in isn't the hard part," I say, joining them.

"You know we're all going to jail for the rest of of lives if we pull this off?" Frank doesn't look too upset by the prospect.

"It's number one on my to-do list," I tell him. "New identities for everyone."

"You're joking," says Margaret. "How am I supposed to work if I have a new identity?"

"Are you serious? You'd like me to let you go to jail just so you have the chance to practice again when they let you out? If they ever do."

Margaret gives a tight, angry shake of her head. She looks down at her pancakes but doesn't eat.

"Couldn't we all, like, wear masks, or something?" Lena asks. "And gloves? Anyway, it's not like we're going to kill anybody. Just–" She stops herself speaking but I hear the thought loud and clear. "Just aliens."

There is an awkward silence as they all wait for my reaction. "Don't give Lena any pancakes, Frank," I say. "She can't eat with that foot in her mouth."

Frank grins and slides over a plateful.

"God, I'm sorry," Lena says. "This must all be awful for you."

"Don't worry," I say. "I passed 'awful' a long time ago. Now I'm so far beyond any place I've ever known there are no sign-posts and no roads. If I can get through this day, and do what I must, nothing will ever matter again."

"Oh God," Lena wails again, her mind a torment of pity and self-flaggellation.

Margaret looks at me hard and says, "We don't have to do this. Maybe there's a better way. We should try and think of some-thing. Something that doesn't involve..."

"Thank you, but anything that would work means destroying the Colony. They won't leave. They couldn't if they wanted to. They should destroy themselves, but they won't do that, either." The shame of it is unbearable. I fall into a morose silence. "I have to do what's right, no matter where that leads me."

Frank brings the conversation back to practical matters, who will do what and how, for which I am deeply grateful. Get through the day. Do what I must. I make it my mantra, my shield against the corrosive self-pity that might yet prevent me.

Then we split up, Frank to find scuba gear and other odds and ends, Margaret to find her sister, and Lena and I to visit my old friend the Clanlord.

Get through the day. Do what I must.

I get Lena a car by walking into a car dealership and taking one. The dealer, with me riding him, invents Lena's completely false identity and sets up a financing arrangement in his own name so that Lena can drive away her brand new SUV.

"You know we just stole this car?" she says, as she pilots the big, gleaming machine out of the lot. She is concerned about being caught, but excited too.

"It's in the name of Colonel David Sturtz, so don't worry, the government will catch up with it as soon as the loss is reported. My guess is that the salesman will be quietly exonerated and the company amply compensated. By the time they do that, however, we will have finished with the car and they can have it back if they want it."

I feel her fleeting regret. "Don't worry. When I've sorted out everyone's new identities, I'll get Frank to buy you one of your own if you like."

She grins, enjoying this new life she has been plunged into as only a closet fantasist could. "Maybe something a tiny bit smaller," she says. "And prettier."

I direct her to my favourite tech store while she dreams of little European sports cars. We buy walkie talkies, dark clothing, infrared goggles, knives, guns, rope, everything we could need for a night-time raid. As a precaution, we pay cash. I make the shop assistants in each store we visit wipe any security footage of the transaction and then forget they ever saw Lena.

It's a busy morning and Lena does well. Nevertheless, while she has lunch in an Italian restaurant down town, I leave her and take a different ride – our waiter – for the next part of the day. Lena is upset and holds the waiter's arm after I have transferred into him.

"Trust me, you don't want to go where I'm going now."

"I don't mind," she says. "I know you'll look after me."

I pull free. "There are some things even I can't protect you from. Besides, I need you to get all the gear back to the apartment and for you and Margaret to help Frank run through the plans again. Test everything, make sure it all works, go over the timings. You know the kind of thing."

She sits back in her seat with a sigh. She's not happy, but she nods and I take my Italian waiter off, through the front door, with the manager calling after him.

-oOo-

The waste ground under the viaduct is exactly the same as when I last saw it. Plastic shanties, a jumble of rubbish, a fire burning in an oil drum, and the derelicts, sitting around or shuffling about. I walk my ride up to them and say, "I want to speak with the Clanlord."

It takes very little time for a group of men to surround me, all touching one another. "Are you brave or stupid?" one of them asks in a voice that rattles like dead leaves.

"I am the killer of Berreg. Take me to your Clanlord." I reach out to grab the man by his shoulder. He flinches, surprised, but I catch him and hold him tight.

And then I am in darkness once more. The stench of sulphur burns my nostrils. Shadows move and menace in the smoky gloom. As before, I am alone with a large male. He brings his ugly snout close to my face and examines me like a morsel of food on a fork. His upper lip pulls back in a snarl to reveal huge, yellow teeth.

"Shall we go?" I ask. I sense that he is working himself up to fight with me and I tense myself, ready to duck under the surface of this collective hallucination.

Perhaps he see my tension. His snarl becomes a sneer. "Little alien," he says. "Little murderer. Invader. How soon you will all be dead. How soon we will grind you all to dust."

In the dimness around me, shadows seem to be gathering, creating a wall of black within the perpetual night of this world. "The Clanlord," I say to remind him. He is so close now that I don't know if I can evade him if he strikes. I want to step back but dare not in case it invites an attack.

A massive figure steps out of the darkness and strides up to me. "I am the lord of this Clan, invader." His great clawed feet crush the cindery earth to powder. The nightmare in my face backs away with a final sneer to allow his lord to approach. Behind the Clanlord, I see four of his females slinking and baring their teeth like a pack of demon hounds.

"You are not the one I spoke to last time I was here." I am not absolutely sure, but this one seems bigger.

"You did me a favour, murderer. By betraying my brother's trust, you revealed his weakness. These are not the times for weakness." I hear sniggers in the shadows. So this is regime change, nightmare style.

"I have come to do you another favour, Clanlord."

He is walking around me, examining me, sizing me up. Every time he moves out of sight my skin crawls.

"Don't tell me. You want my help to gain control of your miserable tribe of weaklings and mindlice." His audience sniggers again. "What's your offer this time, betrayer? More weapons?"

I wonder how many of his people died when the Colony unleashed the silver rain. Perhaps his contempt for what I might offer is not as sincere as it sounds.

"I don't want your help, Clanlord. I have come to warn you, so that you can save your people." He cocks his head like a dog listening to strange sounds. It is a gesture so like that of Earth's indigenous animal life that I wonder at what point these creatures evolved away from the rest. "Tonight, I am going to destroy the Colony. The weapon I will use is so powerful that any of your people within fifty kilometres of the detonation will die. You must leave the area now, as quickly as you can."

With a roar of anger, the Clanlord reaches out and grabs me by the throat. He is so strong I immediately know it is useless to struggle against that grip.

"Do you want them dead or not?" I ask.

He lifts me from the ground and holds me aloft with one hand, roaring in my face like a wild animal. I have just about reached the conclusion that this is my last moment of life, that these creatures are too insane even to consider their own best interests, when he tosses me down into the cinders. He turns away with that odd look of inattention I have learned means he is thinking about what he should do. I climb back to my feet and await his pleasure.

"Why, little killer? Why betray them? Why destroy your own clan?"

"Because they have become an abomination. They have become a disease. They have diverged from the Metacolony and they have outlived their reason to exist." My own vehemence surprises me. Perhaps my own feelings of loss and betrayal have distorted my reasoning. Perhaps I am becoming even more of a deviant than Celedorn. It doesn't matter. All that matters is to put an end to it.

The Clanlord snarls his dismissal of my reasons. They clearly mean nothing to him. "And why help us? We are your enemies. Enemies are for killing. What you are doing makes no sense."

"You are the indigenous cognophytes of this world. You should be protected. It is my duty to spare you harm if I can."

He looks at me as if I am speaking nonsense. Disgust at my apparently childish reasons begins to show in his face. Sensing how close he is to condemning me, his females sidle nearer, drooling with the desire to rend my body.

I need a better argument, fast.

"All right," I say. "I failed your brother. I didn't betray him. I was betrayed myself. But I made him promises and I failed to keep them. My honour has been trampled in the mud. I owe a debt to your people that I must redeem, no matter what the cost.

Those who betrayed me must be punished. Those who trusted me must be repaid. Now do you understand?"

He moves close to me again, and sniffs at me with his enormous nostrils. "Honour, little killer? What could your honour possibly be worth?"

I square up to him. "To me, it is everything. I am an outcast. My people have disowned me. My honour is everything I have left in the world." It is good to be telling the truth. It is not an easy thing to lie to a fellow cognophyte.

Again, he twitches his head aside, pondering this new information. I hope he will lead his people to safety and help me save them.

"Fifty kilometres you say?"

"In every direction. More, to be sure. Can you do that?"

"When will you destroy the invaders?"

"In eight hours."

He hisses with what I take to be irritation. Clearly the evacuation will not be easy.

"We will come with you, to make sure it is done."

"No. I can't take anyone with me. It will be hard enough without that. Besides, no one who is there when the weapon is triggered will survive. The Colony will be destroyed – and me with it."

He looks at me intently for a moment, his face unreadable. To my astonishment, he bows his head to me in an unmistakable gesture of respect. "Win back your honour, little enemy. Die well."

I am alone, in a stranger's body, in a place I do not recognise. My host is wearing rags. I am sitting on the ground on a busy street, a tin plate is at my feet with a few coins in it. A young woman with metal rings in her face and tattoos on her arms takes her hand from my shoulder.

I stand up and accost the first person to pass by. Now my host has a business suit and a wallet full of credit cards. I step across to the kerb and hail a taxi.

Chapter 32

Lena comes down to the lobby to meet me and I pass from the man in the suit into her. The man hands Lena a holdall and wanders away, back to the waiting taxi where he will remember himself. Lena takes me up to Frank's apartment. It is late afternoon and the others are waiting. Nobody looks happy.

"Did you talk to Rachel?" I ask Margaret. She nods. "How is she?"

"She's OK. The CIA's put her up in a hotel not far from here. They're worried she's at risk of reprisals from the Colony. We had coffee."

"You didn't–"

"Give anything away? No. Frank says her phone must be bugged and, even when I thought we were alone, they'd be listening to us with parabolic mikes. I said as much to Rachel, just so she'd be on her guard. She told them about you and the deal you had with the nightmares. That's all. She said you forced me to go with you – and some other guy called Frank she'd never seen before." She gives Frank a tight smile. "We were all victims of your evil mind control."

"Thank her for me when you see her again."

"They want her to join a witness protection programme."

"No need," I say. "I've been working on one of my own." I put the holdall on the table and open it up. Inside is the documentation for the new identities I have been touring government offices and banks to obtain. "It's probably better that she disappears than that she is under the government's eye all the time."

Margaret nods absently, examining her new driver's license. "She's scared. She thinks maybe the Colony will go after her for what she did – or that you will."

"I hope you know me better than that – and my people. We don't do vengeance. We don't bear grudges. That's not one of our faults."

Margaret nods again, but says nothing. Frank ends the silence saying, "You'd better check that we got everything."

The big kitchen table is strewn with equipment and weapons. I can see at a glance it is all there. "And the plan?" I ask.

Frank wheels in a whiteboard from the next room. There are four coloured lines on it moving from left to right, with times marked across the bottom of the board and little labels marking events for each line. The lines start together then diverge and recombine in various places. At the right-hand end of the board, Margaret's, Frank's and Lena's lines are together with the label "drive like hell", attached to them. Mine is out on its own. After the label "kaboom!" mine continues as a dashed line and ends in a question mark.

"You never did tell us how this ends," Frank says.

"It ends as it should. Don't worry." I see Frank and Margaret exchange glances.

"But after you trigger the -"

"Let me worry about that." I say it firmly, which tends to quell humans, who don't like things to escalate into open conflict. All the same, Margaret open her mouth to protest. A light touch and a shake of the head from Frank stops her. She closes her mouth and turns away.

"And you're all familiar with the timings? You've practised using the equipment?"

"We had a full dress rehearsal, just before you arrived," Lena says, because neither of the others seems inclined to speak.

"All right, then. You should all get some rest. We leave at eleven PM sharp."

-oOo-

We take Lena's big SUV and drive out of the city towards the mansion. Lena is scared and thrilled and I have to adjust her neurochemistry to keep her calm and on an even keel. The others look scared too, but I leave them alone. The highways turn to byways as we roll on through the darkness. We take a long detour to approach the mansion from the north, and the silence inside the car deepens with every minute.

When we are almost there, I ask Lena to pull over and stop the car. I tell her to switch off the lights and get out. As soon as this is done, I lean back in. "Come on, you two. I just want to say something before we start."

When we are all standing in the road, our eyes adjusting to the light, our ears noticing the yap and cry of distant wildlife, I say, "You all know I'm not coming back from this, and I think you all know why. I just wanted to take a moment and say goodbye. A short while ago, I saw you all as nothing but rides, or as tools to use in my struggle with the Colony. Since then, I've come to feel a closeness to you all that I never thought was possible.

"You have a beautiful planet and I wish I could stay." I look up at the crescent Moon and they follow my gaze. "You know, when this world has been discovered by the rest of the Galaxy, it's going to be a major tourist destination, and all because of that. People will probably talk about Earth as 'that world with the enormous moon'." I drop my eyes again and, with Lena's hands, reach out to take theirs – a human gesture, but it feels appropriate. "Take care of yourselves. Treasure what you have. And try not to think too badly of my people. Or of me."

I drop their hands and there is a brief silence. I take a step back towards the car and suddenly Margaret is hugging me. She doesn't speak, and nor does Frank, but I feel the wetness of her tears on Lena's cheek. And then Lena starts crying too. My own emotions are as strong as theirs, but I ease us apart and say that we should get going. No one argues. We all get back in the car and drive on in silence.

-oOo-

At a pre-arranged point, Lena stops again. She starts to cry again, still holding the wheel. Frank gets out and goes to retrieve a heavy bag from the trunk.

Thank you Lena, my Vessel, I say, inside her head. *You have been a true friend.* I would not normally pander to her fantasies like this, but I want to give her a parting gift. *Few people would have had the courage or the vision to support me in this mission the way you have. You are a credit to your species. Now I must leave you.*

"Goodbye," she says and reaches a hand out through the window to where Frank is waiting. "Good luck."

Frank takes her hand and I flow into him. Through his eyes, I see Lena teary-eyed and desolate, but I have already felt the pride and resolution in her mind.

I share a brief, silent farewell with Margaret, then Frank sets off across the road, over a fence, and across the fields. Behind us, we hear the car move off.

-oOo-

A ten minute jog across rough ground with that bag over his shoulders is enough to leave Frank panting and tired, so we stop while he gets his breath back. The sniffers found us as soon as we left the car but, as before, they let me pass through without raising the alarm. My contempt for Celedorn ratchets up another notch. Obviously, his contempt for me is at similar levels.

"It's kinda nice, all those things you said." Frank's voice is barely audible, even to himself, but I hear every thought clearly. "I just want to say ..."

I know, Frank.

"Yeah, but let me say it, okay?"

OK.

"That stuff you said yesterday about how I was and how meeting you has changed me. It was all true. I shouldn't have got all worked up about it."

Maybe I shouldn't have just come out with it like that.

"Yeah, maybe. But all this, since you arrived... I..." I bite my metaphorical tongue, knowing exactly what he wants to say. "I'll never get to do anything so important again in my life. Everything else is going to seem pretty ordinary after this. Look, I don't know why you hung around with me, you could have gone from ride to ride and maybe had an easier time of it, but I want to thank you for letting me be a part of it."

My pleasure, Frank. And, just for the record, I hung around because you're a good man to have in my corner, and I needed you.

He thinks about saying more, but he's already said far more than he is comfortable with. He shifts the weight on his shoulders and moves off without another word.

We emerge from the bushes into a paddock where the Treforgan ship is parked.

"Christ, it's big!" Frank whispers. I don't know how it could have been smaller and still carry two thousand of my people in frozen Treforgan bodies, but I say nothing.

We duck under the camouflage netting and head for the main entry lock. The ship is useless as a means of transport, and the Colony keeps it mainly as a kind of warehouse for the supplies and spare tech we brought with us. So it hardly warrants a guard, yet there are two men standing by the ramp, holding hands. Which means they are talking and not paying full attention to their duty.

Frank, I need you to take out one of those guards with the scrambler, but keep the other one conscious. Can you do that?

He draws the gun and checks the power status, just like I showed him. "I need to get a bit closer." Even as he speaks, he is creeping forward. We are underneath the ship now, its black bulk hanging over us, blacker than the night sky. Only the light from the mansion, seeping across the lawns and shrubs, edging through the trees, sifting through the camouflage net, gives us any light at all.

The ship is not large by most standards, a flattened tube twenty metres wide, by a hundred long, give or take, but from this angle it seems gigantic. Frank's crouching journey across its underbelly seems to take forever. We watch the two guards intently as we creep along.

The intention to fire, forms in Frank's mind at the very moment I am about to prompt him to take the shot. I feel certain motor regions of his brain spring to life, moving the arm, sighting along the barrel, squeezing the trigger.

One of the guards twitches and falls to the ground. The other is surprised, jolted perhaps by the contact they had when the scrambler struck. Frank leaps into a flat-out sprint, kicking up dirt as he closes the gap. The still-conscious guard starts to reach down to his fallen companion then realises his danger and looks straight at Frank, already pulling his weapon.

Just hold him tight for a few seconds, I say and we crash into the guard and go rolling across the ground. At the moment of contact, I flow into the guard and race after him.

My opponent is a soldier and trained to expect this. He doesn't stand and fight but races ahead of me, down into his ride's mind, looking for the defences and weapons he will have laid up in preparation. I can't let him reach them. I change my form. I become the sleekest, fastest Earth creature I know, something the host will recognise and imbue with power: a big cat, a panther, white fangs in a body of liquid muscle. I streak along behind my opponent and pounce.

In hand-to-hand combat, I am supreme. I have always been good. I have a natural talent for dealing death, honed now by two years of practice against the nightmares. A fellow mindrider hardly seems much of a challenge these days. After a brief struggle, I stand alone among the ruins of his tattered mind, watching his life melt away to nothing. These remaining shreds of cognition, dissipating like a river mist as the sun rises, were once my brother. I knew him. I trained with him. I killed him.

Well, many more of my brothers will die before this night is over.

I take control of the host to find Frank still hanging onto me.

"You can let go now," I say and we get to our feet. I collect the heavy bag from where it lies on the ground and Frank picks up the scrambler he had dropped. "This is where I leave you, Frank." It is an unnecessary thing to say. He knows the plan as well as I do. Yet I feel as if I need to mark the occasion, even with so banal a statement.

He nods and reaches out a hand. I shake it. "Goodbye," he says. He turns without another word and heads into the trees, towards the mansion.

Chapter 33

I climb the ramp into the main lock and pull the aqualung from the bag. There will be no one inside the ship, so I can take my time, yet I still move quickly. I want this over.

The Treforgan controls are difficult to operate with human hands and feet, but I manage. It is fortunate that the voice interface is duplicated with a manual one, as some Treforgan speech sounds are impossible for humans to make. I set the ramp to retract and the hull doors to close. I tell the ship to prepare for space. The air pumps whine into action, replacing Earth's air with an unbreathable Treforgan mixture. My ears pop as the pressure rises ten percent higher than it is outside. All through the ship, the Earth atmosphere is being pumped out and Treforgan atmosphere is replacing it.

With the aqualung mask in place and the air tanks on my back I can breathe comfortably. The difference in air pressure is small but the partial pressures of the different gasses in the Treforgan air would have left me gasping. In particular, the level of carbon dioxide in the mix would have slowly killed my human host. Along with the change of air, the ship begins to lower the temperature to a cool ten degrees Celsius. My host is not dressed for this but it won't hurt him and, besides, we don't have to survive here for long.

I make my way through the corridors to the bridge and the various command consoles light up as I walk in, holographic displays springing from the smooth grey surfaces. There are no seats and the control zones are too high for a human to use them easily, but none of that matters. Once I get the ship airborne, I need only to fly it thirty-six kilometres straight up.

The navigation console is the one I am most familiar with. Before we left Treforga, many of us were given training in operating the ship to provide backup in case of catastrophe. I volunteered for weapons, which amused my trainer, but I was assigned navigation.

It takes me longer than I expect to be able to program the ship for a takeoff and steady ascent. The assumption in the ship's software is a parabolic ascent into orbit, not a vertical climb that stays directly over one spot on the planet's surface. Instead of being able to give the ship a couple of simple parameters, like orbital height and maximum G, I have to calculate a complete trajectory, overriding many warnings along the way. The maths involved is quite tricky. The rate of climb is necessarily slow to conserve fuel, a mere two tenths of a metre per second per second. Even so, ten minutes is all it will take. Just ten minutes from take-off until I die.

At last, I have the course laid in and can turn my attention to the engineering console. I hear sounds coming from the ship's interior, banging and clanking, as if some machinery has woken up and begun its job. I have no idea what it might mean. I am insufficiently familiar with the ship's systems to know whether I should be worried or not. I want to investigate, but I am eager to finish the job.

My task at the engineering console is to activate the main drive and push it towards an overload. I recall my first lecture on propulsion at the Academy. A dozen of us standing on the bridge of a mock Treforgan starliner and the training officer taking us across to a bank of engineering consoles.

"A starship like this one has two classes of drive." He turned to one of us and said, "Name them."

The trainee answered without hesitation, as he should. "Negative and positive energy drives."

On that massive ship each set of drives was handled at a separate workstation. On this freighter, there is just one console and I study the displays and controls, trying to match them to the little I know.

The negative energy systems produce spacetime distortions so as to generate negative gravity, inertial effects, and faster-than-light warp bubbles. The positive energy systems are there to generate thrust of various kinds, for manoeuvring and forward momentum. I have set the ship to take off and rise using negative gravity and manoeuvring thrusters. I now set about fixing the main propulsion generator to run itself up to maximum and over-load without producing any thrust.

Again, the ship's systems fight me all the way. If this had been a human-built ship, I never would have succeeded. Humans don't trust one another. One of them might do something stupid, or wicked, and damage the ship. Treforgans are not immune to stu-pidity, but they have nothing like the same capacity for wilfully harming one another. Their system security is therefore weak by human standards. If I want to tell the ship to blow itself up, I can. The systems are merely trying to stop me doing so by accident, not by intent.

Again, it takes longer than I had hoped, but I get there in the end. All I have to do now is set the ship in motion.

"Hello, Arramar."

I turn to find a Treforgan female standing on the bridge with me. I was so wrapped up in programming the drive that I hadn't noticed her come in.

"It is Arramar, isn't it?"

The Treforgan is armed. She carries a pulser, a hand-held laser that can deliver thousand kilojoule bursts of infra-red laser energy at ten pulses per second. Against Treforgan bodies, the pulser is an effective anti-personnel weapon, nasty but usually non-lethal. Against a human body, it might as well be a machine gun.

The pulser is pointing straight at me.

"Celedorn?"

"What are you up to, Arramar? You won't get far in this ship. I already explained, we ran it dry. There isn't enough fuel left to get out of this star system, let alone wherever you think you're going."

No, but there is enough fuel to take it to thirty-six thousand metres, where a runaway reaction in the main drive reactor would create a burst of gamma radiation equivalent to that of a two kiloton nuclear bomb.

"How did you find me?" I'm not just stalling, I'm curious too.

"I've had a couple of sniffers trained to alert me if they feel one of our people die. It's a precaution against human incursions more than anything. I don't trust them at all, even though they're notionally our allies against the nightmares. Well, you saw what Sturtz did the other night. They're an unstable, unreliable species.

"Anyway, when I discovered the guards dead, here, at the ship, I suspected you immediately. Unfortunately, I didn't bring any breathing gear with me, so I had to waste time reviving a Treforgan. We kept a few in stasis, just in case. Step over there, would you? I want to have a look at what you've been doing."

I move towards the navigation console as casually as I can. Celedorn goes to look at the engineering displays I have just left. There is no way I can see of overpowering him. His Treforgan host could rip my human one to shreds in moments. All he would need to do is keep me from entering his ride for the few seconds it would take. And I might not even get that close, since he has the pulser aimed at me at all times.

A glance at the engineering displays is all he needs. The overload warnings are large and prominent.

I can see from his expression when he looks at me that he still hasn't quite understood my plan. A gamma ray burst at ground level would be deadly for those nearby but many would survive – certainly long enough to transfer themselves to another ride.

I walk over to the navigation console. His pulser comes up and a finger half-depresses the firing stud. Yet he holds back for a moment, still wanting to know what this is all about before he kills me.

"Allow me to explain," I say. I speak in English and he speaks Treforgan. Hearing the sounds the other makes is easier than producing them. "This is a walkie-talkie." I take hold of the little device, clipped to my shirt. "When I press this button and say..." I press the talk button. "...OK, Frank..." I release the button. Celedorn watches me as if mesmerised. At any moment, he could blast me to pieces, but he doesn't. He just watches my performance.

"You see I have human allies too, Celedorn. One of them has planted a quantity of explosives against one wall of the mansion." From outside, there is a dull thud. I dare say, neither of us would have noticed it at any other time. "That explosion should have brought down a chunk of the wall. The piece just below your gun emplacement on the roof."

I can almost see his mind putting it together. The heavy-duty laser on the roof is the only weapon he has deployed that could have brought down the ship. If Frank has done his job, it should now be safely out of commission. I don't have long. With a sigh, I reach into the navigation console's sensor field and make the gesture that will set the ship in motion.

I say, "Now, we just need to climb to the right height so that when the gamma rays are released, our altitude gives them the chance to cause a cascade of relativistic electrons in the atmosphere. That's what is needed to create an electro-magnetic pulse with a radius of around fifty kilometres. The kind that won't even hurt the humans, but will wipe out every cognophyte within range."

The ship tips and rights itself as it tears free of the camouflage nets. Automatic inertial frame adjustments mean we hardly feel it, but the jolt is just enough to knock Celedorn's ride off balance for an instant, and for me to make a run for the door.

The walls begin to explode around me as Celedorn opens up with the pulser, the deep rumble of its capacitors discharging running below the rattle of vaporising plastics and metals. I am slow and clumsy in the heavy breathing gear but I make it through the door and into the corridor beyond. The shooting stops and the heavy tread of Celedorn's Treforgan host starts up in pursuit.

I throw my ride around a corner just as Celedorn reaches the door. He stops, perhaps listening for me. I drop to the ground and draw the semi-automatic I'm carrying. It's not as deadly against a

Treforgan as Celedorn's pulser would be against me, but if I hit him often enough, it will kill him.

"You're a dead man, Arramar. Either I kill you or the gamma rays will. Why don't you come out and let me put an end to it?"

It is a tempting offer, but the ship will take ten minutes to climb to the necessary height and that would be plenty of time for Celedorn to undo my programming. Sadly, I need to stay alive and keep him occupied until it is too late. I listen for his footsteps but hear nothing. After a while I risk a look around the corner. He is not there. He must have gone back onto the bridge.

Crouching, I sprint for the doorway. I can hear his voice as I approach. "I repeat, emergency evacuation protocol one. If I don't survive this, you know what to do. Find each other again if you can and rebuild the Colony. Survival is all that matters."

I peer round the doorway and see he is standing at the engineering console, attempting to undo my work, while speaking through a comms channel to the Colony below. He glances over his shoulder and sees me. I have time to squeeze off a single shot before his pulser blasts the nearby wall.

I hear no cry and no sound of a falling body, so I probably missed him. I shout, "There's no chance they'll escape, Celedorn."

I know the emergency evacuation protocols. Protocol one requires everyone to drop whatever they are doing and leave the area by the fastest means possible, dispersing and leaving as little trace as they can. I can imagine the pandemonium on the ground as they all run to find any vehicle that will carry them. Most colonists do not live on the property but commute there each day from the nearby suburbs and towns. There will be enough cars vans, buses, trucks, and bicycles for everybody. Yet, even travelling at the best speed they can, it is unlikely they can reach safety before the EMP kills them.

"Some might escape," Celedorn says. "It only takes two to start over again."

I drop down low and peer around the corner again. Celedorn is back at the console, working on cancelling my instructions. I fire a shot into the console itself and the screens blank out. In a rage, Celedorn spins round and blasts away at my position. The wall I am hiding behind shatters and melts under the onslaught and I have to dive away along the corridor to avoid the destruction.

I know I have only delayed him. Any of the other consoles on the bridge can be reconfigured as the engineering station, and I don't have enough bullets for all of them. Yet, if I can delay him long enough, I will have won.

"Arramar, this is madness. Come and help me stop this before it's too late. Do you really want your own people to die? Do you want to kill your brothers?"

"Of course I don't!" How could he even think I wanted this? "And I wouldn't have to, if you had done the right thing when the Vaticinatrix died. A colony without a leader. All of us with no mother. It's an abomination! What were you thinking, Celedorn? What made you do it?"

I start making my way back to where I can see what he is do-ing. I can't let up the pressure on him. He must not be allowed to save the ship.

"We're all abominations, Arramar. You know that. The Vatici-natrix was sick. Her Transformation was botched. All of Her off-spring are tainted. Don't you think I don't know how crazy my ac-tions have been? How terrible the things I have done are by all the ethical standards we both grew up believing?"

"Then why, in the name of the stars above, have you done them? Why go on preserving this motherless Colony?"

I poke my head into the room as quickly as I can and almost have it shot off. He is no longer trying to fix the engines, he is simply waiting for me. Perhaps he has decided that to kill me or persuade me are his only chances of saving the Colony.

"Because the old rules don't apply now. Oh, I know I'm talking like a presatient. I can't help it – any more than you can. Look at you, fighting for what you believe to be right, despite being alone and out of step with everyone else. Look at how different you have become.

"But we're all different now, brother. We're a new thing. An abomination, if you like, but not like anything our people have seen before. That's why they sent us out here into the wilderness, to die. That's why they sent us so far away from the civilised worlds. It's because we're new. It's because we're different. And because of that, the old rules can't apply. We're here alone, no

Vaticinatrix, no Metacolony, just ourselves. We have to make our own rules now, Arramar. Surely you see that?"

I hear a footstep from inside the bridge and I scramble to get away around the next turn in the corridor before he appears. I almost don't make it. I see the Treforgan host appear in the ruined doorway and I throw myself out of the line of fire, my air tank crashing into the wall, its weight making me stagger as I wheel around and keep running.

Chapter 34

I sprint down the echoing corridors, desperately trying to remember the ship's layout, terrified of trapping myself in a dead end. The ship is not large. Fully half of it is taken up with engines, life support, fuel stores. The rest is rack upon rack of stasis tubes, each one empty now that the Treforgan bodies have been thawed and each one's precious cargo transferred to a human host. A glance at my ride's watch shows there are still seven minutes to go. It is hard to see how I can stay alive that long.

Near the bridge there are quarters for those who needed to be awake at times during the voyage – to maintain the systems, or to monitor a course correction. Near the engines are the storerooms that once held essential technologies, tools and materials for establishing the Colony on a new world. The ship was our home for five thousand years, like a giant seed pod germinating in the depths of space.

But the ship I am now running through like a rat in a maze, is an empty shell. The Treforgans are gone, murdered and disposed of once we found human rides to replace them. It was a big job. It took us a long time to bury the bodies in mass graves, using human earth-moving equipment to dig the long trenches, and to shovel the corpses into them. It has never struck me as callous before. I have never before thought of it as murder. Yet two thousand Treforgans were killed so that we could establish the Colony here.

It was a slaughter.

I stagger to a halt in the midst of the empty racks. My ride is growing tired from running around with the heavy breathing equipment on his back. I am growing tired from the effort of controlling my ride for such a long time. Worse than this though, is a deep weariness that has invaded my mind. I am so sick of going on, so tired of just being alive. It feels as though my ride has turned into lead and I don't have the strength any more to move his limbs. I hear Celedorn clatter into the corridor behind me and stop dead. I take a deep breath and turn to face him.

His weapon is trained on me. I let my own fall to the floor. "You can still come back to us, Arramar," he says.

"No. I can't."

He watches me carefully, as if I might be playing a trick on him. As if my surrender is not absolute.

"Help me undo whatever you did to the engines," he says. "We can still save the others."

"Don't you think this has gone on too long, Celedorn? Don't you think we've done enough harm here?"

"I don't want to kill you, brother. I only want to save the Colony. If you don't come with me now, I will have to shoot. Time is running out."

"Then shoot, brother. Maybe you are right. Maybe nothing we ever believed matters any more. Maybe you and the rest can find a new way of life here. All I know for sure now, is that I can't." I raise my arms in a gesture of revelation. "Look at these creatures, Celedorn. Aren't they pathetic? Aren't they sad? Yet they struggle to learn and grow, just like any half-sentient animal does. And what makes us any better than them? What makes us their superiors? Nothing much. That's what. Mind for mind, they are not so inferior. Some of them are not inferior at all. But what we have that they do not, is the Transformation, the melding of two ordinary minds to make something extraordinary, to make a mind so much finer than our own that it has given our species the edge over all others we have ever encountered.

"The Vaticinatrices are our real claim to superiority. Through them, we rise above the body-bound, above the other cognophytes. They are what give us the moral and intellectual power to use these miserable creatures the way we do. Without a Vaticinatrix to sanction and guide what we do, we're just like them. If we inflict ourselves on this planet, we are no better than any little human warlord, conquering for the sake of his own gratification."

Celedorn takes a step towards me. "That's why I needed you and Ekkri -" He stops himself. His chin comes up, an oddly human gesture to see in a Treforgan. "I'm sorry, Arramar. There is no time left."

He takes aim with the pulser, its muzzle pointing at my ride's heart. I close my eyes and wait for death.

There is an explosion that shakes the ship. I stagger and fall against the racks, clinging to them. Celedorn is sent sprawling, his gun clattering away down the corridor. Is it the engines? They shouldn't fail for five minutes yet. Did I do something stupid?

Celedorn pushes himself up from the floor. A second explosion shakes the ship with a frightening violence. I lose my grip on the racks and the corridor seems to slam itself upward into me.

For a moment, the ship tilts and then rights itself. I climb to my feet. Blood drips from my ride's face onto his shirt. A broken nose, perhaps. Celedorn is lying still, a gash on his ride's head where the Treforgan hit the racks. She is now unconscious or dead. All I can think about is getting back to the bridge to find out what happened.

I lurch back along corridors I sprinted through just minutes ago. My ride is still functioning although his coordination is poor. A pain in his temples suggests he too took a damaging blow to the head.

On the bridge, emergency warnings are glowing everywhere. I am grateful that the Treforgans do not follow the human practice of using horns and klaxons to indicate critical situations. I check navigation. The ship has slowed its ascent but is still climbing. I find a spare console and call up engineering. To my huge relief, the main engines are still intact.

Then I see the warnings on tactical. We have been struck by missiles. I rush over to the console and pull up the displays. We were fired on by a ground-based installation, four missiles were sent, two of them struck the ship. Graphics show the extent of the damage. One large and one small hole in the hull. No critical systems have been hit – except the anti-gravity drive.

Damn! I hurry back to engineering to see if I can effect repairs. But the whole system is down. We are no longer climbing under power but are rising ballistically, slowing from whatever speed we had attained as gravity drains away our momentum and drags us back down.

One last hope remains. I run across to navigation again and call up our trajectory on the display. We are still travelling straight up, but we will never make the height I need for the EMP to work. We are at just over nine kilometres and slowing fast. In less than a minute, our ascent will stop and our fall will begin.

I sit down on the floor beside the console and stare blankly at the laser-pocked wall. The ship will hit the ground at a great speed and there will be an enormous release of energy. No doubt the mansion and everything around it for hundreds of metres will be vaporised, a gigantic crater for the media to speculate over, but by the time we hit, almost everyone in the Colony should have made it safely out of danger. I have failed, utterly and completely. The Colony will live on.

A great stream of Treforgan oaths erupts from the doorway and Celedorn charges in. He is upon me before I can even think of resisting him. He flows into my ride like a nightmare, raging and wild, seizing me in an insane fury, and we tumble through the human's mind like a blazing meteor.

He is cursing me for killing our people, calling me a traitor and a name that means someone who enjoys coaxing his ride to have sex. I have no time to explain to him that he has won, and I have lost. His attack is vicious and I fight him off out of pure instinct and training, all the while trying to make him listen to me. But he won't listen. His belief that the Colony is doomed has driven him beyond reason. All he seems to want is my death.

It isn't a fair fight. I am a soldier, and a good one. He is an administrator. Angry at his stubborn insistence on fighting me rather than listening to what he needs to hear, I beat him down, beat him almost to death. Injured and weakened, cursing me still, he drags himself away from me and crawls down into the ride's mind.

I watch him go and my own anger drains out of me. All that is left in me is bitterness and despair, and a sudden regret that I didn't let Celedorn kill me. I could at least have given my brother that small gift, since we will both be dead soon anyway.

I leave the human and enter the Treforgan, climbing free of the tangle of limbs we were in. It is good to be back in the old, familiar mind and body of the species I grew up in. A sense of lightness tells me the ship is almost at the top of its climb. Soon we will be in free-fall as it begins its plummet to the ground.

I leave the Treforgan to her own devices and drift into the lower regions of her mind. I am exhausted from the control I have exerted for so long, from the fighting, and from the dismal emotional weariness that has overcome me. I want to spend my last few minutes among her memories of Treforga. I want to remember the Colony and all my friends as we once were, long ago and far away.

Chapter 35

Slowly, against my will, my ride's distress interrupts my reverie. She is choking, suffocating, and falling, falling fast.

I take a look. She is in the air, confused, desperate, panicking.

For an instant, I am confused too, but it is there in her memory. She came to herself alone on the bridge with an unknown alien on the floor nearby and all the ship's systems telling her it was in atmosphere and about to plunge to its destruction. Not knowing what could have happened, or how she had got there, she did what the displays were telling her to do and abandoned ship.

Human sci-fi films always have spaceships equipped with escape pods, as if space was like an ocean and the crew could man the lifeboats. Neither the reality of the distances involved, the infinitesimal likelihood of rescue, or the economics of dragging so many small spaceships around with you, inclines any spacefaring species to carry escape pods. If your ship fails, you die. Rescue in space doesn't happen.

But Treforgans have wings. They can fly. And they have a physiology that can cope with thin, cold air at high altitudes. If you're a Treforgan and your ship fails while it's in an atmosphere, the best thing you can do is jump off.

So she pulled herself along to the nearest airlock, all gravity gone, and hit the emergency evacuation panel. This threw open the outer hatch and blasted her into the sky at six thousand metres. And that's when she discovered that Earth's air is thinner than her wings were evolved to cope with, and, worse than this, it is not breathable.

For a while, she tumbles through the night sky, terrified and disoriented, gasping for breath, feeling the alien air burning in her lung. It takes many, precious seconds for her mind to take stock of her situation and get past its panic. If she can get to the ground safely, she reasons, there may be people there who can help her. She remembers leaving Treforga. She remembers a charter flight to another world. A vacation trip to Alleb Effo, something she had planned for and dreamed of for years. Could this be it? Had something gone horribly wrong with the landing? If it was, there would be cities down there, people, hospitals. She would be all right if she could only land safely.

Stretching her wings and orienting herself by the streaming air, she manages some semblance of a controlled dive. The angle is too steep, her speed is becoming dangerously high, but she has some control at last.

A light in the sky catches her eye. A huge, bright light. And when she looks, she sees a planet hanging there above her, brilliant and serene. For an instant she is so surprised by the sight of the crescent Moon, its plains and craters so clear, so beautiful, she almost forgets the danger she is in.

But there is no planet hanging in the skies of Alleb Effo. Nothing like this on any world she knows. And then the fear comes rushing back. She is alone on an alien planet. There may be no one down there to help her. Or perhaps there will be more of those little pink-skinned aliens, like the one in the ship. She cries out to the night in her misery.

Until now, I have left her alone. Her fall from the crippled spaceship is unfortunate, but all it does is prolong both our lives by a little. Surely, she cannot survive the fall, and, if she does, Earth's poisonous air will soon finish her off.

Yet I can't help feeling sorry for her, wishing there was some way I could ease her final moments. So I modify her brain chemistry a little, calming her. I put the idea into her mind that she will be all right. I plant the false memory that she knows this world, that there are friends waiting below to rescue her. She sobs with relief. Her joy at the thought of friends and rescue washes through her like a tsunami. At least now she might die happy. Yet her new hope makes her redouble her efforts to control her deadly glide-path.

The guilt I feel at manipulating her this way surprises me. A human phrase comes into my mind. "Little more than animals."

It's how they justify cruelty or negligence of one another because, for some reason, the welfare of animals doesn't matter much. I realise that my people have always treated the body-bound with the same indifference. It has always seemed natural and reasonable because, after all, they don't have the same level of self-awareness as we do. As if that were a sufficient reason to exploit them.

Like this poor Treforgan. She is trying everything she can to slow her descent, fighting for her life. Her life seems to mean so much more to her at this moment than mine does to me. She is alone. For all she knows, she will never make it back to her home and her loved ones. Yet, on the merest chance that she might, she will keep up the struggle, to the very end.

It seems mindless. A reflex born of millions of years of evolution. Yet for her, right now, survival is her sole, overriding purpose. I envy her. I really do. Even though each rasping breath draws more poisonous air into her lung. Even though she is already on the edge of exhaustion, beating her wings against the tenuous skies, with such a long way still to go. Despite all this, the hope of survival fills her with a fierce strength. She will spend herself utterly, if needs be, to win that prize.

Yet I know Treforgans. They are like humans. They live isolated and pointless lives. They fill their days with entertainments and work that they despise, so that they can live and reproduce, so that another generation can do it all over again. What little purpose they have comes from trumped-up religions, arbitrary social allegiances, and their hard-wired urges to mate and bond and feed their children.

It is a sign of how far my mental state has deteriorated that I find myself incapable of seeing any real difference between this brave Treforgan and myself. Without a Vaticinatrix, I am as isolated and pointless as she is. Yet my response to it is to destroy myself and my people. Hers is to find a chance to live.

The rush of air around us is a screeching tornado. I dread to think how fast we are falling. Lights on the ground below have begun to resolve themselves into scattered houses, little ganglia of structure on the pale web of country roads. My ride picks one out and steers towards it.

And I realise something that I have not seen before. While my people bask in the infallible wisdom of the Vaticinatrices, never needing to question the meaning of our lives, or ask why we are here, we are sheltered from the reality of a vast and meaningless cosmos. We are literally children, blindly trusting our mothers to know what to do and to keep us safe. I have never asked myself before whether the Vaticinatrices have doubts, or where They find the purpose in Their lives. And do they – I recoil at the idea – do they lie to us? Do they tell us it will all be all right and that Mummy knows best, because we are helpless children and would be frightened without Their comforting fictions?

A monstrous flash of light illuminates the world. My ride looks behind and we see a massive blister of white-hot gas on the ground, growing larger every moment, consuming everything as it spreads over the fields and forests, the roads and the farmsteads. The ship has hit the ground. The mansion is gone, and with it anyone who did not heed Celedorn's order to evacuate. And Celedorn is gone too, vaporised along with everything else inside that blinding fireball.

I feel the Treforgan's fear rise just instants before the shock wave hits us. I make her pull in her wings and wrap them tightly around her. Then she is tumbling through the air, as if swatted by a giant hand. Deafened and with the air knocked out of her, she takes precious seconds to recover her wits and unfurl her wings again. She can't believe she had the presence of mind to fold her wings. They would have been smashed like a kite in a gale if she had not. It doesn't occur to her to think of how much radiation her body absorbed during that first, bright flash, and I am pleased that she is spared that.

And then I find myself laughing. Not out loud, of course, but in the voice of my own thoughts. I saved her life. I gave her a little while longer to live. And why would I do such a thing? Because I thought about Celedorn dying and finally understood something about why he had kept the Colony going even after the Vaticinatrix had died. I didn't just understand it, I felt it. I feel it now, the thrill of having my own purposes, of giving my own meaning to life, of being more than just a part in something bigger.

Somewhere during this long plummet through the heavens, I have come to a decision. I want to live. I want to survive this night. There are still things I want to do. Many things.

So I start helping my ride. I remind her that the inferno behind us will begin to draw air into it as it burns. I do it subtly. I don't want her to know I'm here. She has enough to worry about.

We catch the wind that feeds the great mushroom cloud behind us. It tears at her wings. She is not built for such airspeeds, but her rate of descent slows a little. Straining to hold her wings out against the howling gale, her spirits lift. Yet even I, without her inborn sense of aeronautics, can see that she won't make it to a safe landing. She is becoming light-headed from the inadequate air she is gulping down. She may even pass out before she hits the ground. And her strength is almost gone. She can barely sustain a glide, yet a landing will require strenuous manoeuvres she has no reserves left to manage.

I curse the irony of finding my will to live at a moment like this.

Very well, she will not survive the landing. My only hope now is to arrange things so that at least I do. And that means finding something soft to land on.

Her night vision is good but the night is dark and the ground is beginning to stream past below us. I murmur encouragement into her mind. I keep her focused on landing close to one of the scattered farm buildings. I try to calculate our speed, the strength of her exoskeleton, the force of an impact with roofs, walls, water, grain towers. None of my rough-and-ready figures look good.

Ahead, I see a reservoir. A big one, hundreds of metres long, with a farmhouse at the end of it. My calculations show that water is our best chance, yet I know even in water, the impact will smash my ride to pieces. Even if she survived, Treforgans cannot swim. She would drown for sure. I make her change direction and head for the water anyway.

And then I remember a film I once saw. I hadn't been on Earth long and I was in the body of a man called Ben. He watched a lot of films and, out of curiosity, I watched a few with him. One was an old war film called "The Dam Busters". It featured an ingenious device, a bomb that was given top-spin, like a ball, and dropped onto water at just the right speed and height so that it bounced along the surface, like skipping a stone.

I try to do the calculations based on my best guesses of angle, speed, mass, and so forth, but the margins of error are so wide that I can't tell whether it would work or not. Spin is the biggest problem. How do I get my ride to spin like a ball?

But there is no more time to calculate. There is no more time for anything. The black, moon-sparkled reservoir is rushing at me with terrible speed and all I can do now is act.

I take full control of my ride, swooping down low to catch the near end of the reservoir at as shallow an angle as I can manage. I push my ride's body well past the point where she would have been unable to stand the pain. I feel the taught skin of her wings begin to tear, but they just need to last a couple more seconds. I push her feet forward and down. I curl her body into a tight ball. I try to get her wings furled around her at the last instant.

And then we hit.

The water seems not to yield. We smash into it as if it were a concrete slab. Everything is confusion and pain. A wing is torn off. The tendons in her legs may have snapped. But we are in the air again. We bounced. We are tumbling along above the water. I dare not un-tuck her head to look, but I'm sure we are spinning too slowly and flying too low.

With a back-breaking crack, we hit again. I have no more control of her body now as we fly into the air again, limbs flailing. The next impact will be our last, but my ride is unconscious before that happens, and so am I.

Chapter 36

"It's a goddam alien that's what it is."

A man is poking my ride with a stick. She does not respond. Her injuries are massive and it is a miracle she recovered consciousness at all. Her lidless eyes see the man edging around her. There is another with him. A woman. Their feet suck and squelch as they move. I guess that we are at the edge of the reservoir, near the farmhouse.

Another miracle.

"We should tell the police," the woman says.

"The hell with that," says the man. "A thing like this could make us rich."

"But the explosion... Maybe this was something to do with it. Maybe it's an alien invasion or something."

"It don't matter. Whatever's going on, we got this. It's on our property and it's ours, not the government's."

"But what if it's important?"

The man pokes me again. "Do you think it's alive?" he asks. "Maybe we'd better tie it up, in case it comes to. Krissy, you watch it now. If it moves, you holler. OK? I'm going to get some rope so I can hog-tie this thing. And a camera. We need evidence."

"Joe, you're not leaving me here on my own."

"You'll be OK. Just look at the state it's in. Only don't let it out of your sight for a minute, you hear?"

"Joe?"

But I can hear his footsteps receding. I am alone with the woman. It may be my last chance. I don't know how long I can keep the Treforgan conscious. I force my ride to speak. Just making a whisper takes all the strength she has left.

"Help... me." I speak in English, rasping out the difficult syllables as best I can.

"Oh good lord!" The woman stares wide-eyed. She looks around for Joe but she doesn't seem to see him.

"Pain," I say. "Dying."

The woman steps closer, her hands fluttering. Again she looks over her shoulder for the missing Joe.

"Please..." I say, not needing to feign the suffering it causes my ride. I realise the Treforgan can feel nothing in her body below the waist. It is a blessing, perhaps, but I am suppressing all her pain anyway. "Closer... Important that I tell you..."

I see the pity in the woman's eyes and I feel a wave of relief. She bends down towards me, reaching out a comforting hand. I am filled with admiration for her species. On how many worlds would you find a creature whose pity could overcome its fear?

The instant her hand touches the hard chest of the Treforgan, I flow into her. For a moment, I simply rest there, appreciating the fact that I am safe again, at once grateful to be alive and appalled at how close I came to extinction. Then I look down at the Treforgan. She is fading fast and may not last more than a few more minutes.

Still in contact with her, I reach in and touch her mind. She is suffering terrible pain and fear. I banish it all with a thought and feel her mind relax. *Everything is well*, I tell her, speaking directly to her. *You need have no more fear. No more pain. I am with you. I will not leave you.*

I feel a thought form in her mind. *Raiweri?*

It is the name of a Treforgan deity. Treforgan superstition is complicated and personal, so it is hard to know what Raiweri means to her without going back inside to have a look. So I say, *I am here. Do not be afraid.* And, with those few words, break another of my people's strongest taboos; I present myself as a god to my ride. But these are strange times and Celedorn was right, we need to make new rules for ourselves now. Perhaps my compassion for this poor creature is more important than any law at this moment.

Am I dying?

You need not fear death. I am with you. There will be no pain. Trust me.

"Krissy? What the hell do you think you're doing?"

I look around and see Joe squelching towards me. At least I see the light from the torch he is shining in my eyes. "Come here, Joe," I say aloud.

What's happening? the Treforgan asks. *I can see lights... strange creatures.*

They will not hurt you. Nothing will ever hurt you again.

"I told you not to mess with the damned thing," Joe says. He bends over us, shining his torch into the dying woman's eyes. I still have Krissy's hand on her chest and I keep her calm. With Krissy's other hand, I touch Joe. Our fields merge and I reach out for his mind. It is nothing at all to render him unconscious. He topples over with a splash and lies still in the mud.

Don't leave me, the Treforgan says.

Never.

It's so hard to breathe.

You'll be free of all this soon.

Will I find my friends?

They're all waiting for you.

She sighs, absolutely certain that I am telling the truth, and breathes no more. Her last few thoughts, as they flicker and die, are of her home and her friends.

After a while, when I can feel her no more, I stand up. Joe and Krissy have a pickup at the farm. That will do to get me back to the city. But first, I need to wake up Joe so he can bury the Tre-forgan and forget all about her.

Chapter 37

The sun is up and the traffic is already snarled by the time I reach Frank's apartment. My sniffers are waiting for me and I greet them all and let them fuss around me for a while. I am riding a young stock broker by then, so as not to alarm the concierge

"Mr. Taylor is out at the moment," Max tells me. He doesn't know when to expect him back. On his desk is a small TV showing news coverage of last night's explosion. An excited journalist is speculating with little information. A banner scrolling below the wide-eyed anchor, says the police have issued a statement claiming there had been an industrial accident.

"Incredible, eh?" Max says, following my gaze. I watch the scenes of emergency vehicles and gabbling people and nod, vaguely.

There are a few armchairs and a sofa in the lobby and I glance at them, thinking about waiting. That's when I notice the woman watching me from the corner.

I cross the lobby and stand over her. "Hello, Rachel."

She stares up into my unfamiliar face, trying to place me. Then she realises who I am. She squirms in her seat. I can see she'd like to stand up and go but, if she did that, she'd have to touch me.

"Get away," she says. "I'll scream if you don't."

I step back. It would be easy to reach out and silence her before she had the time to make a sound, but I only want to talk.

"You're in no danger. I'm not your enemy."

"Yeah, right."

"Do you fancy a walk?"

"What?"

"So we can have a chat. I'd like to catch up. That's all. Is the government still bugging you?"

"How the hell would I know?"

I can't scent any radio transmissions from her, except for the cell phone in her bag. That means she is probably clean.

"We'll both know in about ten minutes if the black cars start rolling up. Are you still working with them?"

She shrugs. "After Sturtz and his guys got blown up, they didn't seem to want me around any more. They thanked me for my cooperation. They're all dickheads too."

I nod towards the door and step back another pace. This time she gets up and we go out into the street. My sniffers take up positions around me. It is reassuring to have them with me again in this world of nightmares.

"I got a call from Maggie in the night. She sounded pretty upset." She looks at me sideways. "She said you were dead. She said you were the one set off that nuke last night, that you killed the whole Colony."

"That's what should have happened. It didn't quite go according to the script."

The Colony is out there somewhere, alive but dispersed. No doubt they are all scared and desperate, trying to find each other. The situation is a mess, but I can see no way of fixing it now.

"A nuke?" she says. "A fucking nuke? You couldn't just poison them or something?"

"It wasn't a nuke. It was nowhere near that bad. Don't worry, there'll be very little radioactive contamination."

"Oh great, I feel better already."

It is striking that she doesn't scruple that two thousand of my people – and their rides – might have been killed, only that the method I used was bit heavy-handed.

"I tried," I said. "I was willing to sacrifice my own life."

"Yeah? Thanks for nothing. And what about the rest of the brain slugs?"

"The nightmares? There's nothing I can do about them." Nothing I want to do about them. They are the dominant life form on this planet. They have a right to be here.

"So we're no better off for all that, are we? Your colony has gone, but the real enemy is still right here, all around us."

I don't bother to correct her about the Colony. On the whole, I prefer it if the government doesn't start hunting them down. They are no longer a threat to the humans. Even if they were, my views on our survival are not so clear cut as they used to be.

"You're no worse off either," I tell her. "The nightmares have always been here." A thought occurs to me. "Did you ever tell the government that I can't ride your sister?"

"Do you think I'm fucking stupid? Do you think I want them locking her up in a lab for the rest of her life while they try to find out why not?"

I wince inwardly at the vitriol in her tone. "Rachel?"

"What?"

"Why are you so angry with me?"

She stops walking and we face each other in the street. "You know why."

"I know the nightmares screwed up your life. I know you hate them and fear them. I know you thought the government was going to eliminate them for you, but they turned out to be working with the Colony. They let you down. They told you to get out and keep your mouth shut, didn't they? They said there were matters of national security involved that you should keep your nose out of. They probably threatened you, too, in case you ever spoke to the press, or wrote your memoires. Am I right?"

She doesn't answer, just looks surly and belligerent. "But why be angry at me? I've been trying to help. I've done enormous harm to my own people. Even before then, all I've done is fight the nightmares. It was me that cleared that one out of you, if you remember."

"My hero."

She looks away quickly and I wonder if I detect a hint of shame in her expression. Perhaps not. She starts walking again, and I walk with her.

"So?" I press her for an answer.

"So I wish you'd never come here. I wish none of this had ever happened. I wish I'd never heard of mindriders and nightmares. And I wish you'd just left me and my family alone."

I fight the temptation to slip into her and find out what she's really thinking. Instead, I hazard a guess. "It's Margaret, isn't it? She said something on the phone last night and it's upset you?"

She purses her lips and keeps walking.

"What did Margaret say? Why isn't anybody back here? Where is she, Rachel? What's she doing?"

She stops again. "She's out there hunting down mindriders. That's what she's doing?"

"What?"

"She was crying on the phone. She said you'd sacrificed so much for us. She said she and Frank – and some other woman – were going to make sure your sacrifice wasn't in vain."

Without thinking, I grab her by the shoulders to get her attention. "Start at the beginning and tell me everything." She gasps in shock and tries to pull free. I immediately let her go, realising my mistake.

Seeing she is in no danger after all, she quickly calms down. "They saw cars and trucks rushing away from the colony last night and they followed them. She said they should have stopped when the explosion went off, but they didn't. They just kept driving. They scattered all over the countryside, onto the freeway and all over the place. It meant some of the colonists had managed to survive, somehow. They could only follow one car so they did. They caught up with it at a filling station."

Telling it seems to give her trouble breathing. Her face is tense and yet more anger seems to be bubbling up inside her. "They pulled up alongside the car and they all – including my sister, including Maggie – they all opened up on the colonists with every gun they had. They killed all of them. Then ran."

She seems to be watching me, waiting for a reaction, but what could I say?

"You don't know Maggie," she says. "You don't know what you've done to her, getting her mixed up in all this. She saves people, for fuck's sake. She's a doctor, not a bloody murderer! You want to know why I'm angry? You know what she said to me?

"She said they had to dump the car and get a new one. She said the police would be onto it before long. She said Frank had the numbers of some of the other colony vehicles and that they would try to find them before they got too far."

Rachel lunges at me and thumps my ride in the chest and arms several times. "She said she was going to finish your work, you asshole! She said she and Frank would make sure none of the others survived."

She stops hitting me as abruptly as she had started and stands there, leaning against me and crying. Tentatively, I put my ride's hands on her shoulders again, offering comfort, for what that's worth. We are attracting attention from the passers-by but it is just idle curiosity, nothing more sinister. I let her weep.

After a while, I say, "We'll find her and stop this. All it will take is one word from me."

She shakes here head. Then, seeming to remember herself, she pulls away from me. "Her phone's dead. I called her back as soon as she hung up. She's probably smashed it or something."

I nod. That would be the sensible thing. "But you were waiting here, at the apartment. You think she might come back."

"She said something about wishing they had the equipment they'd stashed at Frank's place. I thought it might be worth waiting there, just in case."

"It's a good idea. You should go back there. I'll have a look around elsewhere and see what I can find out."

Her conversion from anger to cooperation in just a handful of minutes makes me suspicious, but some humans are like that. Rachel, I know, is needy and emotionally volatile – a legacy of those years of hosting a nightmare, I suppose. The pattern is consistent with her previous switches of loyalty and motive. Above all, I believe she would not act against her sister's interest. But, even then, her choices have not been good in the past. Still, without entering her mind, I must simply trust her. It is difficult, but if I am to respect Margaret's wishes, that's how it has to be.

Chapter 38

She heads back to the apartment and I make a few changes of host, just to be on the safe side. Within fifteen minutes, I am in the local police station, riding a desk sergeant and checking through the computer systems for news of my friends.

The 'drive by' shooting of a group of four people at a service station off the freeway is being handled by the FBI. It takes me another fifteen minutes to get myself over to the local FBI office and into their computer systems.

The Feds don't have much to go on. That the victims all worked at the mansion – the scene of last night's gigantic explosion – makes this a murder with potentially huge significance. But they can find no reason why those four people should be in a car together, apparently fleeing the explosion, and their killers are a complete mystery. The shooters' car was found burning on waste land not far from the crime scene. Eye witnesses saw nothing useful – two, three, or four people, who might have been all women, or all men, or teenage boys – and there was no CCTV footage that could help identify anybody. There are some digital photos of a footprint found near the burning car, which I delete..

While I am there, I look up the files for Margaret, Frank and Lena. Frank's is flagged as a person of interest for Project Pandora. So is Lena's. Pandora turns out to be highly classified and I spend the best part of an hour hacking my way in.

And there is the inside story. Pandora is an inter-agency task force under special oversight by a committee chaired by Senator Keneally. Sturtz's team is part of it, along with CIA, NSA, FBI and other resources. I find transcripts of meetings, field reports, interrogation reports, and briefing papers. It is not clear, from what I can find, whether anybody above Kenealley's level is aware of the existence of the Colony, or of the nightmares, or of the actions being taken.

It is clear that people are scared. Everyone who worked at the mansion, or even visited the place, has been investigated. Many are under covert surveillance. I find reports about a group of four secret missile batteries that have been built around the Colony "to contain the threat of military action by the colonists," and to "provide the option of a pre-emptive strike, should diplomatic channels break down." Which explains how they brought the ship down. There are even press releases and cover stories planned to allow for various contingencies. It is one of these that has been used to explain the explosion of the previous night.

The extent of these machinations and the bureaucracy involved are very impressive. Yet, as Rachel once said, their real concern is with the nightmares. The Colony is viewed as an ally and part of the Pandora project is a "diplomatic mission" to negotiate "an exchange of intelligence and technology with the extraterrestrials."

Well, that is all history now.

As fascinating as it is to explore the extent of their knowledge, it is not getting me any closer to Frank and the others. I erase as much of the database as I can. There will probably be backups that I can't get at, but whatever small inconvenience I can cause Pandora, especially now, seems worthwhile.

I head back to the apartment, changing rides often to make my trail impossible to follow. I pick a middle-aged lady to rejoin Rachel in. I find that, apart from children, ageing females are the kind of human other humans find least threatening.

Rachel is in the same chair as before. There is a small collection of coffee cups and empty sandwich boxes on the table beside her. I give Max a smile as I pass him and he watches me with a mild curiosity as I take a seat next to Rachel.

"Any news?" I ask.

She looks at my ride while she decides it's me, then she shakes her head.

"I'm going to be here until someone shows up," I tell her. "So if you want to take a break, go ahead."

Again a shake of the head. "Max has been fetching me drinks and stuff. I'm OK. What did you find out?"

"That the police have no idea who they're after. Unless they do another shooting, the cops have no reason to suspect any of them." She looks away, overcome with emotion and trying to hide it from me. "I'll keep checking in with the FBI," I assure her. "If your sister does anything else, I'll hear about it and I can track her down through the Feds. If not... Well, she'll be OK, won't she?"

"You don't know that. You don't–" Her eyes widen and she stands up. "Frank!"

He freezes in the middle of the lobby and turns slowly. I see his eyes flick as he checks out the rest of the room. Rachel steps quickly towards him and he reaches into his jacket for the gun he carries. Rachel stops, blinking in surprise.

"I'm – I'm –" she stammers. Frank's eyes are hard and it must be quite a shock to Rachel to see how little he trusts her. Still, she manages to say, "Is Maggie all right? Is she with you?"

"Who's your friend?" Frank keeps his hand inside his jacket.

"It's me, Frank. There's no need to worry. Rachel is just here to see that her sister is all right."

"You? But you're–"

"Yes, I thought I was too. It seems I survived. Do you want to bring the others in now? I assume they're out there."

He pulls a small walkie-talkie from his pocket and says, "OK, it's clear." There is no reply but thirty seconds later, Margaret and Lena walk into the lobby. They both look at Rachel, then at me.

Margaret doesn't get two paces before Rachel has her in a bear hug. I suggest to Frank that we take it all up to the apartment and he starts shepherding everyone towards the elevator. I draw Lena aside.

She looks at me curiously. "It's me, Lena. I'm still alive."

Her mouth drops open. With a squeal, she grabs me in a hug, too. After a moment, she lets me go, but still keeps hold of me, as if I might run away. "But how? We saw the ship go up."

I put a finger to my ride's lips to shush her. Max is not three paces away, watching the whole show. "Would you mind if we let this lady get on with her day?"

"What? Oh, right. Yes, of course. Come on."

I flow into Lena and I leave my former ride in the lobby with a suggestion that she go outside and hail a cab. The elevator ride is a babble of questions, mostly for me, to which my only reply is that I'll tell them everything when we get inside. But before we manage to get into Frank's apartment, Rachel is shouting at Margaret, asking her what the hell she thought she was doing. Margaret is weeping and holding her face in her hands, and Frank is trying to get between them to keep Rachel at bay.

Outside the door, I take over Lena and shout at them all to shut up and get inside. They are surprised enough that they comply. I follow them in and shut the door solidly behind me.

"All right. Everybody just calm down. We've all been under a lot of stress and now we just need to sit down and talk this through. So, please, sit down."

I lead them through to the lounge and they fall into chairs and onto sofas. I take a seat too. In her mind, Lena is so pleased to have me back and so thrilled that I am taking charge of things, that it is quite distracting. Underneath her excitement is relief that their vigilante quest is over. It had frightened and disturbed her more than she could admit to herself.

I let it go. I will get back to that in a while.

First, I tell them everything that has happened to me since I last saw them. I keep them from interrupting until I get right up to the point where Frank walked into the lobby.

"OK, Frank. Your turn."

Frank is looking a little queasy and he keeps glancing nervously at Margaret. She too is looking unsettled and anxious.

"After I left you, I set the explosives and made my way down the drive to the gate house and waited. I saw the bomb go off and the ship rising up from behind the mansion. Then, right on cue, Margaret and Lena came bursting through the gate, guns blazing."

That was me, Lena says in her mind. *Margaret was driving.*

"They picked me up and we drove like maniacs. We timed it, like you said, and stopped at the side of the road and switched everything off so the EMP wouldn't do too much damage. But the time you said came and went. We saw cars and trucks going past but figured that was OK since the pulse was still to come, but it didn't.

"When the ship hit the ground and went off like a nuke, we thought maybe that was it, but there were still vehicles passing and none of them stopped. So we tagged on behind the convoy and watched them. It looked like things had gone badly wrong. We didn't know what to do. We all felt as if we needed to do something, that we should try to stop them just getting away like that."

He glances again at Margaret. In Lena's mind, I see memories of that drive. They are following red tail lights. Margaret is wound up tight and keeps saying, "We can't just let them go. We've got to stop them." She keeps pleading with Frank to do something, to run them off the road, to shoot them, anything. Lena can see that Margaret has lost it, that she's not being quite rational, but Lena feels it too. It can't all just be for nothing. They have to stop them.

"But then we saw they were all turning off, taking different roads, dispersing. In the end, we were following just one car, although I'd got the numbers of a couple of others. When it pulled over for gas, we went in after it."

Again, I see the scene in Lena's mind. Margaret is driving. She pulls up right next to the carload of Colonists. "Shoot them," she shouts, winding down the windows. "Go on. It's our only chance." She has a handgun and she aims it past Frank, through the window, and starts blasting at the four people in the other car. Lena sees the Colonists turn, startled as one of them and then another, is hit. Then one of them raises a gun and fires back. Shouting like a madman, Frank grabs the sub-machine gun that he has been cradling and strafes the other car with bullets. In seconds, they are all dead.

"I ditched the car afterwards and burnt it, stole another car, and we ran. That's probably when Margaret called you," he says to Rachel.

That was also when Margaret started crying, Lena's memories tell me. She cried hysterically, then miserably, then she just sobbed and looked shattered. After that, Lena and Frank had to lead Margaret around like a child.

"We came back for some clean clothes and some rest. Then we were going to head off somewhere. We haven't quite decided where exactly."

"I don't know what made me do it." We all turn to look at Margaret. "I was so scared and so wound up. It was like some kind of fever." Frank moves to comfort her but Rachel does too, and Frank defers to her. "Is that what it's like to be mad?"

Rachel sits beside her and holds her close. "We've all done some stupid, horrible things in the past few days. We've all got blood on our hands."

"But I killed those people, Raich. I didn't know them. They'd never done anything to hurt me. And I just shot them. I was hunting them down. It seemed like I had a right to."

I feel Lena's frisson of horror at the thought that she could have been one of them, ridden to her death without ever knowing it. In Lena's mind, four innocents died along with the four min-driders. I suspect this is what is tormenting Margaret so much.

"Listen," I say, and I have all their attention. "I came back here because I wanted to tell you what I plan to do next. I'm hoping you'll help me.

"I've got more blood on my hands than any of you. What's more, I take on my shoulders the mistakes of my own people that started all this. There are lots of mindriders out there now. I don't know how many were killed fighting the nightmares, and I don't know how many I killed last night, but there could be fifteen hundred or more left alive.

"I need to find them."

Margaret and Rachel look alarmed. Frank looks disappointed, as if he had hoped for more from me. Lena is torn between excitement and dread.

"They are out there on their own, leaderless, in small groups. I have no idea what they will do. My people are not suited to that kind of life. They will try to find each other. They will despair. They will go crazy. My brethren and I are not the most stable family in the Galaxy.

"The nightmares will hunt them down. The humans will hunt them down and try to use them against the nightmares. I want to gather them together and put them somewhere safe. I owe them that."

"Last night you were trying to wipe them out," Rachel says.

"Maybe we were all a bit crazy last night," says Frank.

"Maybe," I agree, although maybe I'm more crazy today than I was then. "Fifteen hundred rogue mindriders is not something you want running around your planet. Their technology may have been destroyed, but many of them have the knowledge to rebuild it. Even without it, they can make a lot of trouble. I need to find them, talk them into accepting my ideas, save you from a dangerous situation, and save them from the persecution that will one day destroy them.

"And I'd like you all to help me."

Yes! The response is immediate and jubilant in Lena's mind. In an instant she is filled with hope and purpose. She is The Vessel again, on a quest to save the world.

Frank stands up and walks away. Rachel is shaking her head. "You can't ask Maggie to do any more," she says. "Look what you've done already."

"She's right," Frank says. His tone is regretful, but I can hear the firmness in is voice. "We've done enough. The cops don't know what we've done. We've got new identities. We should just fade into the background. We're not soldiers. We're not–" He stops speaking, as if he's irritated at the sound of his own voice.

He's trying to protect Margaret, Lena says in her thoughts. *He wants to help, really.* I feel her admiration for Frank. He is a hero to her.

Margaret says nothing. She is watching Frank with troubled eyes. I can't tell if she wants him to stand firm or relent.

After a moment, I ask Lena to stand up.

"I should go," I say. "You're right. I have no right to ask you to do this."

"No. Hang on," Lena says and tries to sit down again.

I take control of her and move towards the door, apologising to her in her mind.

"You have all become important to me. But then, you know that. We said our goodbyes last night." They watch me leave in silence. Only Rachel seems unambiguously pleased to see me go. "I'll send Lena back later," I promise.

Outside, the afternoon is waning. The sky is clouding over and the Sun is out of sight below the high-rise buildings that surround me. The street is full of people and cars and the normal clamour and stench of the city. It is a world with no Colony. An alien world in which I must walk alone.

I whistle up my sniffers and head away from the apartment, letting the crowds and the gathering gloom envelop me. It is a strange world and, for a moment, I shrink from the task I have set myself.

But only for a moment.

Thank You

Thank you for reading *Mindrider*. I really hope you enjoyed it as much as I enjoyed writing it. If so, I'd be grateful if you'd leave a review on one of the book retail sites, your blog, Goodreads, or pasted to a wall on the nearest underpass. To stay informed of when new books of mine are about to appear, please visit my blog and sign up for my newsletter at http://grahamstorrs.cantal-ibre.com.

About the Author

I am a science fiction writer living in Queensland, Australia. A former research scientist, IT consultant and award-winning software designer, I now live and write in a quiet corner of the Australian bush with my wife, Christine, an Airedale terrier called Bertie, and a Tonkinese cat called Minsky.

Other Books By Graham Storrs

My published writing includes three children's science books, and a great many magazine articles, academic papers and book chapters. Since turning my attention to writing fiction I have had many short stories published in a wide range of magazines and anthologies.

I have been writing three series of novels set in my Placid Point universe: the Rik Sylver series, the Canta Libre trilogy and the Deep Fracture series, set eighty, three hundred, and ten thousand years in the future respectively.

My début novel, Timesplash, a near-future, time travel thriller, was a Kindle best-seller. It is now published by Pan Macmillan Australia, as are the sequels, True Path. and Foresight. Both True Path and Foresight were shortlisted for Australia's première science fiction awards, The Aurealis Awards, as Best Science Fiction Novel, in 2014 and 2015.

I also have a couple of other stand-alone novels out there. Heaven is a Place on Earth is a thriller set in a near future dominated by augmented reality and virtual reality technologies, with all the opportunities for deception they bring. Cargo Cult is a sci-fi comedy in the tradition of British sci-fi comedy since Douglas Adams and Doug Naylor. Time and Tyde is a dark comedy set in the present day, about a man stalked by an amoral jerk from the future, or perhaps a man driven insane by a present-day stalker. Either way, it doesn't turn out well.

You can find links to fuller descriptions of all my novels on my website (http://www.grahamstorrs.com). Or just type my name into your favourite online book store and they should all appear.

Contact the Author

I am always happy to hear from readers, so don't be shy. And if you enjoyed this book, don't forget to post your review.

Follow me on Twitter: http://twitter.com/graywave or on Facebook: http://www.facebook.com/GrahamStorrsAuthor

For details of all my novels and short stories, visit http://www.grahamstorrs.com